Killers & Monsters

Three Fates Mafia
Book 2

Clio Evans

To anyone who needs a DILF in their life
(dragon I'd like to f*ck)

Mortals Beware

Mortals Beware:

In this story, you will find the following:

Voyeurism, breeding kink, degradation, double V penetration, fucking a dragon, taking photos of someone without prior consent, spanking, biting, cum inflation, murder, pussy magic, SIZE difference, and more.

If you have any questions, you can reach me on instagram or Facebook, or via email clioevansauthor@gmail.com

Married to the Dragon

10 Years Ago

Serena

"You're a goddess, Serena."

I forced a smile at the woman that was smoothing out my wedding veil, wishing it would hide my tears. I watched her through the lace as she fluttered around me, making sure that everything was perfect.

We couldn't have anything out of place on a day like today.

Everything had to be pristine.

"Ah, no, no," she crooned, wiping the tears away. "Don't let them see you cry. *Don* Avellino wants to see you happy."

Happy.

I'd been happy until a year ago. The night I turned seventeen my entire life was handed to me like a birthday gift with a crimson, bloodied bow. I was informed that a husband had been found, one who would accept me even though I was just the niece of the *don*.

It would strengthen the family.

I'd be doing something good for once.

I'd be helping my uncle.

They'd given me all the reasons why an arranged marriage was a great option, as if I'd had a choice. I was told it was a courtesy to be informed I was getting married instead of being taken to the courthouse immediately.

After my mother died, I was raised alongside *Don* Avellino's daughters. My chest ached for a moment remembering her. She had been such an amazing woman, I hadn't understood how terrible her brother was.

My uncle had taken pity on me by bringing me into his home. But love, in his house, came with strings attached. And the ones tied to those, seemingly selfless, acts were what brought me to today.

I was taught to be the perfect princess, only to be sold like cattle to the highest bidder.

I wondered what my mom would think about this. After she died, my uncle had forbidden me to speak about her. Since then, she'd become a little voice only allowed to exist in my mind.

I hadn't even met the man who would be my husband. I'd see his face for the first time at the altar.

I was nothing but a bargaining chip.

Swallowing the rage I felt, I blinked back the tears. She was right. I couldn't let my mascara run, not while they were watching.

Last week, I celebrated my eighteenth birthday by packing all of my belongings. It had been a terrible day filled with tears and longing and broken dreams. For the past year, I'd been able to mostly forget about the approaching deadline, but the night I officially became an adult, it was the only thing I could think of.

My dress.

My wedding.

My reception.

My husband.

My honeymoon.

To help with my anxiety, I'd sometimes pretend that the man I was marrying was a prince. I'd envision a life where we'd live happily ever after. I'd pretend fate had been kind.

But that was just pretend. I didn't believe in fantasy and was coming to terms with the truth.

This marriage had been arranged by the *don*, so even if the man at the end of the aisle was a ruthless murderer—I would still be given to him.

Because the *don* always got what he wanted.

I drew in a shaky breath, trying not to come undone. One day, maybe my husband would die, and I would inherit everything, becoming a mafia queen myself.

I let out a small chuckle, drawing a wary look from the woman moving around me. I didn't even know her name. One of the many women who were treated like a doormat by *Don* Avellino's men.

Antonio Avellino, my uncle, was one of the most feared men on this side of the world. The rumors I'd already heard about my betrothed were that he controlled the west, and even my uncle had been nervous about meeting him.

That had to mean he was a monster. Not literally, of course. But the type of man that made my uncle nervous was the type of man everyone feared.

This marriage would tie the Avellino family to his, which in turn would help the empire grow.

I was fulfilling my family duty. Doing what I had been raised to do, even as a niece.

My cousins would be married off soon too.

Even though I wasn't his daughter, I had been treated as such since the day I was brought here. I was the oldest, which meant I'd be the first for everything. I was the first to go.

The first to be sold.

Swallowing every ounce of rage, I forced all of my anger into a box in my mind. I turned the key, feeling my shoulders relax and the poise I had been trained to emanate returned. "I'm ready."

"*Bellissima*," she murmured, nodding.

There was a knock at the door and I turned. My cousin, Mia, stood in the doorway, her dark eyes puffy with grief. She was only fifteen and had cried herself to sleep last night in my bed, begging me not to marry this man.

I didn't have the heart to tell Mia it was *her* father who was forcing me to marry him.

She would eventually find out. But for now, I'd rather she remain naive.

"Your father will be looking for you," the woman warned Mia. "Serena is about to walk down the aisle, *bambina*. You should be seated with your family, not here."

"You don't even know him," Mia protested. "I don't understand, Serena. How can you marry him if you've never even met him?"

"It has to be done," I stated.

There was nothing else to say.

I'd been born into this life and was unable to escape. Though it terrified me, all I could do was hope my betrothed would be kind.

He could be the kind of man that would rather see me dead. What if I ended up in a ditch tomorrow?

I tried to drown out the thoughts of death. My mind kept going from childish fantasies that this would be a fairytale to the stark horror that today might be the last day of my life. It wouldn't be the first time something tragic had happened to a new bride in the mafia world.

I drew in a deep breath, forcing those thoughts away. I hoped my uncle had cared enough to arrange my marriage to someone that was at least kind.

Mia pouted, but we were out of time to mourn.

I stole a glance at myself in the mirror, making sure not a single strand of hair was out of place. My dark brown hair was pulled back in a bun with the veil carefully pinned into it. My dress had an off-the-shoulder neckline with intricately, hand-placed, lace, motifs and a diamond necklace glinted at my throat. The long sleeves were decorated with fabric-covered buttons, adding a traditional touch the *don* would appreciate. Beading trailed along the delicate fabric.

It was everything I'd ever wanted in a wedding dress. I'd always dreamed of my wedding day, even planning it out with my cousins when I was younger. We would play pretend with our dolls and squeal when we made them kiss.

Now, this dress no longer represented a bright future, but a funeral for the me I knew.

I grabbed the edge of the sheer veil and pulled it over my face, the entire world shrouded in lace. I crossed the room to Mia and pulled her into my arms, giving her a tight hug.

"I'll miss you," I whispered.

My eyes burned, my heart tearing in half.

Before today, I'd often wondered if I could ever truly love the man taking me away from everything I knew, but it was impossible to figure out. What kind of monster agreed to this sort of thing anyway?

She sniffled and I continued to hold her a few more moments, until I felt the hair on the back of my neck stand up.

My gaze swept to a man who stood at the end of the hall.

My shadow.

Luca Civello.

His dark eyes were fixed on me, watching me. Always watching.

When my uncle had met with me to announce my marriage, he had also promised that he would send one of his own men to be my guard. I wouldn't know anyone once I moved into my husband's house, so having someone familiar with me would be a relief. Luca was hand-picked, having proven that he was far more dangerous than even the *capos* of our family.

I'd never liked him, but at least he would remind me of home.

The opening notes of Ave Maria and the sound of a man's voice echoed through the hallway and a door opened. Mia's eyes averted as *Don* Avellino came toward us, two heavily armed men following him plus one other. Beside him walked his right-hand man, someone we all simply called J.

I didn't like him. The way he looked at me made my stomach curl. I also knew he was the one who had chosen my husband, helping my uncle strike the deal.

"Mia," I hissed. "Go."

"No!" she protested, squeezing me harder.

"*Mia,*" my uncle snapped. "To the chapel, *now*. The cere-mony is about to begin."

I pried her hands away, kissing her on the forehead before straightening and pulling my shoulders back. Mia let out a choked sob as she scurried away, leaving me with my uncle and the other men.

"She just wanted to see me one last time," I said.

"She disobeyed me," he growled.

"Now, now," J *tsked*, his tone unnervingly cheerful. He wore a suit and black gloves, the dye in his hair staining the edges of his scalp. I never understood how he'd become my uncle's right-hand man. "It's your niece's wedding day, *Don* Avellino. We should be happy."

I felt like vomiting.

My uncle held out his hand and I took it, ignoring the chill that ran down my spine.

"This will make our family stronger, *nipote*."

How many times had I heard that statement in the last few months?

"Yes, *zio*," I answered robotically.

He nodded and hooked his arm with mine, leading me toward the doors. Our footsteps echoed over the tiles in the hallway and my heart began to beat faster. I glanced over my shoulder, seeing J standing in the doorway we'd exited, watching me with a sleazy grin on his face.

I looked forward, meeting Luca Civello's eyes again as we passed him. He shook his head, looking away.

The chapel doors were opened for us, and as we approached my stomach did a slow somersault. People turned in their seats, eager to see the bride, and my gaze swept over them to the end of the aisle.

To my future husband.

Only...he wasn't a man.

"Oh gods," I whispered. "*No.*"

I was to be wed to a monster.

Chapter 1
Knives and Avocado Toast

10 years later

SERENA

The curtains of my bedroom windows were yanked open and I groaned as light poured in, disrupting my dark cave. I squinted, opening one eye and glaring at the man who dared to wake me up this way.

Luca ignored me, as always. His back to me, his broad shoulders casting a long shadow. I could see a line of sweat down his shirt, which meant he'd already gone on his morning run and done gods knew what else before the sun rose.

"I want to sleep in," I hissed. "My head hurts." It was true. My head felt like someone was taking an ice pick to it and the beams of light weren't helping.

I grabbed the blankets and pulled them over my head, hiding myself in the mound of warmth. Closing my eyes, I let out a soft sigh.

"No, no," Luca chided. "I don't think so."

I felt a hand grip the blankets and yelped as he tried to tear them off the bed. I held them tight to my body, ensuring he couldn't see me, and let out a fierce hiss.

"I'm naked! And my head hurts!"

"Then don't drink so much wine," he quipped. He threw a blanket back at me, the corner of his mouth almost tugging into a smile. He was freshly shaved, his sharp jaw and high cheekbones now visible. Even sweaty, he was sexy. He had soft dark brown hair that curled around his ears and muscles for days. For weeks. For years. "Breakfast is ready, *piccola regina*."

I blindly reached for a pillow and chucked it at him, but it landed on the floor in front of his feet. Hot or not, he annoyed the *fuck* out of me. I glared for a few moments, then craned my neck, looking at the alarm clock.

"It's not even seven," I protested. "*Luca*," I moaned.

"Up," Luca growled. "You're being lazy. You have training to do and your breakfast is getting cold."

He left before I could argue any further, pulling the door shut behind him.

I sighed, staring at the ceiling for a moment and gathering the willpower to go downstairs.

This had been my home for ten years now. Or prison, depending on how you looked at it. My husband, who I had only seen once in the last five years, was never here. Instead, it was just me, Luca, and the countless bodyguards and men that belonged to the Colchian mafia.

Ian kept this place locked down like a fortress. There were cameras everywhere, which I was certain he liked to look at. Spying on his obedient Italian wife.

"*Serena!*" Luca called, his tone dangerously close to true frustration.

A string of curses flew from my tongue, but I pushed the

sheet back and dragged myself out of bed. I went to my bathroom and changed quickly—pulling on high-waisted palazzo pants and a cropped silk shirt.

I pulled my dark hair back into a bun and glanced at my wedding ring atop a black tray next to the sink.

The diamond gleamed, even through the layer of dust, a reminder that Luca was right.

I had to get up.

I had training to do.

I sailed out of the bedroom and descended the sweeping staircase. The scent of eggs drew me to the right, my footsteps echoing throughout the cavernous house. There were moments I wished I could redecorate, but this place had never felt like my home, so I'd never bothered to ask. Not that I necessarily needed to, I doubted Colchian would care.

The decor was medieval, which wasn't surprising considering my husband was a monster. Not only a monster, but a dragon.

A mafia boss, who was also a dragon, owning a castle in California no longer felt like a stretch of the imagination.

The walls were brick, with stone pillars every ten feet and there was a burgundy runner in the hall leading to the kitchen. The kitchen was open and modern, the only room that was designed in a completely different fashion from the rest of the house.

There was a guard at every door and no matter what I tried, they never spoke to me. Not one fucking word. I walked past one of them, gliding into the kitchen—and then let out a gasp.

Thunk.

A flash of silver, then a knife buried into the doorway next to my head.

I stepped out of the way right as another flew towards me.

"You *sonofabitch*," I growled. "It's too fucking early, Luca!"

Luca didn't care. Someone had woken up on the wrong side of the bed this morning.

"Luca!" I yelled.

"Gotta work for your breakfast like the rest of us peasants," Luca taunted—and then proceeded to throw another knife at me.

This motherfucker.

Thunk. Thunk. Thunk.

Thunk.

I rolled to the floor, dodging right as the bastard launched more knives at me. Where in the hell had he gotten more knives? He normally stopped at five.

The tiles were covered in dents and cracks from what had become a weekly practice.

If I wasn't awake before, I was now. Another knife buried itself in the cabinet next to my head and I snatched it—standing briefly to fling it at Luca before dodging his advances.

I heard his dark chuckle and felt the thrill of our game kick in. Excitement dragged its tantalizing fingertips down my spine, sending a chill through me. I crawled towards the island at the center, only to feel his hand grab my ankle.

"Fuck," I gasped.

He'd snuck up on me.

I squealed as he dragged me back, giving a powerful kick straight to his gut. I flipped over as his hand loosened for a split second and managed to yank myself free.

He towered over me, his dark hair mussed. His eyes simmered with heat, a primal kind that always made me wonder if he wanted to kill me or fuck me.

Luca snarled and lunged for me. I grabbed one of the knives and brought it to his throat as he pinned me to the floor.

"I don't think so," he huffed.

He tightened his hold on my wrist and twisted. I cried out as pain flared, the blade falling to the ground.

He easily overpowered me with his big muscles. It wasn't fair.

I let out a frustrated growl, my ears ringing. I slammed my head up, smashing his nose with my forehead.

I felt a crunch and hesitated, panting as blood dripped onto my cheek, but Luca didn't stop.

His hand gripped my throat, squeezing.

"Luca!" I choked.

My mind began to churn, the high of being pinned under him like this a dangerous and intoxicating thrill.

I'd known him for ten years. And for that entire time, I'd fought the desire that currently had my stomach in knots.

His eyes darkened, his lips tugging into a menacing smile. "Tap out."

"*You—fucker*," I wheezed, but he only squeezed harder.

I slapped the floor with my palm three times and he let go, the two of us breathless. He leaned back, straddling me as his chest heaved. He wiped the blood trickling from his nose, smirking victoriously.

For a moment, I could see *him*, then his expression became stoic.

"Good," he said. "But not good enough. You hesitated."

"You were bleeding," I rasped, wiping his blood off my face

.

He was still straddling me, his muscled thighs pressing against my hips. He was wearing gray sweatpants and I couldn't help but look down. *Why the fuck did my husband let me have such a hot bodyguard?* Luca shook his head, sliding off me before I could actually get a look at what I wanted to see.

I had problems.

One of them was that my dear husband had sent me away

and locked me in a house surrounded by men who were not allowed to touch me. Not allowed to talk to me. Not allowed to do *anything* to me.

The good news was I'd been able to collect an entire arsenal of toys. At least they were always ready to go. I had an entire budget line for vibrators at this point.

Still...

Stop. Thinking about Luca in that way was strictly forbidden. At least until the sun went down and I was alone with those toys.

"If someone was trying to kill you, they would have succeeded just now. Besides, it's not like you to be scared of a little blood." He glowered at me, his brows drawing together.

I studied him. I had tried to put the puzzle pieces of Luca together, but they never seemed to fit. He wore a mask at all times, and although there were moments I could see the man beneath, I often wondered if I knew him.

He was a mystery. A mystery I wanted to spread my legs for, which only made me more frustrated.

If he treated me like a little sister or something, it would be easier to ignore the draw I had to him. But he didn't. He treated me like exactly who I was—the convenient wife of a mafia boss he'd been entrusted to guard with his life.

I sat up, rubbing my throat and glaring at him. "Whatever."

"Not whatever," he growled. "You asked me to teach you, but you don't listen."

"I'm not even awake yet," I muttered, getting to my feet. "I haven't had coffee and I have a fucking hangover. It's not even—"

He moved in a blur, spinning me around. Luca slammed me against the kitchen island hard enough to give me whiplash and I gasped, tears springing to my eyes as he pinned my arms behind my back and held me there.

"They won't care," he hissed, his voice low and deadly serious. "They won't fucking care. I need you to be able to protect yourself."

He held me like that a little longer, his body pressed against mine. For a moment, I imagined what it would be like if he wasn't my bodyguard.

"You fit so well against me," I whispered.

Oh fuck. *Fuck.* That was a thought that was supposed to stay inside my head and not come out of my mouth.

His entire body stiffened and he immediately let go, muttering under his breath. I turned to glare at him, but he was already heading toward the espresso machine.

"Lavender or hazelnut?" he asked, like nothing had happened.

That's how it always was.

Any time there was even an ember of chemistry, we both made sure to snuff it out like it was a raging house fire. Then we'd pretend.

Pretend, pretend, pretend.

At least, that's how it was for me. I had no idea what went on inside his head and he had never let me in. There was a side to him that he didn't allow me to see, and I'd never been brave enough to push him to let me in.

I knew that the Luca who took care of me and the Luca who worked for the mafia were different men.

I rolled my eyes. "Lavender. You're not my servant, Luca. I can make my own coffee."

"Eat your breakfast."

I fought the urge to flip him off.

I knew he was a killer. Once, someone had broken into the house and I'd heard the screams as he'd tortured them. Those screams had followed me into my dreams, forever staining my mind and turning the angel wings I sometimes gave Luca crimson red.

I noticed a couple white hairs nestled in Luca's dark mane. We'd aged. I'd grown up. And yet, we were two adults playing pretend.

When we'd started these charades, it was because I'd been angry and scared. A mafia princess swept away to a place she didn't know, to a world she didn't belong in. Locked in a pretty castle and promptly forgotten.

I got tired of that quickly.

I wanted to be able to save myself.

I might have been raised to play the part of a woman who was no more than a trophy, but that would never be who I was. I was smart and capable of anything I set my mind to. Any talents I had were ones I worked my ass off to create, hours and hours spent practicing to hone a skill set that didn't come natural to me.

I didn't want to need Luca. I wanted him to be able to leave me, eventually, and live the rest of his life in peace. But, until I could beat him in our fights, that wouldn't happen.

Part of me hoped it would never happen.

The espresso machine hissed as he made my lavender latte. I went to the stove and made a plate—scrambled eggs and toast with avocado. Strawberries and tangerines were sliced and ready as well.

I popped a piece of tangerine into my mouth, the flavor making me moan. He really knew how to pick fruit, which I'd always been thankful for because I did not.

I carried my plate to the small table next to a massive window that overlooked the garden and pool. I could see the figures of guards with guns, all moving in their scheduled rounds like clockwork. One would go left, one would go right, one would switch out with another—a synchronized dance.

Luca walked over and set my latte down.

"Aw," I teased, grinning. "You made a heart today."

Whenever Luca made my coffee, he always surprised me with different latte art. I loved it. Any time I tried, the milk made a giant foam blob in the center.

"Yes," he chuckled. Then he took a deep breath, drawing my attention.

He had that look. The one that told me he was about to say something I didn't want to hear. Morning light fell across him, highlighting his muscles in artistic brush strokes. "What?" I asked, frowning.

"I will be gone tomorrow," he said softly.

My appetite immediately soured. Perhaps it was possessive of me, but Luca and I hadn't been apart in ten years. Was that healthy? No. Probably not. But the idea of him leaving made me feel nervous, anxious, and concerned. My stomach clenched, my heart squeezing. "What do you mean?" I asked. "Where are you going?"

He grimaced, then his expression returned to unreadable. "*Don* Colchian has called for me. He's coming to the house tomorrow night and expects me to pick him up. After that, I've been asked to leave for a couple days. He asked that I take some time off."

My blood turned to ice. Ian... was coming here?

This house was far, far away from the city of Moirai. The two times I'd seen him, he had demanded that I come to him. He never came to me. He hadn't stepped foot in this house in all the time I'd been married to him.

"Have someone else do it," I whispered. "I need you here."

I felt a prick of guilt. I'd never thought of Luca needing a vacation. He'd never asked for one, and it hadn't crossed my mind.

"I don't want you to leave me. Stay," I pleaded.

"I can't, *piccola regina. Don* Colchian has given the orders. He called this morning."

That explained why he'd been so rough in our knife dodging practice.

Fuck.

What the hell was my husband doing? No calls, no texts, nothing—for years. Now, out of the blue, he was coming here?

I didn't like it one bit. That either meant something had happened or someone had died.

"He gave me a list of what he wants you to wear upon his arrival."

I grit my teeth and looked away. "What would he do if I said no? Kill me?"

"There are worse things than death, Serena."

I stared out the window, collecting myself. I felt the rage coiling in my gut, a snake that had only become more venomous with age. "I am his wife," I said. "I demand that you send someone else, Luca. If you need a vacation, then we can plan it some other time. A time when he isn't here. That's an order."

My dream was to send Luca away...but maybe that was just a lie I'd been telling myself.

I wasn't sure I could live without him.

My gaze fell down to the coffee, to the heart he'd poured.

"*Serena,*" he whispered, his voice husky.

"Go," I demanded, cutting him off. "Give me the list. I'll see to it later."

"I've already had the clothes bought for you. And the lingerie...and other things."

Lingerie.

My heart beat a little faster. "Give me the fucking list."

Luca stared at me for a moment and then pulled a piece of paper from his pocket, handing it to me. I snatched it away, looking over what was scrawled there.

Three lace lingerie sets, four leather sets, a riding crop, a collar, a paddle, three floggers, a—

What the fuck? This wasn't just lingerie. I may not have been experienced, but I'd watched and read enough stuff to know this was well beyond leather and lace.

What the hell did he think he was doing? Starting a BDSM club?

"This isn't a fucking lingerie list," I seethed.

Luca snatched the list back, shoving it in his pocket. "I took care of it, Serena. You don't even need to worry."

"You took care of buying all of this for me?"

"Yes," he said, flatly.

I stared at my food, my thoughts racing.

Was he coming here to touch me? To do the thing we'd never done on our wedding night?

What if he wanted to get me pregnant?

I reached for my latte, ignoring the way my fingers trembled. I took a sip, forcing my gaze to focus.

"Do you think he wants to sleep with me? Get me pregnant?"

Luca was silent. I felt the tension between us increase, thick enough to be cut with one of the knives that littered the kitchen.

"I won't let him," Luca whispered.

I shook my head, anger making it difficult to drink or eat. "You can't do anything. You wont be able to stop him if he wants to fuck me, because you're taking off for a couple days."

"He won't touch you," Luca snarled. "I won't let him."

"How? You'll be gone."

"Then I won't go," he said. "Fuck. *Serena*."

I blinked back tears. "Why couldn't it have been you?"

Luca went deadly silent, his gaze burning holes into me. "Serena...I don't know what you mean."

Of course he didn't. Fuck. Embarrassment had my cheeks flaming. I was humiliated. He didn't think about me the way I thought about him. It was a one-sided fantasy.

"Leave," I whispered. "I need some time."

Luca turned without another word. I watched him stalk away, his shoulders tense as he ducked through the doorway.

For ten fucking years I had been living this life, and I was done.

I couldn't do this anymore.

Chapter 2
Princess

LUCA

The dragon was coming to claim his princess, but she was *mine*.

She was mine from the moment I had laid eyes on her.

I made it to my room, but my cock was already hard. I turned the lock and went to my bed, my hand already sliding into my sweatpants.

Why couldn't it have been you?

"Fuck," I whispered.

She'd never said something like that to me. Something about today had been different though. It was like she'd known there was something coming.

My blood boiled with rage. I hated him. He'd taken her from her life and left her here to rot.

I should have been the one to marry her. To have her, to love her. But I didn't come from money, and the only thing I'd ever been able to do was stay by her side and protect her.

Asking me to leave her... The dragon knew exactly what he was doing.

Ten years ago, I'd made a deal with him. One that had changed my destiny, and perhaps Serena's too. There'd been so many things that led to that, shadows that followed me to this day, but it had been worth it.

That's what the monster had always been known for. Deals. Making people offer up their souls just for a morsel of happiness. His iridescent eyes haunted me, the way he'd looked at me like I was nothing but something to be pitied.

We'd made a deal and it tortured me.

I gasped, my cock throbbing in my hand as I stroked myself. I grabbed my secret phone from behind the mattress, opening it to look at pictures of her.

Serena.

My *piccola regina*. Little queen.

I watched her every move. I'd been watching over her for a decade, keeping track of everything she did.

At first it had been for protection. When we'd come to this place, I added cameras throughout the property in case someone tried to break in. Even in her bedroom. I was determined to keep her safe, to make sure no harm ever came to her.

But then I'd found myself checking the cameras too often.

Watching as she undressed.

Watching her sleep.

Watching her touch herself.

Fuck. I grunted, finding the picture that had me stroking my cock faster and faster, my breaths coming in soft pants. It was of her smiling, wearing nothing but white lace lingerie in her room.

I'd always wondered what she was smiling about.

What if she was thinking about me?

"Serena," I gasped.

Hot cum shot from my cock, my back arching as I came so hard my vision started to dot. I collapsed back onto my bed, groaning as my cum spilled over my hand and sweatpants.

I wished it was going inside of her.

I moaned. I couldn't think about that.

I couldn't think about actually ever taking her. She didn't think about me like that. To her, I was like family, right?

Why couldn't it have been you?

She didn't mean that. She meant someone like me. Someone who took care of her the way she deserved. Serena was precious, a princess who deserved to have the entire world at her feet.

Not to be locked away and forgotten in a castle.

She belongs to me, Mr. Civello. I'm only allowing you to stay at her side because I believe you will protect her. And you may lust after her, dream of fucking her, of tasting her. But she will never be yours.

Colchian's words haunted me.

I wished I had never made that deal with the dragon. I should have killed him then, but I would have lost Serena.

And I couldn't lose her.

My muscles relaxed and I sighed, throwing my pillow to the side. I took another look at the picture of Serena, running my fingertip over the shape of her body.

The Fates were cruel.

Over the past decade, I'd found ways to keep my desires hidden from her, but it had sent me down a dark path of obsession.

When I was with her, I was her sweet and loyal shadow. I made her food, I made her coffee, I did everything for her. I served her, worshiped her.

But when I wasn't with her, my imagination ran wild.

Desire burned holes into my soul, leaving nothing but a tattered page of unrequited love.

I did things that would scare her, but I couldn't stop...

I pulled my hand from my sweatpants and slid out of bed, heading to the adjoining bathroom. I stripped and turned on the shower, getting under the hot water.

When I was fifteen, my father sold me to Serena's family to pay a debt. I never saw him again, and unsurprisingly, discovered he'd been killed shortly after I joined the Avellino mafia. At first, I was treated poorly, but it didn't take long to prove myself.

I grew up on the streets of Catania, a port city in Sicily. At first glance, one wouldn't know that the beautiful landscape was controlled by one ruthless family, but it was.

I learned how to survive. Joining the beasts who ruled my world gave me the opportunity to finally be able to feed and clothe myself.

Selling me like cheap cattle was the only good thing my father ever did for me.

Then, I met Serena again. The niece of the *Don*, the orphaned mafia princess. She'd been so sad, a broken doll that had to learn to walk in a world that wanted to see her shatter.

She'd never noticed me. She had no idea about the things I'd done to protect her leading up to her uncle sending me with her. She didn't remember the past or what had happened so long ago.

I had begged him to let me go with her.

Well, *blackmailed* him to let me be her bodyguard. His right-hand man had given me info that I had been able to use against him, all in exchange for occasional updates about Serena's life. Once a year or so, I'd receive a call from the infamous J. He'd ask his questions, I'd answer them, and then we'd move on with our lives.

Part of me wondered if he actually cared for her, but I doubted it.

These men who behaved as though they owned the world were disgusting. Her uncle was one of them, and I had brought him to his knees...forcing him to do what I wanted. It had been the catalyst for me discovering who I was.

Ian was next. Eventually, I would discover how to bring him down. I would find his weakness and use it against him. I would twist the knife in his back and watch him bleed out.

One day.

Maybe not now.

But one day, I would rescue my princess from him.

One day, he would wish he'd never met me.

The hot water brought me back to the present and I let out a long breath, running my fingers through my dark hair. My muscles ached slightly, which made me happy. I was rarely sore after the regiments I put myself through on a daily basis.

Serena was improving. Slowly, but surely, I was turning my little queen into a beautiful killer.

My thoughts began to spiral as she invaded my mind, my cock starting to throb again.

This morning had almost broken me.

When I'd pinned her down and choked her, I'd had to use every ounce of self-control. She had no idea how much restraint it took for me not to rip her clothes off and fuck her on the floor.

I could tell she liked it too. She'd liked being choked, liked being trapped under me like that. The way her breaths had sounded, the noises she made...

Lust pumped through me again, making my blood run hot. The dragon would return to us and there was only one thing he could possibly want. The list he'd given me had been specific—outlining all the types of things he wished her to wear.

He didn't see her the way I did.

She was the center of my universe, the reason my world kept spinning.

But to him?

She was only a prize he'd won ten years ago. A toy he could break.

Hot water poured over my shoulders and back. I planted a hand against the shower wall, unable to keep my thoughts at bay as I imagined watching the two of them together.

Would he take her tomorrow night?

It filled me with so much anger, yet my cock hardened all over again.

Would he fuck her in his monster form?

Would he try to get her pregnant?

Tears blurred my vision, hatred building as I gripped my cock and began to stroke again.

It wasn't fair. I wanted to be her first.

I wanted to fuck her.

She's mine.

I groaned, swallowing hard as I imagined filling her with my cock and seed. It was primal and fucked up, but I didn't care. I would wake her every morning with my cock between her legs if I could. I would worship her pussy the same way I worshiped her in other ways, making her cry out for the gods.

But she still belonged to *him.*

A cry tore from me as I came again, tears rolling down my cheeks as cum shot from my cock. I stroked myself until I was completely finished and then huffed, planting my hands on the shower wall.

I needed to get dressed and go back to her. I'd already left her for too long. Even if she was upset with me, I still needed to be at her side. It was where I belonged.

With a sigh, I washed myself quickly, the tension finally

melting some. Within ten minutes, I was dried off and dressed —wearing a nice shirt and pants, with a jacket perfect for hiding weapons.

I stared at myself in the mirror, my gaze sweeping over my appearance. Anyone who didn't know me would see a wealthy, unassuming man. The dimples helped the facade too.

Those who truly knew me were the people who died by my hand.

Those were the souls that got to see me as I really was. The darkness unleashed, the beast who was more monster than human.

But not for Serena.

Never to Serena.

She was the only constant light in my world.

My phone rang on the counter, buzzing against the marble. I scowled at the interruption, seeing the letter 'J' light up the screen.

I answered it brusquely. "Hello?"

"Mr. Civello," the smooth voice said. "We haven't caught up in some time. How is the princess doing?"

"She's doing well," I said, crossing my arms. I was always torn on how much to tell him. Not that there was ever anything out of the ordinary. But ten years of giving him updates on Serena made me feel like I had a babysitter watching my back.

"Any changes?" J asked.

I felt my stomach clench. "Well, today she found out her husband is coming back home for a couple of days and she's not happy about it. Other than that, nothing has changed in the last few months."

"Interesting," he mused. "Of course that bastard won't let her live peacefully."

I could hear men murmuring in the background, followed

by a couple gunshots. I scowled, listening intently. "Indeed." I hated Colchian, but I didn't trust J enough to say so.

"He will kill you if you don't play your cards right," J warned. "I know you want Serena for yourself, Luca."

I gritted my teeth. "Did you have any other questions?"

He let out a dark chuckle, continuing. "Your day will come, Just don't let the dragon kill you first. Keep me updated on her. If anything *strange* happens, let me know."

"Okay." I ended the call and put my phone down, thinking.

Part of me wondered if he knew what I knew about Serena.

Chapter 3
Little Killer

Luca

I had left her alone for an hour, but I refused to give her any more time or space. I was furious Ian was coming back, but keeping ourselves apart wouldn't help anything.

I left my room, pausing in the hall to listen. Her room was across from mine, with the door open I could see she wasn't in there. I looked to my right, watching as one of the guards visibly stiffened.

Maybe they knew the *real* me too.

When I first came to this castle, I made an example of several guards. Part of the deal with the dragon was that I would run the security here, exactly as I pleased.

They didn't look at what was mine. Talk to what was mine. Even breathe next to her. They were to only engage if she were in danger.

Otherwise, they would lose their life. Or one of their family members would. I always made them choose. Over the years, how many chose to save themselves stopped surprising me.

"Serena!" I called, going downstairs.

I had given her enough time to digest the news of the Colchian's return, right? I didn't like to be away from her.

I paused at the foot of the staircase, listening.

"Serena?"

No answer.

Alarm bells began to ring in my mind.

A low growl left me and I stormed up to the guards. "Where did she go?"

"She hasn't left the kitchen, sir."

Wrong. She would have answered me.

I marched into the kitchen. The table was empty, her food barely touched. *Godsdamnit, woman, you have to eat. Why must I feed you like a baby bird?*

"Serena!" I barked.

"I'm here!"

Her voice was faint. I narrowed my gaze and left the kitchen, stepping outside to the terrace. The porch wrapped around the back of the home.

I knew where she was now.

I moved quickly, mentally noting to punish the guard who had so blatantly failed at his duty to keep track of her. I rounded the corner and stopped, my heart skipping a beat.

Serena had a gun in her hands and was pointing it straight at me. Three dead guards were on the ground around her, their bodies unmoving.

Confusion washed over me, but it was brief.

I knew what had happened here.

My little queen had finally snapped.

That shouldn't turn me on, but it did. I'd have to rewatch

the security videos later. The idea of her bringing them down made my cock start to swell.

Stop.

"Serena? What's going on?" I asked, keeping my voice soft.

She stared at me, her dark eyes filled with vitriol. I could feel the rage rolling off her in waves. Her dark hair tumbled down her back, her face speckled red.

I'd seen her like this before.

"You're going to take me away," she seethed, her voice cold. "I'm not fucking a monster. I want to leave this place."

"Put the gun down, Serena." My heart began to beat faster, my blood rushing. The tension from today felt like it was at a breaking point and realization dawned on me.

For ten years, we'd been doing this. Had our game of house finally come to an end?

We squared off. I felt the thrill of it. I felt proud of her.

"Put the gun down," I repeated.

"No," she growled. "Get me the fuck out of here, Luca. I won't do this anymore. I'm not his puppet. I'm not his obedient little wife. I was never given a choice about how my life was supposed to go, but I'm not a prisoner."

Not a prisoner.

She was though. More than I'd ever let her know. But as long as she continued to believe Ian was the reason, it didn't matter. Right? She *should* hate him.

I noticed that her hand wasn't shaking, her gaze was firm, her voice unwavering. Pride swelled in my chest. She stood with blood pooling at her feet, her eyes searing me with a type of heat that made me want to kneel in front of her.

My queen wasn't so little anymore, was she?

"Take me away," she demanded. "That's an order."

I heard guards calling out to one another, the sound of feet on stone as they ran toward us. They were good for nothing.

"Put the gun down," I ordered. "Please."

"Get me out of this fucking place, Luca."

"I can't," I said softly. "Serena, I can't. Ian is keeping you here. And he's coming for you. We can't escape him, but I promise to make sure he doesn't hurt you."

I took a slow step toward her, my hands raised in front of me in surrender. She pulled the trigger, the bullet whizzing right by my head and grazing my ear.

The sting of it went straight to my cock.

"Take me away," she pleaded again, but this time, her voice had a tremble in it.

She would break.

And I would be the one to pick up the pieces.

"You killed three men, Serena. You're a murderer now," I reminded her. *A murderer like me. A sinner like me.* "Why?"

"Because they wouldn't let me leave. I'm tired of this. I'm not going to stay here any longer. I *demand* you to let me leave!"

I lunged for her, snatching the gun like a viper. She cried out as I grabbed her wrist, then she slammed her fist straight into my nose.

Fuck.

My head snapped back, the force of her punch something I'd never experienced before. This was the second time she'd hit me in the nose today, but this felt different. My grip on her loosened and she tore away.

My vision dotted for a moment but I recovered, reaching for her. As she began to turn and take off, I tackled her to the ground, splashing in the pools of blood.

She landed on her side and kicked back, narrowly missing my groin. She was actually fighting me.

Fuck. I was proud. *Good girl.*

I grunted as she rolled me over, slamming me against the

ground and straddling my hips. She clocked me in the jaw, letting out a fierce scream before leaning in close, her lips hovering above mine.

We both froze, our breaths labored.

"I hate you," she whispered. "I hate you, Luca. You were supposed to protect me, but you failed. He's coming for me, he's going to take me, and you won't stop him."

"Serena," I croaked. Hearing her say I failed her hurt more than a bullet could. "*Stop this.* I will make you something else to eat, then we can sit on the couch and watch a show. We'll have an inside day today."

"Don't speak to me like a child," she sneered. "I want to go away."

"We can't, my love," I whispered so softly that only she would hear.

She stared at me for a moment, then her body went limp. I watched as all the energy drained from her, tears filling her eyes.

"What are we doing?" she asked.

Fuck. I hated seeing her like this.

I leaned up, wrapping my arms around her. I glared at the guards who finally arrived and sneered. "Get rid of the bodies then leave us. I want all guards to leave the house for the rest of the day."

"Sir—"

"Would you like to be the fourth body?"

No one argued after that. I could feel their resentment, their wariness. But they knew what would happen if they pissed me off.

Serena's arms wrapped around my neck as I lifted her. Blood covered us, dripping onto the patio. She began to shiver and I knew tears would soon follow. I made a crooning noise and whispered so only she would hear.

"Don't let them see you cry, *piccola regina*."

She went still. My expression hardened as I carried her past the guards, heading back through the kitchen. Bloodied footprints left a trail behind us as I went down the hall then up the grand staircase, taking her to my room.

I kicked the door shut behind us, already thinking about how I was going to convince the dragon not to take his princess.

THREE FATES MAFIA

LUCA

Chapter 4
The Dragon and the Knight

Ian

A knock at the door interrupted my phone call. I frown as it's pushed open, one of my men poking his head in.

Jack knew not to disturb me unless it's urgent.

"Sir," he cleared his throat. "There's a problem at the castle."

Fuck. I held a finger up, signaling to be silent. "Hey Damon," I said to the monster on the other line. "I need to go. Something's come up."

"Fine," Damon sighed. "Good luck. Will you be at the event this Sunday? Everyone is going. The Three Fates are holding an auction and ball."

"Yes," I groaned. "I'm aware. You know I will be there since attendance is required."

Damon chuckled as I hung up, letting out a frustrated breath. It was only Tuesday and already this week had become far busier than I'd planned. Since reading the letter from the Three Fates two days ago, everything had taken a turn. The Three Fates eye had stared back at me, and I had known before I opened it that my life was going to change. And not for the better.

"What's going on, Jack?" I asked. He hesitated and I raised a brow. "Come in and shut the door."

He nodded and did as I commanded. He stood in front of my desk, his Adam's apple bobbing as he swallowed nervously. "Three men have been killed at the castle."

Gods damn it all.

"Three? Why?" I questioned, trying not to sound too surprised. Hearing about three deaths in the mafia was nothing, except when it happened at the castle.

"Well, we don't know what happened yet. I put a blackout on the footage and sent it to you to review before anyone else, as protocol states."

Yes, indeed. Especially the footage at the castle.

"Good. Who was the killer?" Luca needed to stop killing every fucking guard I hired—

"It appears that it was her, sir."

"Her?" I hissed. "Who?"

"Your wife. Mrs. Colchian."

What? I frowned. "Serena Avellino murdered three of our highly trained men? The ones I recruited from the Navy and Special Ops?"

"Yes, sir."

"Serena—the woman who hasn't left the house I gave her in ten years, except to see me twice? That Serena?"

"Yes, sir."

Well then. "Okay, I'll take care of it."

"The men aren't happy, sir. Her personal guard has already been a problem, but with her—"

"I said I'll take care of it. I'll call if I need anything else, Jack. Your job is to make sure no one steps out of line."

He nodded, recognizing I was clearly dismissing him. He turned and disappeared through my office door, shutting it behind him.

Jack was a good man. There was a reason I chose to have him lead most of my men. But sometimes, he didn't read my tone the way I wished he would. Mortals could be annoying in that way.

I stared for a moment, my thoughts already churning.

Serena. My *wife.*

I glanced at my left hand, at the silver band on my finger. I wasn't sure why I bothered wearing my wedding ring, besides the fact that it offered a sort of protection from the women and men who threw themselves at me. Not that I wasn't interested in them, but I was technically married and had morals... even if I was a monster.

My lips pressed together and I turned toward the massive windows that overlooked Moirai bay. I owned a building downtown, and while it wasn't as impressive as the Helm, it was still stunning. I had one floor for my office and another floor that I used as a temporary home on days I didn't feel like flying or driving to my house outside the city limits.

The sun glittered across the water, the clouds calling to me. I felt the urge to break my form, my shoulder blades burning, seeking the wings that should have been there.

I walked back to my desk and sat with a groan. A creature like me wasn't supposed to be stuck in a fucking chair all day. I leaned back, popping my spine before hunching forward.

I would never get used to this form. I was a dragon crammed into a mortal body, running a mafia for three old hags who controlled our lives.

Serena, Serena. What did you do now? I logged on to my

computer. My phone buzzed with multiple messages, rattling on the desk.

I was supposed to see her tomorrow. I knew it would upset her, but I hadn't expected her to murder people over it. Not that it was a big deal to me, but humans usually didn't take it so lightly.

Well, unless you were someone like Luca.

Sighing, I pulled up the security footage from the castle. Three camera angles appeared on the screen. *Gods, she was beautiful.* It had been a long time since I'd seen my wife and she was even more stunning than I remembered.

And now that I knew the truth about her...

I wondered.

Who was the woman I'd whisked away from the Italian mafia all those years ago?

Marrying Serena had given me the opportunity to expand my branch of the Three Fates Mafia and the power to put any enemies in their place. My branch now trafficked weapons, dabbled in cryptocurrency, and oversaw many businesses in the city.

Sometimes I regretted my arranged marriage. She'd been so young, barely eighteen. But back then, she was a tool I, unfortunately, had to use to get ahead in the world. But now?

Now, she was a grown woman.

I watched as she came out of the doors that led to the kitchen. The sunlight caught her dark hair. I leaned in with a frown, seeing red speckles on her shirt.

Was that blood?

A low growl left me, but I let the video continue. I watched as she rounded the corner.

She raised a hand, saying something to one of the guards. He said nothing in response. The others stiffened, but were clearly ignoring her as well.

I watched as Serena shouted then reached for one of their guns. That's when chaos broke out. The guard shoved her backwards and rage burned through me when her head hit the ground hard. She seemed to shake it off quickly, returning to her feet. One of the other guards jumped in—and suddenly golden light flashed, blinding all the cameras for a split second.

What the fuck was that?

Serena stood there, clearly in shock. Three bodies now lay around her, blood staining the gray stones crimson. She still held the gun in her hand.

I took a moment to let my rage subside. There was no point being angry at a dead man, even if he had hurt my wife.

Perhaps I'd let her become a fantasy in my mind, but Serena was a treasure to me. One I hadn't touched, one I sometimes dreamed about, and one I certainly wanted no one else touching.

I watched as Luca appeared, running for her. Their interaction made me grit my teeth. I watched as he tackled her to the ground, watched as she maneuvered herself on top of him, then punched him in the face.

Well, that part wasn't so bad.

I watched as the other guards finally appeared, much too late.

I pulled out a notepad. I jotted down a couple notes, then rewound the video feed.

Most of the guards would need to be replaced or retrained. Their response time was fucking unacceptable.

I had more questions.

With a few clicks, I pulled up the entire camera system and navigated to those in the house. I changed the time frame to a few minutes before the incident, feeling my blood start to boil again.

Luca had Serena pinned to the ground, his hands around her neck.

"What the fuck is going on?" I muttered.

I backtracked further to when Serena first came into the kitchen.

Luca was throwing *knives* at her.

I shook my head in disbelief and watched as she dodged them. Rolling through the kitchen like a damn assassin, avoiding being stabbed by the blades. Their fight came to an end as he rounded the kitchen island, grabbing her by the ankle and bringing her to the ground. She headbutted him, then I watched as he choked my wife, ignoring the way both of my cocks began to harden.

Once she tapped out and Luca let go of her neck, he remained seated on top of her for longer than I liked. Then, as if they hadn't just tried to kill each other, he got up and walked to the espresso machine.

What the fuck?

I'd left her alone with him for too long. This was absurd.

And dangerous.

I realized my talons had come out and were now digging into the wood of my desk. I retracted them, holding in a smoky breath.

There was clearly chemistry between them. Even though I couldn't hear what was being said, the two of them moved like dancers around a flame. One they wouldn't touch, wouldn't acknowledge, but still burned all the same.

I felt a prickle of jealousy.

I'd never pursued Serena. Had never given myself to her. I'd used her, and to smother the guilt I felt, had done my best to give her a life of luxury. I never cared for mortals, but there was something about her that made me want to give her the best—even though I kept her away from my life. Like a shadow, she was always present in my mind. While I tried to ignore that shadow most of the time, it was always there.

I wasn't a good guy. I liked to kill, I liked to torture. I liked to use people's weaknesses to my advantage.

Serena had always been too pure, so I'd done my best to keep her away from the darkness that surrounded me. My life was dangerous and I had brought her into it, unsure if she would survive. But now...?

Maybe it was finally time I treated her like she was mine.

I had planned to go to her eventually... right? My thoughts continually returned to her over the past decade, which was only a blink of time for me. For her, though, it was much longer.

Over the past year, the city of Moirai had changed. With the death of one demigod and the emergence of a new one, the power balance was starting to shift.

Not to mention, the demigod was now mated and married to Damon and the other two men who, together, formed the cursed monster Cerberus.

I'd known those three monsters for centuries and never imagined they might fall for someone like her. I'd seen Damon make mistakes that had changed his life–all because of Melinoe, better known as the infamous M. But, he'd found his happy ending. It was painful to see because it made me long for something I'd never allowed myself to have.

When you'd been alive as long as I had, emotions became more and more stale. Time was cruel that way. Initially, I had disagreed with a demigod being mated to monsters—but their happiness was infectious.

It made me wonder if I really had to be alone.

Serena Avellino had been the prize I'd won for partnering with the mafia in Italy. They truly believed they were ruling Europe now, but that was untrue.

I owned everything.

All of it.

Even their enemies.

I moved them like chess pieces on the board of life and death. It was the only thing that made me feel alive.

Now, I realized that maybe I'd fucked up with her. I had left her alone in the care of a known killer, relying on the fact that he loved her.

But love untouched could turn into obsession.

The way Luca looked at Serena was exactly that.

Obsession.

I could see it from here.

The knight's armor had finally rusted, and he'd become the bastard I'd always known he was.

The time had come for me to rescue her from him, and put her on the mafia throne. Bring her into my world, protect her, and keep our secrets safe.

Especially the one in that letter.

"Fuck," I sighed.

I kept the footage going, then leaned forward again with a frown. I watched as Luca handed her a list, which visibly upset her. Their confrontation ended with him leaving Serena alone in the kitchen.

I could see the outline of his cock growing hard as he walked away.

"You perverted son of a bitch," I muttered.

I chose to follow Luca instead of Serena, watching him rush down the hall and up the stairs to his room. He went inside and I paused the video, looking through the list of all the cameras on the left side of my screen.

"Of course."

None of the cameras showed anything, clearly having been disabled.

All of them but one.

This camera gave me a view of the edge of his bed. More than likely it was one of the micro cameras I'd hidden in the house. Those were harder to detect and couldn't be seen with the naked eye.

I watched as he reached behind the mattress and pulled out a phone. I could see only part of his body, but I knew he was touching himself.

My cocks throbbed in response, a reminder that it had been far too long since I'd taken someone to my bed.

Hell, it had been far too long since I'd taken someone like Luca.

I smiled to myself, thinking about the deal he made with me when Serena and I were married.The things he'd done to seal that deal...

I had to admit—I preferred it when the mortals fucked us monsters instead of fighting us. Made things a lot smoother.

So.

Luca had thrown knives at my wife.

Choked her.

Upset her.

Left her.

Gone upstairs to his room.

And masturbated to what I assumed were photos of her.

Serena had then gone outside and killed three men with a strange flash of light.

Meanwhile, I was sitting here knowing her secret—but wondering if Luca had broken our deal.

I had bigger things to think about.

But I had to know.

I followed them until I realized the cameras had caught up to the present.

If he was touching her, he was doing it right now.

I hated that I couldn't see everything. Hated that only one camera worked.

I waited and waited.

He could be fucking her.

He could be touching what was mine.

What was he doing to her?

Had he taken her, finally, after all this time?

He knew what would happen if he broke our deal.

But maybe...Maybe he didn't care anymore.

Chapter 5
Wash Away My Sins

Serena

I couldn't breathe.

Blood covered my entire body, my clothes were completely soaked. It was sticky with a metallic smell, and clung to me in a way that made me nauseous.

"I'm gonna throw up."

Luca rushed me to his bathroom, plopping me in front of the toilet just in time for me to retch into it. Anything I had eaten this morning came right back up, my mind spinning.

"Gross," I whispered, then threw up again.

What had I done?

I killed them.

Why? How?

I didn't know, didn't understand. Something inside of me had snapped. A rage from some dark, unknown, place within swept over me and I'd killed those men. Their strength had paled in comparison to my own. The light that had surrounded me made me feel like a god.

I gagged, dry heaving at this point. My stomach was completely empty. Luca ran his hand up and down my back, murmuring words of comfort in Italian. I tuned him out, my heart beating so hard that I could feel it in my skull.

Why? Why did I do this?

Killer. Killer. Killer.

I couldn't drown out the dark chant, my thoughts hammering it into my soul. I could feel the adrenaline rush from earlier slowly draining away.

"Serena," Luca cooed softly. "We need to get you cleaned up. I'll start the shower for you—"

"Don't leave me," I rasped.

I reached out and gripped his shirt, tears blurring my vision.

"You can't leave me, Luca."

"You need to shower. We need to get this blood off you and get you into some fresh clothes."

"Then shower with me. I don't care. I can't be alone ri— right now." My words broke, a sob racking my entire body. I squeezed my eyes shut, but all I could see was red.

Killer. Killer. Killer.

Luca cursed. "I can't, Serena. I can't be with you like that. It's inappropriate."

Be with me like *what?* "Luca. You have seen me throw up and cry. You've been there for me when I've had viruses or the flu. Please. Start the shower."

He grabbed my face, tilting it up so I would look at him.

My stomach did a slow flip. In the sunlight, his eyes always reminded me of honey, but right now, they were entirely black. For a moment, I wondered if I was being held by a man or a demon.

His jaw was stiff, his lips pressed into a hard line. Blood speckled his warm beige skin, his dark hair still damp from the shower he'd taken earlier. There was a faint scar through one of his eyebrows. It had always been there but I'd never asked how he'd gotten it.

I wanted to know.

I wanted to know him.

I wanted him.

I sucked in a breath and it sounded like a gods damned lawn mower. "Please," I whispered.

"Fine," he acquiesced. "If your husband finds out, I'm a dead man, Serena."

He let go of me and stood, crossing the bathroom to his shower. I noticed blood was smeared all over the floor while he started the shower, waiting for the water to heat up.

I focused on him, trying to forget everything I'd done minutes before. How could he even stand to be near me right now?

Tears began to trail down my cheeks, a wave of numbness rushing over me.

Luca sighed, tugging his jacket off and tossing it onto the floor. He then grabbed the bottom of his shirt, pulling it over his head, and I felt a deep heat emerge.

Maybe I wasn't completely numb.

He turned away from the shower, facing me, his muscles rippling as he began to unclasp his belt. I inhaled sharply, my gaze falling to his hands.

I was going to see him naked.

Oh, gods.

This was not the time to be getting turned on. I'd just murdered three men, and I was still covered in their blood. Drenched in it. And yet...

Luca watched me, his expression unreadable. His pants fell to the floor, followed by his boxer briefs.

Fuck.

Fuck, fuck, fuck.

I'd seen men online. I'd watched all sorts of things, but there was nothing like seeing someone so damn perfect in person.

He was hard.

The realization sent an electric buzz all over my skin.

"Undress, Serena," he whispered.

I suddenly felt frozen in place. I was a fucking mess right now, it wasn't like he'd want me anyways.

Right?

This was Luca. My protector. The only person I knew from my old life.

I didn't want to fuck up what we had, but I could no longer stop the feelings coming to the surface. This man was the only constant in my world, and he'd been sleeping across the hall from me for ten years.

All the errant day dreams about him came to the front of my mind. All the times that I wondered what it would be like to touch him, to be with him. Would he be rough? Would he be gentle?

I wanted both.

Fuck. I couldn't contain myself anymore.

I slowly got to my feet and began to undress. My hands stopped trembling, all of the rage and fear and horror melting away as I focused on him.

My knight.

My Luca.

Ten years. I'd been with him ten years, but I'd never been *with* him.

He stepped closer to me, stopping once we were toe to toe.

He swept my hair back, helping me undress. His fingertips were hot against me, searing everywhere they touched. My shirt and pants were quickly discarded, but then he paused, unwilling to touch my bra.

"I can't," he whispered. There was a hunger in his voice, a desperation I'd never heard before. "I can't. I made a promise."

"Luca," I murmured. "A promise to who? The man who has left me here to die?"

I reached back and unclasped it, freeing my breasts. His eyes fell to them, his gaze becoming enamored. He sucked in a breath, his cheeks flushing. My nipples hardened as the air hit them, goosebumps rising up. I let my bra fall to our feet and I looked at him.

We both stilled, our breaths becoming harsher.

He shook his head again as I slid my panties down, kicking them away.

"I won't pleasure you," he whispered. "I won't. I can't. *Fuck.*"

Something was breaking between us. I swallowed hard, feeling as though my body were on fire. I felt like I was drowning and he was the oxygen I needed to breathe again.

Luca moved my hair back over my shoulders, his fingertips lingering at my collarbone. I closed my eyes as he dragged his thumb over my skin.

"Luca," I breathed.

He picked me up and carried me to the shower. Steam filled the bathroom as he closed us in, placing me under the hot water. I looked down at the drain, watching as the water ran red.

Right.

I'd killed someone. I'd killed several someones.

"What have I done?" I whispered. "Luca, I'm a monster."

"You're not," he said quickly. He gripped my chin, letting out a low growl. "You're not. Did they attack you?"

"No."

"Did they hurt you?"

"No."

"Were they enemies? Were they—"

"I snapped. I killed them. There was no reason. It all happened so fast. One minute, I was standing in front of them, and the next thing I know, I was overcome with rage. I felt a power surge through me and there was a flash...I took them down in a way I didn't know was possible."

Bloody images from earlier ran through my mind. Over and over again. The overwhelming rage, the burning light. The way that, within seconds, I had taken them down.

"They did something," he said softly. "This isn't you. You're not a murderer."

"I am now."

He sighed, pressing his forehead to mine. "You and me both."

He stroked my jaw with his thumb and I closed my eyes, allowing the hot water to run over me. To wash away my sins.

Meanwhile, all I could think about was Luca.

I looked down, seeing that his cock was still hard.

"You won't touch me?" I whispered.

"No. I won't."

"Can I touch you?"

"No," he snapped. "For fuck's sake. You are *married*."

"He's never touched me. Not once in ten years. I'm pretty sure there are common laws that would make you my husband instead of him..." I swallowed hard, biting my lower lip. "You're bigger than most of my toys."

He let go of me like I'd burned him, stepping back with a

frustrated noise. "Wash all the blood off your body, Serena. I can't handle this. I'm telling you no."

Tears filled my eyes again, but I nodded. "Okay. I'm sorry."

Fuck. I'd made him uncomfortable.

I turned around, embarrassed now. What the hell was wrong with me? Of course he didn't want me. Not only was I married to a monster, I was now a murderer. Guilt made me feel like I was roasting over coals, but then Luca grabbed my wrist— yanking me back around to face him.

Steam drifted around us, drops of water rolling over our muscles. I bit my lower lip, the pain keeping me from breaking down.

"You aren't allowed to hide from me, *piccola regina. Ever.*"

He cupped my face as I began to cry, his lips almost touching mine.

"We will figure this out together. Okay? We will. I will."

"How?" My voice cracked as he wiped away a tear. " He's coming for me. And it feels different this time."

I knew it was.

I could feel it in my bones.

The end of one era and the beginning of something new.

"We need to wait and see," Luca said softly. "We need to see what he wants. He's never hurt you or even touched you."

"That's true," I agreed. "*No one* has ever touched me."

I wanted Luca to be the first.

I trusted him.

"I wish it was you," I confessed. "I wish it was you I was married to. I wish you didn't have to guard me. I wish I didn't have to be married to a monster."

"The Fates are cruel," Luca sighed. "But at least I get to be around you, *piccola regina.* That's all I've ever asked for."

I wanted to yell. I wanted to scream at him to fight for more. To *demand* that I belong to him and him alone.

But no.

He was right.

And by tempting him, I was hurting him.

Colchian was a mafia boss. He was a monster far older than either of us. When I had first been brought here, I had spent nights doing research on him. Finding out everything that I could.

He had the kind of money I could hardly fathom. And he hoarded his wealth. Stayed out of the public eye.

The only way I would ever escape him was through death.

Luca sighed and pushed me back under the water. "I'm going to wash you now. Is that okay?"

"Okay," I whispered, my thoughts returning to the very thing I should not be focusing on.

Death.

Murder.

Killing.

What if I killed my husband?

I would inherit all of his wealth.

I would be able to choose Luca.

He reached around me and squeezed shampoo into his hands, lathering it up and working it through my hair. I let out a soft moan as he scrubbed my scalp, all while I thought about killing my husband.

Fuck.

It could work.

"Close your eyes."

I obeyed him as he pulled me back under the shower head, rinsing the soap away. He wiped my eyes for me, letting out a contented sigh.

"Do you like this?" I whispered.

"Yes," he answered. "Very much. I live to serve you, *piccola regina.*"

I closed my eyes as he ran conditioner through my hair, the feeling of simply being touched by him was making my pussy start to throb. I felt my cheeks blush, but didn't care.

I had wanted this for so long. Dreamed of it. Of someone simply touching me, caring for me.

Loving me.

He poured body wash onto a loofah and began to lather me up. Pleasure spread through me as he attentively rubbed me all over. I fought the urge to laugh as he very carefully avoided my breasts and anything below my waist, unless it was my thighs.

I let out a nervous giggle, opening my eyes as he knelt in front of me. He ran his hands along my legs, looking up at me like I was the center of his world.

I parted my legs ever so slightly and watched as he realized that his face was right in front of my pussy.

I'd never seen Luca truly blush until now.

"You'll be the fucking end of me, Serena Avellino," he huffed.

Fuck. I tipped my head back, embracing the heat. His touch became scalding, leaving trails of longing behind.

I watched as the last of the blood swirled down the drain. I was finally clean.

"Luca," I groaned. "I'm going to kill him."

He chuckled as he rose to his feet. I stepped back from the water so that he could wash himself too.

"I'm serious," I said. "I'm going to murder him. I'm going to murder my husband."

Luca all but rolled his eyes.

"Luca," I hissed. "I'm fucking serious."

I stepped closer to him, but froze when I felt his cock brush against me.

The *noise* he made.

He shoved me against the shower wall, pinning me there,

keeping his hips pushed back so his throbbing cock wouldn't rub against me.

"Sorry," I rasped. "That was an accident, but you're not listening to me."

"You can't fucking kill him," Luca snarled. "That is absurd. Insane even."

"Do you want me? Or am I imagining things?"

He went silent, staring at me like I'd lost my mind.

"Serena..."

"Do. You. Want. Me?"

"More than anything," he admitted softly.

I drew in a shaky breath, feeling my soul melt. "Then we have to kill him," I whispered. "That's the only way."

"The only way for what?"

"The only way you get to have me."

He shook his head. "No."

"Yes," I said. "Tomorrow. He'll be here. He'll come for me. And I will kill him."

"It's a bad plan."

"Haven't you been training me for this?" I hissed.

"I've been training you to protect yourself," he snarled.

I rolled my eyes and turned away from him, opening the shower door and stepping out. I snatched a fluffy towel and wrapped it around myself, tiptoeing around the trails of blood we'd left.

I left the bathroom as the shower was shut off, Luca's curses following me.

I went to his bed, looking around. I had hardly ever been in his room. The door had always been locked and I had never cared.

It was simple. Much more minimalist than my own. In fact, if I didn't know Luca, I certainly wouldn't know anything about him by his living space.

"Serena." He came to the doorway.

Fucking hell. He had the towel wrapped around his waist, water dripping down his chest and abs.

"I'm going to do it," I said, crossing my arms over my chest. "I'm going to slay the dragon."

"You've truly lost your mind today," he retorted.

I chewed on my bottom lip, looking away from him. Perhaps focusing on murdering my husband wasn't the healthiest way to cope with what I'd done today, but oh well.

"I want you," I said. "I've wanted you for a long time. I've dreamed about you. I've touched myself and called your name. You're the only person who has ever truly known me. I can't lose you. I won't lose you."

I looked up at him, feeling everything click into place.

"Tomorrow, my husband comes home to me, and I'm going to kill him and take everything he owns."

Chapter 6
The Colchian's Castle

IAN

It'd been twenty-four hours since I found out my wife murdered three of her guards. Twenty-four hours since I'd watched the security footage.

Over and over.

I'd watched him take her into his bathroom.

A man who had sworn he would never touch her.

Now, as I slid into the back seat of the car waiting for me, I wondered what exactly I was going to do. Normally, I had a plan for everything, but the Fates had other ideas, didn't they?

The car door shut, blocking out the California night sky.

"How's my wife, Luca?" I asked, keeping my tone as even as possible.

I enjoyed the way the man sitting across from me recoiled. Over the last decade, he'd done a good job of mastering his expression, but I could feel the fury emanating off him in waves.

I stared him down, unable to keep my thoughts from returning to the video footage of him and Serena.

"She's been difficult the last 24 hours," he answered.

I kept my face blank and continued to stare at him, waiting to see if he'd squirm.

He wasn't a boy anymore, that was for sure.

Luca Civello was the human who had begged to stay with my wife. I could still recall his desperate pleas.

He would do anything for her.

The broken princess.

I chuckled to myself. "Tell me about her," I commanded.

The car lurched forward, the tires crackling over pavement as the driver began the hour-long journey to my castle. The private airport we had landed at was used by the Three Fates Mafia, although I wasn't sure anyone other than Perseus frequented these runways.

The only elder demigod who was half decent. I didn't hate her as much as I did the others.

"What would you like to know?" Luca asked.

"Everything. Tell me about her. What does she like? What does she do with her days?" *Does she murder men regularly with magic, or was that a fluke? Do you fuck her every morning? Have you filled her with your worthless seed?*

"She is smart and hardworking. She's recently taken up martial arts and is excelling at sparring. She sometimes paints, although she's not very good at it. Most days, we wake up and work out, I make her food, and she does whatever pleases her."

"You consider that hardworking?" I asked. "That sounds lazy to me. I've given her everything she wants and she doesn't have to work for it. She's spoiled." I was pushing him on purpose, and it was working.

Luca was silent for a moment and I noticed he was clenching his jaw. "She works hard at what she wants."

I cocked my head, pinning him with my gaze. I felt a ripple of energy from him and fought the urge to chuckle. After all this time, he hadn't changed, except he was now more bitter.

That would make destroying him so much easier.

"Does she want to leave the castle?"

Luca glared at me, his hands tightening into fists. The highway was quiet, punctuated by the hum of another passing car. Lights occasionally highlighted his face, casting long shadows over the bridge of his nose and cheekbones.

He hated me, and he clearly loathed that I didn't care what he thought of me. And why would I? Luca was the type of man I hired to do my dirty work and then had to kill because he'd done it too well. The only reason I let him stay with Serena was because of how devoted he was to her.

Too devoted.

I would hold my tongue and feel out what was going on with the two of them before throwing any accusations or punishments around.

"Of course she wants to leave. Her *husband* abandoned her."

"My wife has everything she needs, doesn't she?"

"She doesn't have someone she loves."

"Of course she does," I chuckled. "Doesn't she love you?"

"No," he muttered. "Of course not."

Liar. A good liar, but still a liar. His poker face might have worked if I hadn't watched how he'd run to his room with a hard-on just from speaking to Serena.

It was eating me alive not knowing if he'd fucked her.

I leaned forward, smoke blowing from my nostrils. I paused once my face was right in front of his, drawing in his scent. I could smell his cum and wondered how many times he'd touched himself thinking about her.

Had he broken our deal? I had expected him to. And

maybe I wanted him to, as the punishments I had in mind for such an act were exciting—this new feeling of jealousy making the thought more intense.

I'd been around for a long time. It was difficult to find things that intrigued me anymore, but Luca and Serena...

My mind wandered to the letter I'd received this week from the Three Fates, *that* had definitely piqued my interest. In fact, it had pushed me to action. I needed to know the truth. They claimed my wife was not mortal. That I was married to someone that was a creature of some sort. It was time to return to the castle.

The Fates were good at what they did, which meant all the paths that had crossed over the last decade had led to these moments. The strings had finally tangled, the three of us pulled into a knot.

If Serena wasn't a mortal, was Luca? Shaking my head of these thoughts, I came back to the moment.

"Have you touched her?"

"No," he answered. "I haven't. As we agreed long ago."

Our agreement. The deal that we had struck, a screaming mouse caught in my trap, begging for a morsel of cheese.

"She's still a virgin then?"

"She has...toys."

"But she's never been fucked by another person?"

"No," Luca confirmed. "As you said in the deal."

I studied him and concluded he was telling the truth. Which meant the scenario I'd had in my mind hadn't actually happened.

I leaned back in my seat, letting the darkness hide my smile.

So he hadn't slept with her.

My wife was still untouched, even with Luca always by her side.

Serena, Serena. Little killer. A mafia princess who had been locked away from the world—although I certainly hadn't been the one to turn the key.

I needed to know more about her.

I needed to *understand* her.

I had seen Serena twice in the last decade, but I would never forget the first time I met her or our wedding night. She had been so frightened and angry, but she'd refused to let it show. I respected her fortitude.

"Are you scared of monsters, wife?"

"No," she lied. *"I've met many monsters more frightening than you. And don't call me that."*

"Call you what?"

"Your wife."

"But you are, Serena."

"Just get this over with, Don Colchian."

"Ian," I corrected, smoke puffing from my breath. I tipped her face up, ignoring the dried tear streaks on her beautiful face. She was too young, too naive. *"Get what over with?"*

"The wedding night," she whispered.

I lifted my clawed hand, wondering how she would react to my full dragon form. Large enough that I could clutch her entire body in one clawed hand. She would be too small to take either of my cocks.

"I won't be mating you," I said. *"So you can relax."*

"What? What will you do with me then?"

I felt Luca's gaze on me and I let go of the memory. "Does she hate me?" I asked.

"Yes," Luca admitted. "Why shouldn't she? And why have you come for her? You're a monster—"

A low growl left me, one that had him straightening in his seat. "Don't mistake me allowing you to speak as an opportunity to insult me," I hissed. "Mind your manners, Luca, or else I might have you for dinner."

He went silent, although I could feel his glare. The two of us stayed like that for the rest of the trip, all while my thoughts returned to the past.

I had come to her because of the letter.

Suddenly, it felt as though the golden wax seal was burning a hole into my chest. A scrawled note from the Three Fates was tucked inside my jacket pocket, an invitation as much as a warning.

Dear Colchian,
Your wife is not mortal.
Sincerely,
The Three Fates

That was all. And if she was not mortal... What was she? And why would the Fates send me a note like that? What did they want me to do?

They were stringing me along, like always.

I pulled my phone out, checking my messages. I had a text from Ashley, the new demigod mafia queen. Well, *new* in my time. A year passed in the blink of an eye for me.

To my dismay, she'd managed to weasel her way into a friendship with me. One that wasn't entirely horrible. She'd also done me a favor by sending me a list of lingerie to buy for my wife.

Ashley: *Good luck and don't be a dick. Remember that women like to be treated well. I'll see you Sunday. Oh, and bring her to the event because I'm tired of being the youngest woman there. She can distract me from starting a war with Jason.*

I snorted. The event on Sunday. I wasn't sure that was the right place to bring Serena. I still had time to decide, though. It was an annual auction and dinner that the Three Fates Mafia hosted, and it was attended by the politicians and representatives of Moirai. It was a game of charades, and one I'd never enjoyed.

"We've arrived," Luca said gruffly.

The car slowed to a stop in front of my home. I had forgotten how lovely the view was, admiring the valley below and the forest beyond.

It was refreshing to not be surrounded by the sounds and scents of Moirai. Luca opened the door and slid out, holding it for me. I winked at him, which made him glare.

I stood, towering over him. My mortal form was one I enjoyed well enough, and as I turned I caught my reflection in the window. Silver hair and a neatly trimmed beard, tan skin that was taut over muscles. My giveaway had always been my iridescent eyes. I could never be *completely* human looking.

"So, when are you leaving?" I asked.

Luca immediately tensed, which I didn't think was possible given how stiff he already was. His eyes darkened, glowering at me, his lips pressed together. "About that. I'm not going on vacation."

"Yes, you are," I said. "I need to be alone with Serena. Without your interference. I assure you no harm will come to her."

"I don't trust you," he growled. "And I won't leave her. My life is dedicated to protecting her. I will stay at her side like I always have."

"You either leave or I will have you taken care of."

He cursed, looking away. He shook his head as he worked through his options. Planning, plotting. I was already certain he wanted to kill me, and if he thought he could do so in one night, then he was more stupid than I originally thought.

"At least let me stay the night," he requested.

Another plea.

I shook my head, feeling irritated. Everything about this man infuriated me. He was different from when we had first met...

The things he'd done to make sure he stayed with her.

I doubted Serena was aware of the second phone. Or the deal he had made.

I found myself smiling.

"Tomorrow morning," I said. "You will leave for three days. You will leave her with me. She will be safe and sound, but you will take some time to yourself. Hell, maybe go fuck someone."

His eyes burned with hatred.

"Understood?"

"Fine," he conceded.

I took a step closer and tipped his face up, forcing him to look at me. I knew he was used to being the tallest in the room, the strongest too.

But not when he was with me.

"Good boy," I said softly. "I like it more when you're obedient."

His jaw stiffened and I knew he was seconds from telling me to fuck off.

I was enjoying this entirely too much. What was next? Dinner with Serena? I wondered how much she had changed since I saw her last.

I walked past Luca, ignoring the men who flanked us. "Has dinner been prepared?"

"Yes, sir," Luca said.

"Great. Make sure Serena is there. I won't tolerate her being late."

"I'm sure she is waiting for you like a good wife," he muttered.

I paused at the grand door. It was open for me, and I was met with the warmth of the foyer. I stepped inside, taking in everything.

I hadn't been here in so long.

My gaze swept up the grand staircase. Sure enough, at the top was my wife—and she was even more stunning than I remembered.

Chapter 7
Wife

Ian

Serena stood, wearing a long black dress with a plunging v-neck. Her dark hair lay in waves around her shoulders, her lips painted a bright red. Diamonds clung to her neck and my ring glittered on her slender finger.

I could suddenly feel the weight of mine. It had managed to be a shield for me over the years, but not with her.

Something had changed in me. I was finally seeing her for the woman she was and not the eighteen-year-old girl I'd met at the altar. She already belonged to me anyway, so why couldn't I have her? She was my wife. I was her husband.

I should have never left her alone. I had abandoned her, even if I had given her a life of luxury. I felt a possessive streak flare inside of me, the dragon within craving her.

I needed her to want me.

Serena held my gaze for a few moments and then started descending the staircase. Her steps were slow, measured. Her grace and poise were something to behold, and I found myself enchanted.

Maybe she was a witch. Maybe she was casting a spell on me right now.

A smile twisted my lips—until Luca rushed past me as she came to the bottom step. Ruining my reverie like a fucking asshole. "Your shoe," he said softly, kneeling in front of her.

Serena grabbed the handrail, lifting her heel onto his knee. I watched as he grabbed the strap around her ankle that had come undone, buckling it again.

Jealousy began to slowly rise within me.

She offered him a smile. "Thanks, Luca."

The icy mask she normally wore when I was around melted, warmth blooming when she looked at him.

Luca stood and stepped to the side, turning to face me. He went from being the sweet and protective bodyguard to enemy number one within a matter of seconds.

"Serena," I said. "It's good to see you."

Her name felt strange on my tongue. For years now, she had been a shadow of a thought, but now...

I needed to know her.

"You look well," I said as she approached me.

"Thanks," she replied, her voice tight. "It's strange to see you after so long, but you haven't changed."

I leaned forward and she visibly stiffened as I kissed both of her cheeks, breathing in her scent. She smelled like fresh gardenias, a soft floral aroma with a delicious creaminess that reminded me of coconut.

I wanted to lap her scent up.

As I kissed her cheeks, I looked past her, seeing Luca's murderous expression. I also noted the couple strands of silver in his hair, I had somehow missed that small display of his mortality. Eventually he'd die. I fought the urge to grin at that thought.

"Take my arm," I said, smiling at her.

Her shoulders pulled back, her arm sliding into the crook of mine. Her expression became unreadable as I guided her down the hall.

Just like I'd seen on the video feeds, the guards didn't so much as look at her. There was a tension around them that bordered on fear. I could smell their sweat, could hear the way their heartbeats quickened.

Was it because of me? Or her?

I felt a cloud of darkness following us and glanced over my shoulder.

It was Luca.

Interesting. He was like an eternal darkness following her sunshine. A mad dog drooling over its favorite toy.

I looked forward again as we continued down the hall to the dining room. I noted some of the extra cameras, ones I had not authorized.

Anger rose in me again. I would be having a word with him later about how fucked up and not okay these additions were. Apparently, I'd let a pervert live and take care of my wife. I should have paid more attention.

We entered the dining room and I noted the layer of dust. A stale scent lingered and an emptiness clung to the room. Above us was a chandelier that probably hadn't been lit in years, the stone walls radiating a chill.

The oak table was long, our places already set. Mine at the head of the table and hers to my left. I guided Serena to her seat, pulling the chair out for her.

"Thanks," she muttered as she sat, immediately reaching for the wine.

I fought a smile again as I sat at the head of the table, and then frowned as I realized Luca was still following us.

"Mr. Civello," I said, trying to not sound annoyed. "I do believe my wife is safe in my presence, you may leave. Take the evening off. We don't need guards hovering around us."

Luca froze, his dark eyes sliding to her. I turned my attention to Serena as well, pleased to see her nod ever so slightly.

"You can go, Luca," she said. "I'll be fine."

The vein in his temple ticked, but he nodded. "As you wish."

We watched him leave. The guards down the hall visibly relaxed as he walked past them.

"Hmm." I frowned.

"Is there something wrong, *Don* Colchian?" Serena asked, raising a perfect brow.

Up close, she was even more beautiful. The way she looked at me was intriguing. She hated me, that much was clear, and I wondered why. What had I done to make her feel this way?

I shifted in my seat, studying her.

"No," I said, smiling. "There's nothing wrong. And call me Ian, Serena. How have you been?"

She pressed her lips together, giving me a hard look. "I've been fine, *Ian*. What are you doing here?"

Straight to the point. I could appreciate that, although it was not the behavior I expected from this woman. For a moment, she reminded me of Medusa. A woman who'd been cornered her whole life, who now struck with a venom that could make empires crumble.

I raised a brow and leaned back in my seat. "Can a husband not visit his wife?"

"You haven't visited in years," she said, glaring at me. "I've seen you twice in the decade since you swept me away from

Italy. You've kept me here, in this castle, and I don't understand why. "

"Well, you could have visited me," I argued.

"And *you* could have visited *me*."

I reached for my glass of wine, taking a measured sip. We were both quiet. One of our servers came to the doorway with a tray, setting out a basket of bread, followed by two starter salads.

She snorted, shaking her head as she grabbed her fork. She eyed the salad in front of me doubtfully. "Do you even eat regular food?"

I blinked, the question was absurd, but then I remembered she didn't really know me. I *had* only seen her twice in the last decade. She had no way of knowing about my food habits. In her mind, I was a monster.

"I do eat regular food," I said, picking up my fork. I stabbed a tomato with it, holding it up. "I'm a monster, not an alien."

"What's the difference?"

"You tell me. I'm not so different from you, it seems."

"Oh? And how is that?" she quipped. "You're the *Don* of a mafia branch, a dragon, and a murderer. I fail to see any similarities between us."

She was sassy tonight. Much more than how I remembered her. I was amused by the streak of fire I saw in her eyes.

Drawn to it like a moth to a flame.

"Well, for one, neither of us are mortal."

She stabbed a tomato with her fork as I spoke, and I winced as juice shot straight onto my face. She gasped, covering her mouth, her cold demeanor wavering.

For just a moment, I saw a glimpse of the woman I wanted to know.

"Oh, fuck," she said, and then let out a small giggle. "Sorry, excuse my language."

Now, I laughed. I couldn't help it.

"You can say *fuck*," I teased. "We're adults."

She mumbled under her breath and picked up her cloth napkin, reaching for my face. The movement surprised me, and I forced myself to stay still as she wiped it away.

She seemed to have surprised herself too. Serena paused and I watched her expression as she realized she was touching me.

It was intimate in the most innocent of ways.

Fucking hell. I realized that I wanted to worship this woman.

She leaned back, setting the napkin down. I cleared my throat and she looked away, a blush creeping over her cheeks.

An awkward silence settled between us again.

Why were my hearts beating so fast?

"What do you mean when you say I'm not mortal?" Serena finally asked.

I studied her, wondering if she knew. She had to know, right? If she wasn't human, then of all people, she would be aware of it.

After yesterday, surely she had realized. Humans couldn't kill three highly trained men with a flash of light.

Should I have known? Usually, I could sense when someone wasn't a mortal. They had a unique scent to them, different than humans.

I decided to be honest with her.

"I received a letter from the Three Fates," I said. "They only said that you are not a mortal. So, I decided to come visit and find out exactly what you are."

I grabbed my glass of wine, taking a sip of the sweet red. A bit too sweet for my taste, but—

"So, you're not here to get me pregnant?"

I almost choked on my wine. Coughing, I set it down and leaned back as I fought for air. *"What?"*

"I should be offended by that reaction," she snorted. "Isn't that why you're here?"

"No," I responded.

"But, all the lingerie! Plus the collars, and floggers, and—"

I had finally recovered. "Is that not what a husband buys his wife?"

"No!" she shouted, standing up. "You gave Luca a list long enough to stock a BDSM club."

A low growl left me and I stood too, towering over her. She didn't cower, didn't flinch. She stood tall, her dark eyes piercing me.

Both of us had our hands planted on the table, glaring at each other.

"And how would you know what's in a BDSM club?" I asked.

"Because I read books and watch porn," she snapped. "How else should I get off? My husband refuses to touch me and no one else is *allowed* to touch me."

"I've never refused," I said. "I just haven't offered. But when I do, you won't say no."

"Yes, I will," she snapped. "I don't want you to touch me. *Ever.*"

"You say that now," I chuckled. "But you won't resist. You'll want me, even if you hate me."

"A *husband* does a lot of things," she sneered. "But gifting me lingerie after you've left me here, locked up and alone, for *years* is not one of them."

A snarl ripped out of me and I gripped her jaw. My hands started to shift, black claws emerging from seemingly human fingers. I pulled her close, enjoying the way her breath hitched a little too much.

"I've never locked you up," I whispered. "Have you ever wanted something you couldn't have?"

She winced, her words failing her.

"Answer me," I growled.

"No."

"Have you not been provided all the food and material items you could possibly want? You get to spend your days in a beautiful home where every little thing is done for you. Your bed is made, your meals are cooked, your home is cleaned. I have given you everything you could ever want over the last ten years."

"No," she answered, swallowing hard. "No, you have not. And don't act like I should be grateful to you. Yes, you have given me material things, but you've never loved me. You never will. I was eighteen when you married me and then you stuck me in a house I didn't choose, one I'm not allowed to leave. I have been imprisoned here. I would rather be on the fucking streets and able to make my own decisions than be a doll for a man to dress up and play with whenever he wants."

I was baffled by her. She kept saying I had confined her here, but I'd never done that. I never said anything about her having to always stay in this house.

"I've done so much for you," I said. Covering up murders was at the top of the list.

She yanked her head free, not even wincing as my claws cut her cheeks. Blood welled up, the scent invading my nostrils.

Her blood smelled delicious.

My cocks began to harden, my breaths quickening. "I can't love you, Serena."

"You never tried," she said. "And if you won't love me, then why can't I see other people?"

I snarled and lunged for her, but she twirled out of the way with the grace of a ballerina.

The monster in me didn't appreciate that.

Fuck it.

My suit began to rip as I shoved her against the dining room wall. Nevermind that the jacket alone cost four figures, I let it tear as the monster came out to play. I shifted, allowing my half form to emerge, a beast untamed.

Her eyes widened as my head became that of a dragon, my skin transforming into hardened scales that were silver to black. My wings burst free, spined branches with velvety onyx flesh pulled tight like drums.

My claws wrapped around her throat, pinning her. I could feel her heart pounding, the vein in her neck pulsing.

Then I caught her scent.

The arousal.

I narrowed my eyes, breathing her in.

She was temptation, embodied in a woman.

"You are *mine*," I growled, my voice deep and gravely. "You may hate me. You may be disgusted by me. But you are mine, Serena, you always will be."

"I will never be yours," she seethed. "*Let me go.*"

My claws tightened and she struggled for breath. Her scent became more heady, a drug that made me want to bend her over the table and take her.

I let the fantasy play out for a few seconds.

Would she want to take both of my cocks at the same time?

I leaned in, the blood streaking down her face reminding me of tears. My long tongue was forked at the end and I flicked it out, licking the streaks of red.

She let out an involuntary moan I knew she hadn't meant for me to hear.

This woman. My little wife.

Why had I kept her at a distance?

The taste of her blood hit my tongue and I closed my eyes, letting out a primal noise. She tasted unlike anything I'd ever had before, except for—

Fuck.

I let go of her suddenly, as if she'd seared me, taking a step back.

There was no way. No fucking way.

I felt the bonds snap into place, a fire starting in my chest.

I now knew two things.

One... Serena was my mate. My true mate. It took every ounce of control not to fall to my knees, to keep tears from falling.

I'd been searching for so long.

And two...

"You're a demigod."

Chapter 8
Dragon I'd Like to F*ck

SERENA

"You're a demigod."

Half dragon, half man—my husband stood in front of me, staring at me as if I were the monster. His tan skin had turned to silver and black scales, his wings spreading behind him.

My husband was a DILF.

Dragon I'd like to fuck.

Calm the fuck down. I did my best to refocus on what he'd just said, and not the realization that I might be into monsters. That was a problem for future me.

"What are you talking about?" I asked, bewildered.

A demigod? I knew what a demigod was, but they weren't real. Ian shook his head, letting out a frustrated noise. "It's impossible, well, it should be impossible. But, of course, that's what you are. The Fates are fucking with all of us. I need to hide you."

"What?" I snapped. "I am already hidden! For a whole decade you've kept me here away from the world."

"I never locked you up here," he snapped, shaking his head. "And this is different. This is..."

I still was not over seeing a silver fox of a man turn into a fucking dragon. Or, partial dragon.

Either way he was hot, which wasn't fair. In my mind, I'd built him up as something horrible because it was easier to hate him that way. It was easier to plot his murder that way. I'd seen this form before, right? But the way I remembered him was completely different.

He was no longer a scary monster who had taken me from my family.

My pussy gave a light throb and I mentally screamed at myself. *What the hell is wrong with you?!*

I forced my gaze to move away from what was left of his pants, and the bulge there.

This was the result of being touch starved. Even dragon dick started to sound fun.

"I'm not a demigod, Ian," I said. "Truly. I was born just like any other human."

"And your parents? The ones who died when you were a child?"

I felt my throat constrict, my heart skipping a beat. "Do not speak of them," I whispered.

"Answer me," he demanded, stepping closer.

I pressed my back against the wall, holding my head up high. "What about them?"

"Did you know them?"

I hated him. I hated him for asking me this. For bringing family up. Since leaving Italy, the only family I'd spoken to were my cousins, both of whom were supposedly happy. But aside from them, everyone else was dead to me, including my uncle who had refused to speak to me after he married me off to Ian.

"I knew my mother," I said, fighting back tears that began to burn. Memories of her came flooding in. Her gentle smile. Her scent. The way she held me when I cried. How she promised she'd never let anything bad happen to me. *Sei al sicuro, bambina. You are safe, child.* "My father died before she did. I never knew him."

"Do you know anything about him?" Ian asked. He started to pace, his clawed hands clasped behind his back.

"To speak of him was forbidden," I explained. "When my mother died, it was forbidden to speak of her too. Per my uncle's command."

Ian nodded. I could see his mind racing, his iridescent eyes burning with something I couldn't put my finger on. Hate, perhaps? Maybe he hated me as much as I hated him.

Maybe he was thinking about murdering me too.

"That explains the murders, then," Ian said softly.

I froze, my heart stopping.

He cocked his dragon-like head to the side, his scales shimmering. "Oh yes. I know about the killings that happened yesterday. I watched the video several times."

"It was an accident," I whispered, wishing I could disappear.

"No, it wasn't," he said, smiling.

"Am I to stay like this the entire time we talk?" I bit out. "Bleeding and pinned against a wall? Or can we discuss this civilly?"

"You want to talk civilly about the fact that you killed three men?"

"Like you haven't," I snapped. "Don't give me that. I know what kind of world you live in. It's the same one my uncle tried to shield me from. It's the same one that brought us together. I fucked up yesterday, yes, but you, of all people, don't have a right to rub it in my face."

Ian stared at me. I felt like I was made of glass, that he could see right through me. He let out a soft hum, giving me an apologetic look. He then began to shift back into the form of a man, his scales disappearing. His wings vanished and his face became recognizable again.

His human form was too damn good looking.

"I'm sorry. I lost my temper, Serena." He grabbed one of the cloth napkins from the table and came to me, holding it up. "Please, let me heal these."

I nodded slowly, holding my breath as he gently wiped away the blood. He then ran the pad of his thumb over the cuts, a warm zap following.

He leaned in closer and all I could do was stare at him. He had colorful eyes, and a neatly trimmed silver beard that I had the urge to touch. He was covered in muscles, his skin smooth. There was hair on his chest, trailing down to the v at his hips.

Warmth and pleasure spread through my body. He pulled his hand away. "Good as new. There's still some blood but I'm sure you can wash it off later."

"You have magical abilities?"

"Some," Ian said. " Are you hungry, still?"

"I've lost my appetite," I whispered.

He had just healed me with *magic*. All I could think about now was what else could my dragon husband do? What if he could brainwash me? Or turn me into a mouse? Or—

"Then we can speak in the study. Come," he said, turning for the doorway.

I hesitated for a moment, ultimately deciding to follow him.

The two of us walked through the house, my eyes never

leaving him. There were two faint lines on his shoulder blades, and I realized that was where his wings emerged.

What am I doing? I'm not supposed to be acting friendly towards him. After everything he put me through...

He led me through a couple rooms, ones I hardly ever used. It was a big home and at least half of it was covered in dust. Even with the cleaning crew, it was impossible to keep up with.

If I had chosen my own house, I would have picked out a small cottage. Or maybe an apartment. Part of me loved the idea of being in the city and part of me wanted to live in the woods, just me and ten cats.

We came to a door with a dragon carved into it. He opened it, ushering me inside.

This was his office, one of the few places I actively avoided. I never used this space because it reminded me too much of Ian. I let out a sigh as I looked around at the shelves of books. It was a small library, with two plush chairs, and a fireplace behind the massive oak desk.

I stared at the painting above the fireplace, realizing it was a dragon in a forest, its massive tail wrapped around a silver tower. A woman stood at the top, a knight at the bottom.

"Would you like a fire to be lit?" Ian asked.

"Sure," I said, curious.

Ian leaned forward, parting his lips. Fire billowed from them, igniting the wooden logs in the hearth. I gasped as embers floated around him, the fire beginning to burn.

He cleared his throat, running his fingers through his silver hair.

"You never come in here," Ian stated.

"Correct."

He nodded, giving me a soft smile. "Can you close the door?"

I closed it softly, still trying to grasp everything that was happening. There was so much to unpack, so many questions I wanted to ask.

"I know you hate me," he started. "You have a lot of reasons to, I suppose. But, I don't intend to hurt you. I have always wanted to keep you safe, Serena, which is why I kept my distance."

Well, I intend to hurt you. I felt a prickle of guilt but ignored it as I sat down in a chair across from his desk. Ian took the other, regarding me thoughtfully.

Warmth began to fill the room, and it was welcomed. Light played over us, flickering as the flames grew more steady.

"Tell me about demigods," I began to ramble. "Tell me everything. To even think that a demigod exists is absurd. Does that mean there are gods and goddesses too? I don't believe I'm one, but..."

"You are," he said. He sounded so sure of himself. "And yes. There are gods and goddesses, each with designated powers. They oversee different parts of our world, from the rage you feel to the grass that grows, each of them unique in their control. They have been around for thousands of years. They're fickle and you can't trust them."

"That's great," I muttered.

I could barely wrap my mind around what he was telling me.

"They suck at their jobs," I said, thinking of everything wrong with this world.

"Well, they each have their faults. And I don't know who you descend from. That, we will have to figure out. If you belong to one of the majors... I don't know what we'll do. We will need to keep your identity secret. Gods have killed their own children before, it's not unheard of."

Even better. "We?"

"Yes. Now that I know this, I will be rearranging my plans. I need to stay with you."

I leaned back in my chair, my thoughts racing. I had many more questions for him. Aside from the pent up anger I felt for Ian, there was a curiosity that had been festering for a decade.

Who was this monster I had married?

I shouldn't care. Learning more about the person I was supposed to kill certainly wouldn't help me feel better, but I couldn't resist. For so long, he'd practically been a figment of my imagination, and now, here he was. Breathing fire into my life.

"You've grown up," Ian murmured, his tone surprising me.

"I have," I said. "I'm no longer an eighteen year old girl with stars in her eyes."

"I can see that. Although I don't think you had stars in your eyes when we met. I'm not sorry for keeping you away from my world. It's a bloody one. It's dangerous."

"Is it any different from the one I grew up in?"

"Yes," Ian said. "You're no longer the niece of a man wanted dead by many people. You're the demigod wife of a monster, which puts a bounty on your head from the gods, Fates, and monsters alike."

I shook my head, his words settling over me. Ian wanted to protect me, which felt absurd. In the two times we'd seen each other over the last decade, we'd never spoken for this long. It was only ever an exchange of pleasantries followed by me pretending to be happy. A trophy wife who smiled and loved her life.

"You keep saying these things like I should be grateful to you," I said. "But I'm not. If you were going to keep me out of your life, fine. I never needed to be in it. But you never let me pursue my own life. I've been stuck here. Luca has been stuck here."

"He wanted to be," Ian leaned back in his chair, assessing me. "Begged to be."

"I doubt he begged," I snorted. "He's not the type to do that."

"You're wrong," Ian said, his lips tugging into a knowing smile. "And what do you mean I've kept you here? You keep saying that and I have no idea what you mean."

"Here. In this house. I've never been allowed to go anywhere, never been allowed to travel."

"I never put those rules on you," Ian said, frowning. "*Never*. In fact, you have a credit card, in your name, which allows you to travel anywhere in the world you want. My only restrictions on your travel were for certain cities where my known enemies reside."

What?

I had difficulty finding the words to say. He had to be lying. "No. You said I couldn't go anywhere. Couldn't date anyone. Couldn't be touched."

"I *did* say the last two things," Ian confirmed. "Because if you were seen cheating on me, that would impact my reputation. If it's any consolation, I haven't been touched since our wedding either. I haven't kissed or fucked someone in a decade. And, if I'm being honest, I didn't actually expect you to obey that rule. But I never said you couldn't leave this house."

"No," I whispered. "I've always wanted to travel. All I do in my free time is watch travel shows and dream of escaping."

Ian gave me a sad, knowing look.

I was unable to keep sitting, so I stood. I hugged myself, pacing back and forth in front of his desk. The only sound was the back-and-forth swish of my dress, my heart beating faster.

"What about the guards? They aren't allowed to speak to me."

"I never said they couldn't."

He was lying. He *had* to be lying.

I didn't know if I believed him. But, if he was telling the truth, then it meant...

Had Luca been lying to me?

"*Serena!*"

Chapter 9
Liar Liar

SERENA

My blood rushed in my ears, my entire world splitting at the seams. Yesterday I had been so sure I would take any chance I could to murder my husband, but now I wasn't sure what to do.

Was he telling me the truth about Luca?

Luca pounded on the door from the outside, the wood rattling. I jumped, surprised by the sudden intrusion, and then my ankle gave.

I would have fallen, but Ian was there, swooping me up into his arms.

"Fuck," I hissed, pain shooting through my leg. "These fucking shoes."

"Are you okay?" he asked, worried.

"I just rolled it," I mumbled, becoming painfully aware he was holding me like a princess. I blushed as I realized I was gripping the shreds of his suit jacket.

He let out a soft sigh, taking me back to my chair. He sat me down carefully, grabbing a footstool so I could prop my ankle. I winced as he touched me, but he was gentle.

Way more gentle than a monster should have been.

Fuck. His fingertips brushed over my skin, the crackle of electricity between us running straight to my pussy. I could barely hear Luca shouting now.

"Serena!"

"Stay," Ian said. "I can heal you—"

"Some ice is fine," I squeaked.

Ian rose and quickly crossed the study. "I know you don't know me, Serena, but I promise I'm not as terrible as you think."

He opened the door and Luca rushed in, his chest heaving. He shoved Ian back with a growl.

"Can I fucking help you?" Ian demanded, smoke curling from his mouth. "She twisted her ankle and needs ice."

Luca started to reach behind his back, and I knew he was going to pull out his gun or a knife.

"Luca," I said quickly, trying to stand up.

Which was a terrible idea.

I stumbled, cursing the gods and these fucking heels and the designer who made them—only to be picked up again by Ian.

"Let her go," Luca ordered.

Ian's chest rumbled. My eyes widened as an electric shock ran through me, melting every thought.

Luca noticed, and that was bad.

Very, very bad.

"Don't you fucking touch her!" Luca growled, reaching for Ian.

To everyone's surprise, I slapped his hand.

Luca hissed, pulling his hand back. "What?"

"Stop it," I said. "I rolled my ankle, I'm fucking humiliated, and I need you to *stop*. He isn't hurting me. I promise."

"Let me have her, Ian."

"No," Ian said, his arms tightening around me. "She rolled her ankle because your barbaric pounding on the door startled her."

For fucks sake. This was a mess.

Luca tried reaching for Ian again, but I slapped his hand once more.

"Luca," I snapped, trying to draw his attention. "Stop this. Stop!"

Ian laughed, his voice becoming cruel. "Mr. Civello, if you attempt to touch me or my *wife* one more fucking time—I'm going to gut you."

"No," Luca sneered. "You can't touch her. You don't know how to take care of her like I do."

"I *can* touch her," Ian said calmly. "She belongs to me. Not you. As much as you'd like."

I frowned, my gaze darting between the two of them. Luca stiffened, his expression becoming crazed.

"You can put me down," I said. "Please."

Ian hesitated for a moment, he and Luca locked in a glaring contest.

"Put me down."

Ian slowly lowered me, his hand settling on my lower back, keeping me steady.

"I need to get these shoes off and I'll be fine," I said.

Luca fell to his knees faster than I could blink, his fingers gently unhooking the heels.

Fucking hell.

The same searing heat I'd felt from Ian returned, but this time it came from Luca.

Yesterday, he took care of me. I'd snapped into a million

pieces, had become a murderer—but he'd pieced me back together and given me exactly what I needed. Someone to lean on, to rely on.

I'd also wanted him in a way that I'd never allowed myself to before. I'd made a decision to change our lives, but now...

Did I truly know him?

Was my husband lying to me?

Or had Luca been deceiving me this entire time?

"Luca," I whispered. "I can take them off."

"As can I, *piccola regina*."

Ian's hand heated, his body emanating rage as Luca carefully slid my other heel free. I shrank three inches and was now surrounded by two tall and brooding men whom I wanted to ride until sunrise.

Luca looked at me and I watched as he realized there was dried blood on my face.

"You motherfucking—"

Ian moved in a blur. I gasped as Luca was body slammed to the floor, crunching like a bag of ice. Ian choked him, holding him down with ease like I'd never seen before.

No, no, no.

"Stop," I begged. "Stop, you're hurting him. He's only trying to protect me! Both of you are being fucking morons!"

Ian ignored me until I started to walk towards the door. Both of them immediately turned their attention on me like ravenous vultures.

I gritted my teeth. "If you hurt him, I will never give you answers to anything. And I will never give myself to you, Ian. *Let him go.* For fuck's sake."

Ian sighed, embers leaving his mouth as he released Luca slowly. He leaned back, glaring down at Luca.

"You're lucky I don't have you killed," he said, his

demeanor completely different than it had been with me. "You would never see her again."

Luca growled and shoved him off, rolling to his feet. "Threaten me again and—"

"Am I getting the ice myself or is one of you going to do it?" I interrupted.

Both of them were silent.

"Go," Ian commanded. "Luca, take care of her. Get her some ice and get her settled upstairs. I want you to come back to my office in an hour. I need to speak to you alone."

"Promise me you won't kill each other," I demanded, giving them each a sharp look. "Both of you."

Neither of them said a word.

Gods, I was going to lose my mind.

"Luca," I whispered.

"I promise," he gritted out.

"I promise as well," Ian said, crossing his arms.

"Good," I said. "Take me away, please."

Luca came to me and scooped me into his arms, like Ian had before. His warmth was a different kind than Ian's, one I was familiar with.

The thought of Luca lying to me felt like I was being stabbed in the heart.

He carried me from the room and down the hall, taking me towards the kitchen. I laid my head on his shoulder, breathing in his smoky scent.

I wanted him so much it hurt, but I had to know the truth.

"Did you lie to me?" I whispered.

"*What?*" he gasped, stopping in the middle of the kitchen.

I looked up at him, fighting back tears. "Was Ian the one who said I couldn't travel? Or was that you?"

His expression gave him away. He'd always had a good

poker face and I usually struggled to read his expression, but I saw it.

The flicker of guilt. The panic.

His body stiffened, his breaths shortening.

"Answer me," I demanded in a harsh whisper. "And don't you *dare* fucking lie."

"I had my reasons," Luca said tightly. "It was for your own safety—"

"FUCK YOU!" I shouted, shoving hard against his chest. "Are you kidding me? Put me down."

"No," he growled.

"Put. Me. Down."

"That almost sounded like a threat," he said wryly.

I shoved against him harder this time, but he only grunted, carrying me to the kitchen island. He sat me on the counter top, boxing me in and using his hips to push my knees apart. I pushed him, my rage taking over and making me feel like I was falling apart. Spiraling and tumbling down a dark hole.

I felt like I'd been punched in the gut. I could barely breathe, my vision dotting.

He grabbed my face and I raked my nails down his arm. He didn't wince, both of us going still as I felt his cock throbbing through his pants.

"Fight me," he whispered. "Go on. Keep fighting. Because if you stop, I'm going to fuck you like I should have years ago."

"You're a liar," I sneered, tears filling my eyes.

I wouldn't let him see me cry. I held them back, let them burn.

He was unmoving, a wall of muscle. His anger rolled off him in waves, heightening my own rage.

"You *lied* to me," I said again. Every word was agonizing. "You're the only person I've ever trusted and you betrayed me. I should have never let him stay with me."

"I *had* to lie to you," he rasped. "And even if you'd sent me away, I would have come back to you. I belong to you, Serena."

"Let me go," I said, my voice growing eerily calm.

"No," he huffed, squeezing my jaw tighter. "What do you want me to say, Serena? That I'm sorry? I'm not sorry. I'm not sorry at all. I have *loved* you since the day I met you. My purpose in life is to keep you safe, which meant keeping you secret from the world to make sure no one found out about your abilities."

"*What?*" I whispered. "What the hell are you talking about?"

"Do you not remember that day in the alley?" he murmured, letting go of my face. He pressed his forehead to mine, his lips parting. "The day you wandered off from your mother. It was summer and unbelievably hot. You were wearing a red sundress with tiny white flowers all over it and the sun was setting. I found you sitting on the steps crying, and I was going to help you find your mother. While we were searching, a man attacked us. He wanted you. And you killed him, and then your mother came."

Tears filled my eyes. I blinked, searching my memories. It was fuzzy, but I knew the day he was talking about.

How many times had I dreamed about that boy as a girl? My knight in shining armor.

"Luca." I was a broken record, my mind spinning.

"My father sold me to the mafia shortly after that day. And when I saw you, not long after your mother died, you didn't recognize me."

"Oh my god," I said, shaking my head. "How... that was you?"

"Yes. I've been with you ever since. I made it my mission to become one of the best killers, to build up my strength, so I could protect you. I became the best I could be, so I would be worthy of you."

I shook my head in disbelief, leaning away. Tears streamed down my cheeks now. "But... but why would you lock me up here? You know I haven't been happy here. I've never been allowed to live and *you stole* that from me."

"I kept you safe."

"You kept me broken."

We stared at each other now, our world crumbling at our fingertips.

"I protected you the only way I knew how," he said. "I love you. I've loved you for so long and—"

"This isn't love," I choked out. "You broke my wings and stole them from me. I've been living a lie, all because you wouldn't let me do what I wanted. I trusted you and this whole time you made me believe things about Ian that weren't true."

"No. No. I—"

"I want you to leave."

"Don't," he choked out, his voice breaking. "Serena, I love you. I —"

"*I want you to leave!*" I shouted.

"Luca." Ian's voice broke the two of us apart.

Luca's hands curled into fists as we both looked up.

Ian glowered at him. "I changed my mind. I want to meet with you. Now."

"I'm having a conversation—" Luca argued.

"*Now.*"

"At least let me get her upstairs," he pleaded.

"I'd rather fucking crawl." I said.

Luca looked at me like I'd shot him through the heart. He stared for a moment, and then shook his head stalking towards Ian. I watched as my husband stepped to the side, giving me a warning look.

He raised his hand and I gasped as I felt the pain disappear in my ankle.

"Sorry," he said. "Magic will at least keep you from getting your pretty knees dirty. Go to bed, sweetheart."

With that, he left me alone, taking my bodyguard with him.

Luca was a fucking liar. The last ten years had shattered right in front of me. Who could I have been if I would have had the freedom I deserved? Who would I be now that I knew the truth?

Chapter 10
Deal or No Deal

Luca

I felt my phone buzzing in my pocket but ignored it.

I would never pick up a phone call from J again. Not after seeing how much pain I'd fucking caused Serena.

Everything I'd done had been to keep her safe. To make sure she lived.

But all of it was crumbling because of the bastard now shoving me into his office.

Ian was already half-shifted by the time I turned around. I heard the office door lock click before I was slammed to the floor, a clawed hand covering my mouth.

Both of us were breathing hard. Ian's wings spread behind him, a low growl rumbling in his chest.

"If you scream or shout, I will kill you," Ian whispered. "Got it, Luca?"

I nodded. I hated him. I hated everything about this, especially the look I'd just seen on Serena's face.

He removed his hand from my mouth, keeping me pinned beneath him. "Why did you do this to her? I had no fucking idea, Luca. No wonder she hates me. Was that your motive? To make sure she would hate her husband? What about my text messages to her? My emails?"

"She never saw them," I admitted.

I couldn't tell him about J. I couldn't give him more reasons to force me out. To take me away from Serena.

Desperation pumped through me.

Ian bared sharp teeth at me. "Are you fucking joking?"

"No," I said. "No. I wanted her to hate you. I wanted her to leave you. I've been planning this from the beginning. To steal her from you and take what is *mine*."

"Why?" he whispered. "Years ago, you begged me to let you stay with her. I didn't need you, but I allowed you to stay on as her personal bodyguard because I could see how much you cared for her. But this? This isn't caring for someone, Luca."

"All I've done is care for her. I love her more than you will ever be able to. I've done *everything* for her."

Ian leaned back, still seated on top of me. I swallowed hard, ignoring the way I enjoyed being under him. I hated him but couldn't help thinking about what I'd done for him so long ago.

Some things you never forgot.

Ian let out a low chuckle. "Your arousal amuses me, Luca. You like being shoved to the floor and made to feel weak, don't you? Have you fucked anyone since you persuaded me to let you live with my wife?"

"Fuck off," I said. "I'm not answering that. It was a one-time thing. The fact you even made me do that..." The things I'd done to get what I wanted.

"I never made you do anything. You were very willing," he taunted. "Then the answer is no. Interesting. No wonder you're going crazy. A young man like you in his prime, and no hole to fill."

"Get the fuck off me," I muttered.

"Only if you promise to stop being a bastard."

"What do you want?" I sneered.

Ian slid off me, shifting back into his human form. I pressed my lips into a hard line, wishing my cock didn't respond to his dominance.

Ian leaned back on the floor, sighing as he studied me. "I should have known better than to trust you. I kill men like you regularly. Eat them for breakfast; build my throne with their bones."

I rolled my eyes and sat up.

"She will hate you," Ian said.

"She won't." She would never hate me. I was hers, and she knew that. She knew that I loved her.

Yesterday, she had finally seen *me*.

Some of my secrets had been revealed today, but she would understand.

Everything that I did, I did for her.

Fuck. The thought of her in my shower, wet and covered in blood...

I'd wanted to fuck her so badly. It had taken every ounce of strength to stop myself, to keep me from touching her.

All because of this bastard.

"I have an offer. One that you might not like, but it will still... help us both."

"And what's that?" I bit out.

"As wrong as it was of you to keep her from exploring the outside world, I'm glad you did. She is not a regular human. She's a demigod. Guessing by your actions over the last decade, I'm assuming you knew she was different."

I nodded, thinking of the alley.

"If anyone besides us discovered that, her life would be in danger. Demigods and monsters alike would hunt her. Hell, even the gods would want to find her and kill her. I don't know who her father is, and I worry he may be one of the less kind gods."

"So she *is* a demigod?"

"Yes," he said. "I received a letter from the Three Fates. Do you know who they are?"

I'd heard of the Three Fates. Aside from what I'd learned through myths and legends, I'd never been able to get information on what they did now. But I did know that the mafia Ian ran was a branch of a much larger organization, one ran by the Three Fates. My understanding was that it was led by monsters, and they all controlled the city of Moirai. They controlled other parts of the world too.

What I knew of Ian was this—he was ruthless, cruel, and controlling. Even though he'd shown restraint and patience tonight, I knew there was a side to him that was a terrible and ruthless beast.

Just like me.

As mortal as I was, there was a darker part of me. A part that coveted my princess and would do anything for her. I would kill for her in the blink of an eye, raze this entire earth for her.

"We have to keep her safe," Ian said. "And that means we must move her from this home. That also means you're not going on vacation, so there's my peace offering."

"And where would we go?"

"To Moirai."

"That's idiotic," I said. "You want to keep her safe and away from your world. Why would you take her closer to it?"

"Because no one will attack me there," Ian sighed. "My men are well trained, and I have friends who will protect her from forces *you* would be powerless against. I've thought through all the options. Knowing how the Fates are, even if I take her far away, something will happen to bring her back. This is about thinking one step ahead of them."

"What's in it for me?" I asked.

"You get to remain with Serena. I'm not doing you any fucking favors. I pay your salary, provide you with a place to live, you eat for free in my home. What more could you possibly want?"

I sighed, tipping my head back and staring at the ceiling. The fire was still burning in its hearth, turning the ceiling a golden orange and creating shadows that danced along the shelves.

Serena.

I didn't know how to show her that everything I'd done had been for her safety.

"I want to be with her," I whispered.

"She's *mine.*"

"You've never touched her," I argued. "You've never wanted her."

"I do want her," Ian said. "And I will claim her. She belongs to me, Luca. She is more than a wife to me. She is my mate. I plan on making her fall in love with me and breeding her until my cocks are raw."

Rage and jealousy tore through me. "She *belongs* to me."

"That will never be true."

Then, as Serena had said before she started to think better of him, there was only one option.

I would have to kill the dragon.

But not yet. I needed to wait for the right moment.

"Who do you think she would choose?" Ian asked.

I looked at him, wishing I could take him out now. "Me. Obviously."

Ian gave me a doubtful look. "I don't know, Luca. She just found out that you've fucked her over for the last decade of her life. It doesn't bode well for you. Plus you only have one cock. I have two."

"I only need one," I said, getting to my feet.

"So, do we have a deal then?"

"What?"

"Are you going to help me protect her?"

"Always," I said. "But I'm not doing it for you. I'm doing it for her. Am I free to go?"

"No. One more thing." Ian got to his feet, stepping closer to me. I went still, feeling a wave of electricity run through my body. My cock gave a helpless throb, and once again, all I could think about was what we'd done together... "I know you hate me," he whispered. "But why don't you come to my bed tonight?"

"No," I replied quickly, ignoring how my cock began to harden.

"Are you sure?" Ian asked, smirking.

"Yes." This son of a bitch.

"Well. The invitation is there," he said. "Now. Go and cool off. And perhaps give Serena some time to process everything."

I got up and went to the door, leaving him without another word.

I went down the hallway, noting that the guards' positions had been shuffled around. I crept upstairs, stopping in front of Serena's door. I leaned in and pressed my ear against it.

I couldn't hear anything, but I knew she was in there.

Fuck. I'd fucked up. Anger pumped through me, and I closed my eyes, wishing she wasn't so upset. I could understand why she was, but I wouldn't have changed anything that I had done.

I pressed my palm against the door, wishing she'd let me in.

I wouldn't ask her, though.

I sighed and backed away, going to my door. I slipped inside my room, leaving the door unlocked.

Everything had gone wrong.

Yesterday, I'd seen a fire in her that I had never seen before. The need to burn down the world around her, to show Ian she didn't belong to him. But the pain I saw in her eyes when she realized he wasn't the only monster in her life had damn near brought me to my knees.

I lived to please her. To serve her. I loved her more than I loved myself.

I hated hurting her.

But, the things I knew.

The secrets I kept.

Ones from before Ian.

I sucked in a breath, stripped to my boxers, and tossed my phone onto the side table. I ignored the missed call notification, ignored the fact that J wanted information from me.

No more telling him about Serena.

Not after the disaster this evening had been.

I didn't know him well enough. All the details I'd given him over the years had seemed harmless, but when we spoke earlier it'd felt different.

I drew in a deep breath, my head falling back. I stared at the ceiling, wishing I could go to her. That I could show her how much she meant to me.

How much I wanted her.

The thought of touching her, of fucking her...my cock hardened in response.

I reached down to touch myself but stopped, feeling guilty.

I went to my bed, reaching for the second phone I kept hidden behind the mattress. I pulled it out and began looking through my countless photos of Serena.

Ian had been so shocked to learn she wasn't human.

But, deep down, I had known the truth for a long time.

I knew before anyone else, aside from her mother.

It was such a relief to get this long-held secret off my chest. Such a relief to reveal that she was the reason I was who I was.

My throat constricted as I looked at a picture of her. The one I always landed on. She was smiling and looked like she didn't have a care in the world. She looked happy.

"I'm lost." A little girl sat on the stone steps, tears streaming down her cheeks. She wore a cherry red dress, her dark hair pulled back into a braid. She looked all shiny and new like she didn't belong here.

I glanced around, feeling nervous. I wasn't strong enough to protect her if I needed to.

"What's your name? Where did you come from?" I asked.

"Serena," she cried. More tears rolled down her cheeks. "I want my mama."

I held out my hand, offering it to her. "I can help you," I said. "But we need to go. The sun is setting soon, and it's not safe for you. Okay?"

She sniffled and nodded, holding out her hand. I took it and helped her stand.

Then I heard a shout.

The hair on the back of my neck stood up. "Come on," I said, tugging her along.

We started to run, and I heard another shout, closer now. We had to move fast.

I took a turn down an alley and cursed. It was a dead end.

"Give me the girl."

Serena squealed, wrapping her arms around me as we turned. A man stood at the alley entrance, towering over us.

"No," I said, keeping my voice firm. "Our mom will be here soon."

The man laughed, taking a step closer. "A piece of trash like you isn't related to her. Give me the girl, or die."

He pulled a knife out, then lunged. Serena screamed, her arms tightening around me, and I felt a burst of energy around us. I flew back as light burst from her. I squeezed my eyes shut, feeling like I would burn up.

She fell to the ground, silence settling over us. I pushed myself up and ran to her, seeing the man was dead. Blood pooled around him.

She blinked her eyes open and began to push herself up on the elbows. I covered her eyes with my hand, "No, little queen. Don't look."

"Serena?!!!"

A woman's voice echoed down the alley and Serena tore away from me. "Mama!"

I let out a deep breath, the memory ending in my mind.

She could be angry at me. I knew that I hurt her, but it was to keep her safe.

She would come around.

She would realize how much I fucking loved her.

After that day, I'd sworn to become strong enough to protect anyone who needed me. I would never allow myself to be so weak again. I couldn't stand the thought of not being able to protect her.

And when I had met Serena again, this time as the niece of *Don* Avilleno, she had needed someone to protect her again.

Chapter 11
A Proposal

SERENA

There wasn't enough monster porn on the internet.

That's what I discovered at 3 a.m. last night after not being able to sleep for several hours. The first couple I'd spent crying off and on, then all my thoughts had gone down a horny rabbit hole.

Now, the sun was bleeding into my room, indicating it was almost time to get up. I still hadn't come, and all I could think about was what it would be like to ride a dragon.

I craned my neck, watching as the clock turned to 7 a.m. I waited, expecting Luca to invade my room like usual. The minutes ticked by, and I expected him to storm in, call me lazy, then throw knives at me.

None of that happened.

I sat up in bed, feeling a wave of sadness and anger. If he had kept me locked up all this time, what else had he hidden from me?

Also, how the hell was I supposed to go about murdering my husband if I couldn't trust my accomplice?

I got out of bed, changed into a black t-shirt and skirt, then left my room. The smell of bacon made my stomach growl, and I remembered I hadn't eaten last night.

I rounded the corner expecting to see Luca at the stove but was surprised to find Ian instead. He stood with a small towel thrown over his shoulder, his back muscles even more delicious in the daytime. He wore gym shorts, and I couldn't stop my gaze from wandering.

Gym shorts were right up there with gray sweatpants in my book. I sucked in a breath, trying to ignore the little lick of lust I felt.

"No throwing knives this morning, please," he said without looking back at me.

That made me grin despite the growing realization that I wanted to bone the dragon I was supposed to slay. *Slay. Not lay.*

Was that even the plan anymore? Ian coming here had ruined everything. My entire reality had been shattered.

I cleared my throat, wishing I could douse these flames of desire with some fucking holy water or something. *Something* that would make me stop feeling this way. "Where's Luca?" I asked, catching myself swaying my hips as I walked toward him.

I leaned around him, snatching a piece of bacon off a plate. He gave me a playful growl, which only made me smile.

"You can't stop me from eating the bacon," I said. "Luca never makes bacon except on holidays."

"Oh yeah?" Ian chuckled. "You know, you could cook for yourself. Then you could have bacon every day of the year. You should try it sometime."

"I have cooked for myself before, thanks," I snapped,

leaning against the counter to his left and watching him. "But I'm not very good at it."

"I'm sure if you practiced you would get better," Ian said, looking up at me. "I'm convinced you could do anything you wanted to, Serena."

I swallowed hard, studying him. Fucking hell. It was hard to hate him with a face like that. He was too hot for his own good. He winked at me, returning his attention to cooking breakfast.

The pan wasn't the only thing sizzling now.

"To answer your question, I haven't seen Luca this morning. Perhaps he slept in."

"He never sleeps in," I said. "Not unless he's sick."

"I'm surprised you're so eager to see him, given last night's revelations."

Eager wasn't the right word, but I didn't correct him. I wanted to ensure Luca was alive and kicking because I still needed to find out how much he'd done over the last decade.

All the secrets...

What else was he hiding from me?

I thought about that for a moment, wondering if the man I loved was someone else entirely

I hoped not.

"Well, I want to talk to him."

"Maybe he's packing," Ian suggested. He pulled the pan off the stove, moved it aside, then opened the oven and reached in to grab a pan.

"Wait, you're going to burn—"

He pulled the tray out and set it down, raising a brow with a smirk. "Worried about me, honey bun? A dragon can hardly be burned by your little oven."

"Shut up," I scoffed, eyeing him suspiciously. "*Honey bun?*"

Well, I could rule out death by fire or burning.

"Don't call me that. And what do you mean *packing?*" I asked.

"I'm taking you to Moirai. How about sugar plum instead?" Ian replied casually. "And I canceled Luca's vacation so he could come with you. Despite last night, I figured you would be more comfortable with him."

Both of my brows raised. "Really? We're going there? Also, you absolutely cannot call me sugar plum. That's terrible. Surely there are better nicknames than that."

"Yes," Ian said. "I need to keep you close for your safety. After thinking everything through, I'd rather us be there. The Fates always get their way, so we might as well give them what they want. We'll stay at my apartment. It has several rooms, so I'm sure you'll find one you like. What about *little killer?*"

Little killer. The way he said it, you would have thought he was calling me princess. Butterflies erupted in my stomach, and I could only stare at him. "Are we... are we going to fly? And no. Why do you need a pet name for me?!"

"Yep," Ian answered. "Come eat breakfast, Serena. I can hear your stomach growling." He motioned for me to sit at the breakfast nook. "You're my wife. Isn't that what couples do? Give each other silly nicknames."

"We aren't like other couples," I grumbled, taking a seat. "Our marriage was a business deal. You don't love me. You haven't spent any time with me, besides the two brief visits over the last ten years."

"What about baby cakes, gummy bear, peaches, bubbles, sunshine, apple of my eye—" he continued, ignoring my comment.

"I'm going to vomit on you."

He laughed. I liked his laugh.

Excitement washed over me, followed by a wave of anxiety.

The only times I'd left this place was to visit him, but this would be different.

Ian made me a plate with biscuits, eggs, and bacon then set it down on the table in front of me. He piled food onto a plate for himself and joined me.

He was easy to be around when he was like this. He was almost pleasant when he wasn't trying to pick me apart or play twenty questions.

An uncomfortable silence settled over us, the kind that was charged like an electrical storm.

Stop thinking about his dick. You're not fucking him.

My dreams had been naughty last night, leaving the imprint of *what if*. Not to mention, the monster porn I *had* managed to find all had one thing in common—monster dicks.

What if Ian wasn't the monster I believed him to be?

What if my husband was actually someone I could love?

"Let's eat, then you can pack, then we'll leave," Ian said, breaking the silence. "What if I call you princess?"

"I'm not a princess," I quipped, arching a brow. "I'm a queen. And I prefer to be treated as such."

He raised a brow, a slow smile tugging at his mouth. Every time he grinned, I wanted to do everything I could to keep it there. He had an addicting smile, especially because he was usually so serious. "Is that why he calls you *little queen*?"

I blushed and nodded, trying to steer my thoughts elsewhere.

I was finally getting to leave this place, but then what? I didn't know what it meant to be a demigod and certainly didn't know which god was my parent.

But staying here certainly wouldn't give me the answers I needed.

"Alright," I sighed. "Sounds like a plan. I'll go with you to Moirai."

"Good," he said. "Additionally... I have a proposal for you."

"A proposal?" I asked.

He watched me cut two biscuits in half and lay bacon on each side. "Yes..." he drifted off, scowling as I spooned apricot jam onto the bacon.

He let out a low hiss as I reached for the Tabasco sauce.

"Are you judging me?" I asked, fighting back a smirk as I poured a few drops on top. I could only smile as I mushed the two biscuit halves together.

His expression almost sent me into a fit of laughter. Still, I managed to remain completely serious as I took a bite.

"I can't believe I'm about to say this while you have jam dripping down your chin," he said, shaking his head. He let out a deep chuckle. "I want to fuck you, Serena."

Shit. I swallowed hard and *wrong*, sending me into a coughing fit like I was about to die. The Tabasco sauce hit the back of my throat, and tears sprang to my eyes. I grabbed a napkin, covering my mouth as I fought to live against the bacon, jam, and hot sauce sandwich.

Ian sipped his water cooly, waiting for me to finish dying. Finally, I caught my breath, tears streaking down my cheeks.

"Fuck me," I wheezed.

"Indeed," Ian said. "That's exactly what I mean."

"What? *Why?*" I asked, my voice sounding ragged like I'd chain-smoked a pack of cigarettes.

"Why else? I want you," he said, smirking. "I want to touch you. To kiss you. To fuck you. I want to do it all. I'm attracted to you, Serena. All night, I dreamed about coming to your bed and making you come over and over again. I dreamed about shoving my forked tongue between those pretty legs and devouring you, little queen."

Fuck. Fuck, fuck, fuck. His words had my pussy throbbing and my breaths shortening.

"So my proposal is this. Sleep with me. Be with me. I have a decade to make up to you. I want to treat you right, to show you that I am not so bad. And then, I will let you be with Luca."

I blinked, wiping away the tears.

Part of me wanted to say no. That I would never touch him. He was a monster, after all, and I was supposed to be plotting his death.

I will let you be with Luca.

I didn't want anyone to let me do anything. I wanted to be in charge of my own world. That was why I'd lost my mind a couple days ago and murdered those men.

But, if he let me be with Luca...

It was why I'd wanted to kill him in the first place, and now that reason would be gone.

Did I still want to be with Luca, though? I had so many questions for him. I needed those answers before I let my relationship go any further with him, even as friends.

"I... I will consider your offer," I said softly.

"Good," he said. "I need an answer by midnight."

"Why midnight?" I asked. "Is that when you turn into a pumpkin?"

"What? No," he said, his expression growing serious.

I couldn't tell if he knew I was joking or not.

"Fine," I agreed. "Midnight." That would give me time to think everything over, to try to let logic win over my pussy.

"May I do something that might persuade you?"

My heart skipped a beat. My body seemed to know what it wanted before my mind did because I nodded.

Smoke curled from his nostrils, his gaze becoming heated. "May I touch you?" he whispered.

Fuck. I'd never felt like this before. Suddenly, I couldn't think. Every sane part of me short-circuited, and every nerve ending came alive with the electrical sensation of need.

"Yes," I whispered.

He slid from his chair, coming around the table to me. I watched as he knelt, his hand sliding down my calf to the ankle I'd rolled last night. He began to rub it, and I immediately groaned, my head falling back.

"Fuck," I whispered.

He massaged it and then worked his way back up my calf, over my thigh. My breath hitched as he slowly pushed my skirt up.

"Ian," I whimpered.

"Spread your legs for me."

I turned in my chair, shuddering as I spread my thighs for him. He hiked my skirt up further until my crimson lace underwear was visible.

"You're perfect," he whispered, then leaned down.

I cried out, my pussy throbbing as his lips pressed against my clit through the lace in a gentle kiss. That soft pressure alone made me want to come for him, my entire body feeling alive and desperate.

His fingers traced over me, and I groaned, my head falling back.

I'd never been touched like this.

He looped two fingers around the thatch of lace and tugged it to the side.

"Oh fuck," I whispered. "Ian."

"Call me sir when I'm pleasuring you," he whispered. "Spread your legs wider, little queen."

"Yes, sir," I mumbled, parting my legs as far as possible.

He leaned forward, the tip of his tongue flicking over my clit.

I gasped and found my fingers curling in his silver hair, holding his head to my pussy.

"Do you want my tongue inside you?"

"Yes," I whispered. "Please. Please, I need this."

"I know," he grunted.

Leaning back, he let go of my underwear and licked his lips.

And that was all he did.

Holy fuck. This fucker had just given me the lady blue balls of the century.

He pulled my skirt down carefully, fixing the fabric so it draped perfectly. He winked at me and stood, returning to his seat.

"*That's it?*"

"Yes," Ian said. "A teaser. For both of us."

We stared at each other for a few moments. I felt like I was burning alive.

"Morning."

I looked up as Luca came into the kitchen. He looked like he hadn't slept, dark circles under his eyes.

I glared at him, all of the anger from last night coming back in full force. "I need to pack," I said, standing up.

"I already took care of it for you," Luca said, coming to the table.

"Great," I muttered. "You didn't have to do that. I can pack for myself. I can also cook for myself. And make my own lattes. In fact, I can do anything and everything for myself."

Luca stole the biscuit off my plate and shrugged. "I rather you not have to lift a finger over menial tasks, *piccola regina.*"

With that, he took his moody ass outside, leaving me with Ian wondering what the hell I was going to do.

Between the two of them, I was falling apart.

Chapter 12
Flight to Moirai

IAN

I owned a fleet of jets and planes and had countless men who worked for me. I paid them well, they did a good job, and there was an understanding. They knew if they ever fucked me over, I would kill them, their family, and anyone they had ever loved.

It was harsh. But it was how it had to be.

Still, I found myself wondering if the life I'd chosen was indeed a good one. Was I ever truly happy?

Sitting across from Serena, I realized that I'd never been happy. Not until now.

The flight to Moirai was different than any other I'd ever had, all because of Serena's excitement. Our seats faced each other, two and two. I watched as she leaned against one of the windows, staring at the city below as we descended; her eyes lit up with pure joy.

Luca sat next to her and across from me, his discomfort evident. He hated flying, and based on the sweat accumulated on his forehead from the last couple of hours, I realized he might even be scared of planes.

It made me happier than it should have. I liked knowing one of his weaknesses.

For the next five minutes, I thought about all the ways I could torture him just by knowing he hated planes. Meanwhile, I was confident he was thinking of all the ways he could try and kill me.

Serena blew out a breath, letting out a happy hum. My attention returned to her, my brittle soul basking in her sunshine.

Since my breakfast with Serena, I had been hanging on by a thread. I'd thought about what I wanted last night and decided I wanted her.

I needed to have her, taste her, touch her... The little tease had been as cruel to me as it had been to her, but I'd certainly made my point.

Her scent was like nectar. I wanted to drown myself in the essence of her little pussy, to feel her clench me so tight that my seed filled her.

I knew that she wanted me, even if she would rather see me dead.

"It's so big," Serena whispered in awe.

My thoughts were already in the gutter. I wanted to hear her say that about my cocks with the same sort of innocent reverence. Every word from her mouth had me craving her more and more.

Serena grinned, leaning back in her seat. "I can't believe I get to go to Moirai. No thanks to you," she said, glaring at Luca.

Luca sighed, closing his eyes. "I don't want to talk about that right now, *piccola regina.*"

"Maybe you kept her locked up for ten years because

you're afraid of heights," I suggested, enjoying both of their expressions.

Serena gasped, her glare becoming even sharper, while Luca groaned, his knuckles turning white as he gripped the seat tighter.

"Is that true?" Serena asked.

"That's not *why*, but I don't like flying," he said between clenched teeth. "We'll talk about this another time."

"When?" she asked.

"*Another time.*"

"Serena," I said, my voice dripping with false pity. "Why don't you hold the poor man's hand?"

She raised a dark brow and all but rolled her eyes at me. But then, I watched as she slid her hand into Luca's and the way he immediately gripped it. My wedding ring glittered on her finger as she held his hand, her gaze lifting to mine.

"Good girl," I said before I could stop myself.

Luca's eyes flew open, burning with anger. Meanwhile, Serena blushed, offering me a smile before looking away. I caught the scent of her arousal and looked in the opposite direction, cursing myself.

"We're thirty minutes out," I said.

Luca shook his head. "I'm going to the bathroom," he said, ripping off his seat belt. "I'm about to vomit everything I ate today. Call her a good girl again, and I'll throw up on your fancy suit."

I watched in amusement as the massive bodyguard squeezed through the aisle, making his way to the front of the plane, then crammed himself into the bathroom.

Serena sighed. "I had no idea he was scared of flying."

"Me neither," I chuckled. "The very worst that can happen is we crash and die. Well, he would die. You and I would likely be fine."

"Charming," she muttered. She tilted her chin up, eyeing me.

After a moment, I saw something wicked there, a gleam of mischief.

"I wonder how long he'll be gone for," she said, her voice taking on a suggestive tone.

"Serena," I warned, lowering my voice. "I don't know what you think you're up to, but no."

She quirked a brow, unbuckling herself. I watched her slide a hand over her thigh, curling her fingers under the edge of her skirt. The pleats were bunched as she hiked it up, repositioning in her seat. She put one leg over the armrest, and my mouth fell open as I realized she didn't have panties on.

"Tell me if he comes back," she whispered. "I'd hate for him to catch you looking at my pussy like this. But you fucking left me wet earlier, after I stayed up until 3 a.m. watching monster porn, and that isn't fair, Ian. So, I want you to know, two can play that game."

Holy fuck.

My cocks immediately hardened, my breath hitching as she slid her fingers down. I watched as she dipped a finger inside her pretty pussy, her essence glistening. Taunting me. Reminding me that I could have taken her earlier, but I hadn't.

Did she say she watched monster *porn?*

Fuck. My cocks began to throb, desperation seeping into every cell of my being.

"Serena," I whispered. "Pull your skirt down."

"No," she said, giving me a teasing smile. "I'm wet, *husband.*"

Fucking hell. A low growl left me, and I watched as she shoved two fingers inside her pussy, her head tipping back with a moan.

I couldn't look away. No matter how much I wanted to try

to ignore her, I couldn't. She was being a brat, and she knew it. All I could do was watch the way she worked her fingers inside herself, her other hand finding her clit.

She cried out, and I felt the back of my neck turn hot. I glanced back, remembering I had guards seated in the back of the plane.

I unbuckled myself quickly and stood, reaching for a curtain that would offer us more privacy. I tugged it free, meeting the curious gazes of some of my men.

"Do not disturb us," I snarled. "And put on some gods damned headphones. If a single one of you fucks listen to what's about to happen, I will personally burn you alive."

Their faces paled, and I watched as headphones were pulled over their ears, eyes averting.

I closed the curtain right as Serena let out a sharp cry, her breath becoming ragged.

I rushed over to her and grabbed her jaw, forcing her to look up at me with a snarl. Her breath hitched, her eyes still burning with defiance.

"Come," I whispered. "Come for me, now."

"I'll come for myself," she rasped. "Not for you."

I glowered as she grinned up at me. Her eyes fluttered, a groan leaving her pouty lips. I could feel her heart beating wildly, could smell the rush of her arousal as her orgasm crashed into her.

She was so pretty when she came. Her gaze darkened with sated lust and her breathing calmed as she relaxed against the seat. I released her jaw, leaning down and adjusting her leg so she was seated correctly again. She yelped as I yanked her skirt back into place and buckled her seatbelt.

"Don't do that again," I whispered. "Or else I'll fuck you so hard, you won't be able to walk straight."

She gave me a low feminine chuckle, batting her eyelashes innocently.

Serena Avellino would be the death of me.

"Maybe that's what I want," she whispered. "Maybe I want you to fuck me so hard I can't walk. *Sir*."

A groan interrupted what I was about to say, and I looked up as the bathroom door shoved open. I curled my hands into fists, feeling my knuckles whiten as I plopped back into my seat right before Luca returned to us.

"You okay?" Serena asked.

"I'll survive," he said, sweat dripping down his face. "We'll never speak of this again."

"Oh, no," she laughed. "I will be reminding you about this daily for the rest of your life."

The plane began to descend, and Luca mumbled some curses, closing his eyes again.

"We're about to land," I said, watching the ground grow closer.

Within a few minutes, the wheels touched down, and the plane came to a rumbling stop. I signaled my men to leave first, so they could ensure there were no unwanted visitors at the airport. Maybe it was paranoia, but I didn't want anyone to know I had brought my wife to Moirai.

Luca immediately yanked off his seatbelt and stood, blowing out a breath. "Alright," he said. "We made it. Great."

"We're not at the gates yet, dumb ass," I said. "Sit back down."

Luca sneered at me and flopped back onto his seat, color finally returning to his face. He looked past me, raising a brow. "Why are the curtains drawn?"

"Because I wanted them to be," I snapped.

Serena giggled softly and then looked away, her focus returning to the city. I could still *smell* her and wished that I didn't need to breathe. It took every ounce of control to keep my cocks from hardening again.

Our captain spoke over the intercom, informing us that we had arrived in Moirai and our car was waiting on the runway. I mentioned we'd be at the apartment within the hour.

We came to a complete halt, and I unbuckled then stood. I yanked open the curtain, ignoring the looks I got.

"Our bags will already be in the car," I said. I turned and offered Serena my hand.

Serena unbuckled quickly and, to my pleasant surprise, slid her hand into mine. "Lead the way," she said, standing.

Luca made an unrecognizable noise as I tugged her along, escorting her to the door. The co-pilot was already there, unlatching it for us.

"Mr. Colchian," he greeted me, giving a respectful nod.

I returned it and began descending the staircase leading to our car. Serena followed me with Luca behind her.

The city skyline drew my attention, the sky slowly starting to dim. The puffy clouds were various shades of peach, the neon lights of Moirai becoming brighter.

The three of us walked to the car.

"I want the window seat," Serena insisted.

"I don't want to sit next to him," Luca hissed.

"Too bad," she said.

I took the middle seat, fighting the urge to laugh. Luca squeezed in next to me, turning his head to glare at me.

I met his gaze and raised a brow. "Keep looking at me like that, and I might decide to make you suck my cock."

Serena gasped, swiveling in her seat to look at us. I enjoyed her shock and how Luca scoffed at my words entirely too much.

He looked away, but I could see a blush creeping up his neck.

Serena swallowed hard and looked away, but I felt her reaction, too.

There was no hiding from me.

I leaned back in my seat, smirking the entire drive home. I realized I enjoyed teasing Luca almost as much as Serena, which made me wonder...

Would he take me up on the offer I'd made last night? Would he ever willingly come to my bed?

What about Serena? I'd also offered her a deal that would bring her to me at midnight tonight.

"This city is so pretty," Serena whispered.

She stared out the window just like she had on the plane, watching the cars, people, and buildings with contagious excitement. I ducked my head, looking over her shoulder to see what she saw. I'd never cared much for Moirai, but hearing her small gasps was changing my thoughts about the city.

I wanted to show her the whole world.

First, I had to show her I was someone she could love.

My thoughts surprised me. Is that what I wanted? After all this time, did I really want someone to love?

I liked the idea more and more the longer I was around her.

Luca, on the other hand...

I wasn't sure what to do with him. Not yet, anyway.

The driver pulled into a parking garage and drove to a heavily guarded entrance near the back. This entrance was only meant for me and other Three Fates Mafia officials. After someone had accidentally hit Madeline's Bugatti I'd paid for the damages and opted to have our own section for parking.

"Is this where you live?" Serena asked.

"Yes. One of the floors is my home. Well, one of my homes. And the floor above is my office."

"So what about all the other floors?"

"Some of them are leased to companies I own. Some of them are used for other things."

"Is there enough space for you to change into your full dragon form here? Or do you have to go to the roof for that?"

"I have a floor specifically dedicated to being able to change." My nest with all of the treasures I had collected over the years. "I can show you sometime."

"Absolutely not," Luca snapped.

"Why?" I chuckled. "Are you scared of dragons, Luca?"

"No. But it wouldn't be safe."

"Hmm, I thought we'd gotten over this. Serena is always safe with me. You, however, are not. Who knows, maybe I'll turn into a dragon and roast you like a marshmallow."

Serena giggled, Luca glared, and I grinned as the car pulled into a parking spot.

Luca exited the car quickly, walking around to Serena's door. I leaned across her, reaching for the door handle at the same time he arrived to open her door, both of us gripping the handle.

We glared at each other through the tinted glass.

"Ian," she whispered.

I huffed and let go.

One point for Luca.

"I'm ready for a hot shower," I muttered. A hot shower where I could stroke both of my cocks until I came.

All while thinking about her sucking on me.

"And pizza," Serena said. "Oh! Will you take me to get ice cream?"

Ice cream?

I frowned at her. "Why?"

"I want to go to an ice cream stand. Or a hot dog stand!"

"Those are both bad for you," Luca said. "I can make ice cream—"

"I don't want fancy ice cream," she said. "I want the same stuff everyone else eats, and I want it in a waffle cone with sprinkles. Please?"

"Sure," I said. "Now, let's go. Out."

"You promise?" she asked.

"Yes," I hissed. "Woman, get out of the car."

She smirked and slid out of the car. Luca slammed the door shut and I got out on the other side. The driver popped the trunk.

"I can have your luggage brought up, sir," he offered.

"We can take them ourselves," I said. "I have a big strong bodyguard who's on my payroll right here. I'm sure he won't mind."

Luca glared at me, and I fought a smile.

One point to me.

THREE FATES MAFIA

SERENA

Chapter 13
Midnight Magic

SERENA

I stared out the massive window of my room, watching the city below us. I felt like a god being this high up. The sun set over Moirai, the sky varying between peach and magenta hues. I crossed my arms and leaned against the glass, listening intently to the conversation between Ian and Luca in the living room.

"I have an errand for you, then I'll leave you alone," Ian said.

"I'd like to remind you that my job is to protect her," Luca hissed.

"I know that. I need you to meet up with a friend, Ashley. She has an important item for me. Also, if you see any signs of werewolves or a three-headed beast, run."

"That sounds insane," Luca growled.

"Oh, come now. You'll be fine. You're a big boy."

The two of them grumbled back and forth for a few more

moments. Ultimately, the conversation ended with Luca slamming the door.

Leaving me alone with Ian.

I turned and went to my bed, plopping down on the fluffy blankets. They smelled clean and were soft.

After what happened on the plane, I couldn't concentrate. I felt a desperation I'd never felt before, followed by a needy frustration that nothing was taming.

I was going to sleep with him.

I had gone back and forth with myself for hours now and kept coming back to the same conclusion. Between now and yesterday, I'd started to like my husband.

It didn't hurt that he was hot. Or that he very clearly wanted me.

I looked over at the clock on the bedside table. It was already 9 p.m. Three hours until I had to make a decision, but it was already made.

I sighed and slowly sat up, gasping as I realized Ian was standing in the doorway of my room. I had turned off all the lights so I could watch the city glow, and now the darkness clung to him, only interrupted by the iridescent flames that burned in his gaze.

He watched me the same way I watched him. With hunger. Need.

"You have three hours," he whispered, his voice hoarse.

"I've already decided." My heart began to beat faster as I swallowed hard.

"And?" he asked. "What have you decided, little queen?"

Was I doing this? Was I really going to sleep with this dragon who had— "I want you."

He blew out a breath. "Are you sure?"

"Yes."

"Then come with me, wife."

I usually felt a bolt of anger when he reminded me I was his wife, but not now. His ring was on my finger, and soon his cock would be filling me, and I'd get to cum from riding a dragon.

A dragon who was my husband.

I slid out of bed, the cold wood floor making me tip-toe. I walked quickly to him, and he lifted me up in one swift motion, my arms wrapping around his neck as he pushed me against the wall.

"Serena," he whispered. "I'll be gentle."

"I don't want you to be gentle," I rasped. "I want you to take me as a monster would. As the *real* you."

He let out a low groan and I felt him begin to shift, his clothes tearing beneath my hands. Wings spread behind his back, his head becoming one of a dragon.

Heat speared me to my core as I parted my lips, his tongue snaking out and intertwining with mine.

I gasped, drawing back for a moment, and he gave me a fanged smile.

The end of his tongue split into two.

"You okay?" he chuckled.

"More than," I answered.

We started to kiss again, my entire body relaxing as I gave in to him. All of the tension melted between us, and I groaned as I wrapped my legs around his hips, grinding against him.

Ian let out a low growl and carried me down the hall to his bed, kicking open the door.

I needed him inside me. I needed to feel him on top of me, to finally release the way I'd been dreaming of for so long.

He laid me back on his bed, our tongues dancing as he pinned me beneath him. I ran my hands under his shredded shirt, pulling the fabric free and tossing it to the side.

He grunted as my fingertips traced the dips of his abs, the feeling of his scales sending a shiver through me.

"You're so warm," I moaned.

Smoke curled from his mouth, and I groaned as he dragged his claws down my chest. My shirt sliced in half, and two of his claws curled over the edge of my pants. He popped the button, yanking them down quickly.

My entire body felt like it was on fire. I looked down between us, gasping as I saw not one, but two, cocks.

"Two?" I whispered.

"One for each hole, little wife."

"Oh fuck," I mumbled.

My reality was proving to be wilder than my imagination.

He suddenly pulled back and clapped three times. Several lights in the room turned on, bathing us in a romantic amber glow. I let out a surprised laugh, then my attention returned entirely to him.

Now I could see him, and he was perfect.

His naked body stood in front of me, his silver-to-black scales shining, leading my eyes all the way down to both of his cocks. Both were hard, precum dripping from the tips and protruding from what looked like a slit.

"What..." I drifted off, flushing. I didn't know how to ask him about his anatomy and didn't want to say anything wrong. But my curiosity was peaked, and my eyes gave me away.

Ian smirked, his forked tongue running over his bottom lip. "It's where my cocks stay when I'm not hard. Dragons aren't like humans, little queen."

He slid his hand down, stroking the cock on top, his eyes darkening. The sight of him doing so tore a moan from me.

"Show me how you like to be touched," he said. "Show me how to please you, and then I'll make you feel like a goddess."

His eyes never left me as I slid my hand down my body, feeling myself like I had a million times—only this was different. Being watched by him so intensely sent butterflies through my stomach, my breaths becoming harsher as I dragged my fingers over my clit.

I realized that I liked being watched. There was a power in it I'd never felt before. Knowing I was the center of his entire world in this moment added an erotic edge to what we were doing, leaving me craving more.

I circled my clit, feeling how wet I was for him. "I want you," I whispered.

"I know, baby," he murmured, his gaze feasting on my pussy. "Keep touching yourself, sweetheart."

I bit my lower lip, my pussy fluttering as I circled my clit. My breath hitched as he stroked his cock, watching me. Devouring me. I felt like I was being worshiped on an altar, and he was kneeling before me, begging me to show him what felt good.

That was true power.

Now that I had a taste of it, I'd never look back.

"Good girl," he purred.

I slipped two fingers inside of myself, moaning as my body responded. I arched against the bed, pleasure spreading through me.

"I want to taste you," he rasped.

I nodded, a plea slipping from my lips. "Please."

He crawled onto the bed and leaned down, his hands sliding up my thighs. His claws dragged over my skin, the sensation making me shiver. I slid my fingers back to my clit as he lowered his head between my thighs. The double tip of his tongue ran over my pussy, immediately making me cry out.

Everything felt like fire. Like lust and need.

He grunted as I began to rub my clit faster—and then he plunged his tongue inside of me.

A cry tore from me, my entire body feeling electrified. I gasped, bucking my hips against him as an orgasm crashed into me. He pinned my thighs down as I came on his dragon tongue, rapture overcoming me.

My breaths shortened as I sank into the blankets, then I felt his tongue thrust.

Fuck.

He chuckled, his chest vibrating as he pulled his tongue back and then pushed it back in. I gripped the blankets with a moan.

His scent and warmth surrounded me. He looked up, letting out a low groan. "You taste like heaven, little queen. Your pussy was made for me."

"I want you inside of me," I whimpered. "Please."

I needed him inside of me.

He grabbed a bottle of lube from his nightstand and returned to the bed, kneeling at my feet.

Like me, he couldn't fight the force of need drawing us together.

"I wanted to make this special," he huffed. "This is your first time, after all. I'll try my best to be gentle. I'll make it up to you later, but right now, I need to breed your pussy and make you mine. Do you understand?"

"Yes, sir," I rasped.

"Good girl," he praised. "You remembered."

I watched as he picked up the bottle of lube and poured a generous amount onto his hands, then mine. He gave both of his cocks a slow and deliberate pump, covering them with lube. I spread the cool gel over my pussy, pushing some inside. Getting ready for him.

I was nervous, I realized, but this felt right.

Being with him was right.

"I can't wait anymore," I groaned. "Hurry."

Ian leaned over me, planting a hand next to my head.

"We'll start with one cock, little queen, and if you can take it, I'll give you both."

"Thank you, sir," I whispered.

He cursed under his breath, embers escaping and floating around us.

"Don't catch me on fire," I teased.

"I won't," he huffed.

I felt the head of his cock press against me and looked down between us, watching as the lower one began to spread me.

Fuck. I gasped as he slowly began to fill me, the ridges along his cock hitting parts of me that made my toes curl. I reached up and gripped his shoulders, bracing myself as I took more.

"Ian," I moaned. "Oh fuck. You're so big."

This was completely different from the toys I used. The experience of having someone pin me down, their body hot against mine...it was unlike anything I'd ever done before.

I moaned again, all sorts of noises leaving me as pleasure washed through me.

"You can be as loud as you want, little queen," he rasped. "Scream for me. Cry for me. All your noises are so fucking hot, I could come from listening to you."

I cried out in response, clenching around him.

"I want it all," I moaned. "*Please.*"

"Anything for you, little queen."

He pulled his hips back then thrust forward, filling me completely in one swift motion. My entire body buzzed, his cock pulsing inside of me. I cried out, my nails digging into his scaled muscles.

His massive spiked wings spread behind him, his groans blending with mine. He dragged his hips back and then pumped forward, his cock thrusting into me. I could feel every ridge, every movement— and all of it was perfect.

I held onto him as he fell into a harsh rhythm, a low possessive growl leaving him as he continued to pump in and out. Euphoria flowed through my veins, pleasure sending me closer and closer to the edge.

My breaths turned into pants, his thrusts becoming hurried.

"I'm sorry, baby," he grunted, fucking me harder. "I can't—fuck—take it slow. I have to breed you, little queen."

His words made me cry out, and I realized two things.

One, I had a breeding kink.

Two, I had a monster kink.

An orgasm crashed into me, merciless in the way it pulled me down into absolute ecstasy.

"Fuck," he gasped. "You're squeezing my cock so hard."

"Give me the other," I whimpered.

"So eager," he grunted. "Finish taking this one first."

He shoved my thighs back, the angle changing in a way that had me howling with need.

If he changed positions right now, I would murder him.

"Right there!" I cried. "Fuck! Don't you fucking stop!"

Ian laughed as he thrust inside me, his claws digging into my skin. Whatever spot he was rubbing right now made me feel like abandoning everything I knew.

The head of his cock hit as deep as he could go, the ridges continually rubbing me, driving me closer and closer to coming again until—

"*Oh fuck.*"

I came again, clenching around his massive cock. I saw stars, my mind spinning as I melted around him.

"I'm coming," he growled.

He gave one final thrust, then hot cum began to shoot from his cock.

I felt it inside of me, the warmth spreading. I collapsed under him, panting. My entire body tingled, my eyes closing.

He kept coming, his moans sweet. "You took me so well," he whispered.

I nodded, unable to form an intelligible sentence yet.

He chuckled, leaning down to kiss me. I parted my lips for him, moaning as our tongues met. He drew back, smoke curling around us.

I stared up at him in wonder, my heart beating quickly.

"I'm going to take care of you," he whispered reverently. "I promise."

"Take care of me by giving me your other cock," I huffed.

He was still buried inside of me and still hard too. His cum kept filling me, and I felt it start to drip out.

"There's so much," I whispered, amazed.

"You want the other?" he asked. "I thought you were going to fall asleep."

"No," I gasped. "No. I just had to come back to earth first. What's the point of having two if I don't take them both?"

He chuckled, his tongue dragging over my cheek. He thrust his hips, drawing a long groan from me. "You're fucking perfect," he said. "Everything I could ever dream of."

His words sounded like a confession. Before I could respond, he pulled his cock out. He rolled me onto my side and settled behind me, fitting my body snugly against him. I felt the heads of his cocks against me, and he adjusted them so they fit together, his arm wrapping around my body while the other gripped my thigh.

His cum spilled out and he growled. "I'm going to fuck it all back inside of you, little queen."

I whimpered, my pussy pulsing. I wanted him to breed me all over again, to fuck me until my voice was hoarse.

"Are you ready?"

"Yes," I said. "Now."

He nodded and then shoved both of his cocks inside of me.

Fuck. He was already huge with one of them, but with both... I arched against him, but his arm held me tight as his cock stretched me more than I had ever been stretched. I gasped, raking my nails over his seatbelt of an arm. There was a hint of pain as I adjusted around him, but then all I felt was pleasure.

"Thank the gods you're a demigod," he rasped. "I can feel your body accommodating me. Your pussy is gripping me so fucking tight, baby. I'm going to fill you all over again."

Fuck this man could talk dirty. Man, monster...

All my thoughts crumbled to dust as he began to fuck me. His body was hot against mine, my ass pressed against him as he began to rock, filling me with both of his thick cocks.

It was so wrong to enjoy being fucked by a monster this much, but I didn't care. Fuck, I didn't care about a gods damned thing except coming around him again.

"Harder," I gasped.

"Harder and I'll fucking ruin you," he growled.

"You can try."

He growled at the challenge, smoke curling around me as he began to fuck me harder. The sound of our skin slapping together filled the room, the intense pleasure becoming more intense coupled with the stinging pain of his claws digging into my skin.

The two of us fell into a harsh rhythm, my mind completely melting as he fucked me over and over, his cocks spearing me until we both moaned. A brutal orgasm crashed into me at the same time he buried both of his cocks deep inside me, the heat of his cum filling me again.

He grunted and suddenly rolled over onto his back, holding me on top of him.

"What are you doing?" I gasped.

He gripped both my thighs. I was lying on top of him now, his clawed hands holding me in this position, all the while his cocks continued to fill me.

"Getting you pregnant," he grunted.

That should have horrified me. Right? I shouldn't have wanted that. I should tell him no, should pull off his cocks...

Instead, I drew in a soft breath, relaxing against him.

He let out a dark chuckle. "Do you wish he was here right now?"

"Who?" I whispered.

"Luca."

Oh. Oh, fuck. He'd fucked me hard enough that I'd almost forgotten Luca's name.

Guilt flared through me, but Ian growled.

"Don't feel bad. He'll have his turn, won't he?"

"Would you ever let him..." I trailed off, appalled about the question I was about to ask.

"Finish your question."

My cheeks became iron-hot, embarrassment pumping through me.

"Finish. Your. Question."

"Would you ever let him fuck me with you?"

"Yes."

There was zero hesitance, which shocked me. My pussy pulsed at the though of them both fucking me. Of Luca taking me and then Ian, them taking turns making me come.

Fuck. Now I couldn't stop thinking about it.

Ian slowly lifted me and I gasped as his cocks pulled free. In one swift motion, he rolled me beneath him, pushing my legs back again so that all the cum would stay inside.

"You're going to carry my babies," he said. "You're going to be my mate. My wife. And I'm going to give you every single thing you've ever wanted, including Luca."

"You already promised me Luca," I teased.

"I did," he said. "Now I'm promising you the whole world."

I pressed my lips together, staring up at him.

"You can't tell him about this," I whispered. "Don't tell him I agreed to sleep with you so I could be with him. I want to tell him."

"No? You just asked me if I'd let him fuck you with me, little queen."

"I know. I know, it's...he's going to be upset."

"He'll get over it," Ian said. "He likes me more than he lets on."

For a moment, I thought Ian would add on to that, but then he stopped. He let out a soft hum and slowly began to shift back into his fully human form. After a few moments, I was looking at the man I'd told myself I should hate.

I couldn't hate him, though.

He leaned down, cradling my face gently.

This was the same man who had taken me from the life I knew. That had put fear in my uncle's eyes.

But when he was with me...

I leaned up, kissing him hard. His silver beard rubbed against my face as he deepened our kiss, a soft moan leaving him.

I didn't know what my life was turning into, but I knew I couldn't stop.

I was starting to fall for Ian—and now I had to make sure Luca didn't try and kill him. I needed to change his mind about my husband, but I wasn't sure how.

Chapter 14
Secrets

Serena

It was almost midnight when I left Ian sleeping and snuck down the hall to my room. Luca still wasn't home, which was starting to worry me. After the buzz of lust had worn off, my thoughts had returned to him.

Even though I should be mad at him.

There hadn't been a night in the last ten years where he'd been away like this, which made me uneasy. Maybe we were bad for each other. Maybe I should have let him go—but I couldn't.

I paused outside his bedroom, glancing back at Ian's door. The lights were off now, and I could hear his snore drifting through the apartment.

I smiled. It was silly, but knowing that the mafia monster snored while he slept was cute.

My heart beat faster as I crept closer to Luca's door. He hadn't come back, right? What if he'd come back and we hadn't heard him? What if...

Everything was becoming so complicated. The secrets all of us had made navigating the world around me difficult. I wanted Ian and had been with him tonight. Hell, I could still *feel* that I had been with him tonight.

Fuck it.

I gripped the doorknob and turned it quietly, slipping into Luca's room. It was colder in here than the rest of the apartment, and I pulled Ian's stolen dress shirt tighter around me.

He definitely wasn't home yet.

I let out a breath and crossed the room to the bed. Like his room at the castle, there were hardly any signs that someone had been in here, aside from the wrinkles on the bedspread.

I was tired of everything being so untouched. Our lives, our secrets, our hearts. Everything was like this fucking room. Neat, orderly, wrapped up with a little bow.

Not anymore.

I flopped down on the blankets with a heavy sigh, my mind racing.

I could touch him now.

What if he came home and found me naked in his bed?

What would he do?

The thought turned me on more than it should have.

"Fuck," I whispered.

Ian had already made me come several times. He could go for hours, and the only reason we stopped was because I was getting winded. The monster's stamina was insane.

Still...

I rolled over onto my back to touch myself. I slid my hand over my stomach, a soft moan leaving me. Everything with Ian had been perfect. He'd brought out a new side of me. All I could think about now was riding him or riding Luca.

So much had happened this week, but sleeping with my

husband was one of the highlights. That and now being able to be with Luca.

Would he be mad if he knew what I'd done? Ian was my husband, after all.

I sucked in a breath as I ran my fingertips over my clit. I was still sensitive, the feather-light touch feeling like something so much more.

"Luca." I moaned his name quietly and felt a rush of heat, my cheeks flushing.

How long had I wanted to do that?

All of the things I'd imagined him doing to me...

I moved closer to the center of the bed so I could spread my legs wider, but I stopped when I felt something hard against my ribs. I scowled, realizing that whatever it was, it was hidden under the blankets. I moved and reached my hand under, grabbing it.

A phone.

Weird.

Why was there a phone here?

I tapped the screen and it lit up, displaying a passcode screen.

What would Luca use as a passcode? More importantly, why did he have a second phone?

So many questions ran through my mind. I stared at it, wondering. What would he have to hide?

I paused for a moment, scolding myself. I shouldn't be looking through his stuff. Then again... he knew everything there was to know about me. Hell, he had bought me lingerie, cleaned blood off me after I murdered those guys, seen me throw up and... He'd seen everything.

I wanted to know more about him.

I tried a random combination which, of course, didn't work.

"What would you use?" I murmured.

Most people used birthdays for passwords, right? That's what I had read somewhere before. They used something familiar and easy to remember.

His birthday was in September. Maybe he'd used that. I typed in his birthdate and was given the same error.

Luca doesn't care about himself. He cares about you.

Surely not.

Biting my lower lip, I typed in my birthdate. 041795.

The screen unlocked and I cursed. "Luca," I whispered. "What is wrong with you?"

Excitement ran through me, though. What if I learned more about him through this? It was a massive invasion of privacy, but he would forgive me. Right? Eye for an eye, or something like that.

I scrolled through the phone but didn't find much. No text messages, no numbers, no apps. No emails. Nothing. I frowned, tapping the photos folder—and then my heart stopped.

"What the fuck?" I hissed, sitting up.

My face was there, on a photo album.

I drew in a breath and opened the album, my stomach clenching.

Thousands of photos.

"Oh my god," I rasped.

Holy fuck.

"Luca," I whispered. "What the fuck?"

Some of them were of me clothed, but many were not. In the shower, getting dressed, on my bed.

Playing with myself.

There were over *ten thousand* photos of me.

This sick motherfucker.

Fuck.

My hands started to shake. The rage I felt boiled up and

then settled into something hard. A shield around my heart, one that no knight in shining fucking armor would be able to penetrate.

I wouldn't show my cards yet.

No.

I forced myself to take a deep breath. I closed the album, turned the phone screen off, and slipped it under the blankets. Putting it back where I had found it.

Luca fucking Civello was a dead man.

He was going to beg me for fucking mercy.

"He loves you."

I jumped, turning around to see Ian standing in the doorway. His eyes burned in the dark, his expression unreadable.

"He's been watching me for years," I whispered. "I never said he could take these photos of me. He never asked. He never—fuck." I covered my mouth, my thoughts reeling.

"Serena," Ian said softly. "He loved you when we met, and I told him he could never touch you. If anything, this is my fault. I made him obsess over you. He's not a good man."

"I love him too. And I hate that. I hate myself for that."

Ian let out a noise and crossed the room, coming to me. His hands gripped my waist as he tugged me close.

I leaned into him, letting myself feel everything. Every ounce of rage, every morsel of anger.

"Say the word, and I'll have him killed," Ian whispered. "But I don't think you want that, even knowing his darkest secrets."

"If he had asked me..."

"Would you have said yes?"

No. Maybe. I didn't know. I'd wanted Luca for a long time, but the side of him I'd seen this week... the dark, depraved, obsessive hunger. All of it centered around me.

"I created a monster when I told him he could never have

you, and you're the only one who can bring him back. But it's your choice."

"You would have him killed?" I asked.

"In the blink of an eye," Ian chuckled. "If that's what you wanted. Don't you remember, Serena? I would do anything for you." He tipped my face up, making me look at him. "You're mine, little queen. You're my wife, my mate—and I intend to show you what that means."

"I don't want you to kill him," I admitted. I swallowed hard, thinking.

Earlier this week, I'd been talking to Luca about murdering the monster who held me in his arms now. Now, I was talking to the monster about murdering the man who had guarded me for a decade. Who had loved me even when I hadn't known.

Luca had been watching me for years. It was an obsession and I'd never noticed.

Or maybe I had noticed.

"I want to handle it," I said. "You don't need to interfere. I can handle my own problems. That's what I want more than anything, Ian. I don't need a man to solve things for me. Luca has made it clear that doesn't work out very well."

Ian cupped my face and kissed my forehead. "I can do that," he sighed. "Even if my instinct is to kill him."

"Thank you," I said, closing my eyes.

Luca was my problem.

"Can I tuck you into bed?" Ian asked.

"Yes," I said, feeling that flutter of excitement return.

"Excellent," he chuckled. He scooped me up, drawing a squeal from me as he carried me out of Luca's room to my own bedroom.

Carrying me to my bed, he gently laid me down. I giggled, kissing him as he pulled the blanket over me, wrapping me in it.

"You look good in my clothes," he teased.

I grinned, relaxing into the bed.

"You can always sleep with me," he said softly. "If you want."

"Maybe one day," I replied. "I still... I need time. You aren't who I thought you were."

"I am who you thought I was," Ian said. "But I can be much more than that too. I run a mafia, little queen. I'm a monster. I've killed mortals, fought gods, and devoured demigods just like you."

I raised a brow. "I think you did devour me..."

He snickered, planting another kiss on my lips. "Go to sleep, love. Tomorrow is a new day."

I watched him go, then closed my eyes, letting sleep take me before my anger kept me awake all night.

Chapter 15
Revenge

Luca

The city of Moirai made me jumpy. The sounds and busyness had me side-eyeing everything, cautious of every person who hustled past me.

I made my way to the building known as the Helm, craning my head back to look all the way to the top. It was the tallest in the city, and at the very top was supposedly where I needed to go.

My pocket started to ring, and I cursed under my breath, fishing it out. I moved out of the crowd, leaning against the building.

J.

This bastard. At some point, I had to confront him.

I was feeling feisty, so maybe today was that day. I wasn't the type to run from my demons.

"Hello?" I answered, looking at the faces of people as they passed by.

I hated cities. There were so many people, even this late at night. I'd much rather be back at the castle on the coast, far away from the loud bustle of this place.

"You've been ignoring me."

"I've been busy," I snapped. "You only call once a year. What do you want?"

"Where are you right now?" he asked, his voice lowering.

I knew that tone. I knew exactly what kind of bastard he was too.

Which meant I needed to get rid of him.

"None of your business," I said. "We're not doing this anymore, J. If you want to talk to Serena, call her yourself. I'm not your messenger boy."

"The only fucking reason you're alive right now is because of me," he sneered. "Her uncle wanted to slaughter you. Are you really going to throw everything I did for you in my face? Did the dragon get to you?"

The dragon. For years, I'd heard how bad Ian was. How terrible and evil. How he would take everything from me.

I didn't need J for anything, especially not handling Ian.

"Fuck off and lose my number," I snarled, ending the call.

I was so fucking done with everything. Between the increased calls from J, me pissing off Serena, the flight from fucking hell, and Ian sending me out like his personal errand boy—I was ready to explode.

I checked the gun hidden in my jacket, double-checked the knives, and then entered the pristine lobby through the Helm's front doors. I headed for the elevators, then stopped when a voice called out.

"Sir. *Sir,* you need a badge to go up."

I turned, irritation working through me. There was a man at the counter, and he raised a brow expectantly.

There were other guards in the room, I realized.

Fine.

I went to the desk, offering him a dry smile. "Sorry. I'm here to meet someone and was told to go up the elevator."

"Sure. What's your name?"

"Luca," I said.

"ID?"

"I'm not giving you my ID," I said. "Just let me go up and I will be out of your way."

"That's not how it works here."

I turned around, meeting the eyes of a bald man a couple inches taller than me. He wore a suit, tattoos covering his skin. He arched his brow expectantly.

"Who the fuck are you?"

"Luca," I said. "Ian sent me."

"Ian did, eh? He didn't say anything about you."

"I'm here to meet Ashley, not whoever the fuck you are."

We squared off. He was a strong-looking bastard, but if I—

His eyes flashed, burning with the same eeriness Ian's sometimes had.

For fucks sake.

"Ashley is my *wife*," he snarled. "What the fuck do you want with my wife—"

"*Aaecus.*"

We both looked up, and I heard Aaecus let out a breath.

A blonde woman stood a few feet away, wearing a sequined crimson dress and silver heels. She looked like a gods damned movie star, her hair falling in loose waves and bright blue eyes.

"Fucking hell, baby girl," Aaecus groaned, his demeanor going from guard dog to puppy. "I'm going to have to murder half of Moirai tonight with you looking like that."

She grinned and walked over to us, offering me a soft smile. "You must be Luca. Ian sent you later than I expected, and I have other plans. Here it is, though."

She held out her hand and I held out mine, ignoring the very possessive growl of the mighty tattooed Aaecus.

Did all monsters fucking growl?

I curled my hand around the object she gave me, raising a brow as I looked down at it. "What is this?"

"Pomegranate seeds," Ashley said. "Straight from the Underworld. Do I want to know what he wants them for?"

"I don't have a clue," I said, frowning at the vial. Pomegranate seeds filled it completely, the deep magenta juice coating them. I tucked it into my jacket, giving her a grim nod. "Thanks. Sorry to interrupt."

"No worries," Ashley said, hooking her arm into Aaecus'. He was like a sated lion now, watching me through narrowed eyes. "Are the three of you going to be at the event on Sunday?"

"Why would he be there?" Aaecus grumbled.

Ashley only smirked, patting his chest. "Ian's partners should be there, right?"

"I'm not his partner," I said quickly.

"Oh? I thought you were with his wife."

Where the fuck had she heard that?

"I'm her bodyguard," I gritted out.

They both cocked their heads, and Aaecus snorted. "Alright. If you say so. Let's go, baby girl, before Minos blows up our group chat with dick pics."

I watched the two of them leave and shook my head, bewildered. I pulled my phone out and saw the time, cursing under my breath.

It was getting close to midnight already. This errand had taken way longer than it should have, and that meant I'd left Serena alone with Ian.

If he touched her...

I tucked my phone away and sped through the lobby, pushing the front glass door open.

A shout had my head snapping up right as a black car sped by, the window rolling open.

Fuck.

I dove to the ground as bullets began to fly towards me, the glass doors shattering and a chorus of screams and panic following. *Pop, pop, pop.*

I rolled to the side, more bullets hitting the brick wall behind me. I got back up and ran, diving behind a parked car as more bullets flew.

Fuck. More screams. Blood. A couple people hit the ground, and the bullets kept flying until I heard the screeching of tires as the car barreled away.

I sat there for a moment, but only a moment. That's how long I gave myself to breathe before I started moving again. I ignored the sounds of people crying, screaming, dying—taking off down the sidewalk and ducking into an alley.

Fuck. Someone had tried to kill me.

Was it Ian? Of course it was. I was on his turf now, in his world.

That son of a bitch. I was going to murder him. I should have the moment I picked him up from the airport. I should never have let him even speak to Serena.

I tipped my head back, looking up at the sky. I couldn't see the stars here, and I hated that. It made me feel trapped.

"Dead monster," I muttered.

I walked down the alley, coming out on another street. Sirens sang into the night sky, the flash of red and blue splashing over me as police cars and ambulances weaved through traffic. A guy on a motorcycle was trying to park.

Perfect.

I stalked over to him. "Hey, bud."

He looked up as I swung my fist into his gut, letting him fall against me as his breath rushed out.

"Good boy," I chuckled, taking the key from him before he could find his composure. I gave him a hard shove, sending his ass to the sidewalk. "Thanks for the ride."

"Hey!" he wheezed, but I was already getting on the bike.

I put the key in, cranked the engine, and sped off into the traffic before he could get another word in. I needed to get back to Serena fast—before Ian realized he hadn't managed to kill me.

Chapter 16
Mate

LUCA

I walked through the front door and closed it carefully behind me, not wanting to wake Serena.

The apartment was dark and quiet. I stood still and listened, looking down the hall to my right. Serena's bedroom was on the left, mine across from hers, and Ian's bedroom was at the end.

I needed to do this fast.

His door was cracked open slightly, a golden crescent of light stretching over the hardwoods.

I slowly peeled off my jacket and set it down, kicking off my boots. I pulled the gun from my belt and crept down the hall, silent as I came to Ian's door.

Unlike the fucking assholes who had just tried to murder me, my gun had a silencer, which meant I wouldn't disturb Serena. She needed her sleep.

I also didn't want her to wake up and find her husband's blood on my hands.

I could explain it to her. I could show her that he was bad for us, bad for her. I could do exactly what we'd sworn to do earlier this week before he'd swayed her with his toxic words.

My heart pounded in my chest, my throat constricting. Still, my hands didn't shake.

I needed blood.

His blood.

I came to the door and paused, listening for him. I felt a cold deadliness wash over me, the calm before the storm. It was how I always felt when I was about to murder someone.

"Come in."

Fuck. His voice made me grip the gun tight, my finger feathering the trigger. I could feel every nerve in my body, every ligament and muscle, urging me to walk in and immediately shoot.

I could.

But no.

I wanted him to see me. I wanted him to know that the hit he'd put out on his wife's bodyguard had failed and that I would take her from him.

That I would be his end.

"Are you just going to stand there, Luca?" His voice held soft amusement. I hated that.

I slipped into his bedroom, shutting the door behind me, and pointed the gun right at him.

Ian was in his half-dragon form, lounging on his bed. He leaned against his headboard, the blankets gathered at his waist. The heads of both his cocks were out, his clawed hand gripping them both.

He snorted. "What's this about, Luca? Are you going to try and shoot me?"

"You *shot* me!" I hissed.

"I don't know what you're talking about."

His demeanor was so calm, utterly unaffected by the gun I had pointed at him. In fact, he let out a soft moan, stroking one of his cocks. His hand glided up and down his shaft, precum dripping from the head. His scales glinted in the lighting of the room, reflecting like tiny metal chips.

"Stop that," I snarled.

It didn't help that my cock perked up, all my blood starting to drain from my head. Why couldn't I put a cap on my desire around him? Or my feelings? All the coldness vanished, sinking into a low, throbbing heat that erased my urge to kill.

It made me want to fuck him.

"Why?" Ian whispered. "Luca, I didn't shoot at you. I don't know what the hell you're talking about."

"I was attacked," I said. "A car drove by outside of the Helm, rolled down the window, and proceeded to unleash a fucking machine gun on me."

"I doubt it was a machine gun. But I can assure you, that wasn't me or my men. In fact, I put an order out to my organization that no one is allowed to attack you. Not even me. "

"And the others?" I growled.

"Well. Did you run into any werewolves?"

"No," I snapped. "I did, however, almost get into a fight with the tall tattooed motherfucker with Ashley, but she intervened."

"Did she give you the seeds?"

"Yes," I hissed.

"Good. Put the gun down, Luca, and come here."

His command left me speechless.

He tilted his dragon head, his jaws parting in a fanged smile. My cock hardened completely in response, and I found my resistance slipping.

"Lock the door," he said softly.

I swallowed hard and lowered my gun, cursing under my breath. Fuck.

"I didn't try to kill you," Ian said. "Tomorrow, I will find out who did. Now, come here."

I pressed my lips together, my thoughts going blank for a moment,then I reached behind me and turned the lock.

"This is a bad idea," I whispered. "I fucking hate your guts."

"I don't like you either," Ian grunted. "So take off your pants."

I undid them quickly and kicked them to the side. In one swift movement, Ian was across the room, slamming me into the wall. I parted my lips for his dragon tongue, grunting as a fiery need spread through my body.

It had been way too long since I'd been touched.

For a moment, I felt guilty that Serena didn't know what this felt like.

She would find out, though.

Soon.

Fuck the dragon, then murder him. Then you can have her.

Ian growled as my cock came free, gripping me in his scaled palm. I groaned, tilting my head against the wall as he broke our kiss.

He dragged his claws over my shirt, ripping open the fabric. The sound of it being shredded sent a chill down my spine, the delicious kind. His tongue flicked across my nipples, drawing out more heated grunts from me.

"You're so sensitive," Ian teased. "I'd think you were a trembling little virgin if I hadn't fucked you before."

Fuck.

My breath hitched, my hips thrusting forward as he began

to stroke my cock. I needed release at the hands of another, even if those hands belonged to a monster.

"Do you remember our first time?" he chuckled.

How could I fucking forget? That time I fucked a dragon so I could save my girl. It wasn't exactly something you could pretend never happened, though I tried to.

Ian shoved me to my knees. I hit the ground with a heavy thud, grunting as I looked up at him.

He cupped my face, his claws digging into my jaw.

"When were you going to tell Serena about your second phone?"

I felt like I'd been punched in the gut. I went very still, a growl leaving me. "I don't know what you're talking about."

Ian let out a humorless laugh. "I have cameras everywhere at the castle, knight, including one in your room. I've seen you jack off to pictures of her. What I can't understand is why you brought the phone into my home. Did you think I'd let you stroke this mortal cock to pictures of my wife? Really?"

"Fuck you," I growled, my heart beating faster.

No one had ever known about that. It was a secret, one I intended to take to my grave. But now Ian knew.

"You're a whore," Ian whispered. "And a bastard. Do you think she ever knew? Or was that the fun of it? Wondering if she'd catch you looking at her."

My cock throbbed in response despite the hatred I felt for him. I tried to pull my face away, but his claws tightened, drawing blood.

"You could've had the real thing," he whispered. "But you keep fucking up. Now, touch me," he taunted. "And maybe I'll keep this between us."

My hatred burned, but I couldn't fight the hunger taking over. I was starving for this, starving to be fucked. All the rage and adrenaline from the night was funneling straight into a needy passion that only he could satisfy.

He was right, though.

The photos of Serena. All of them. I'd always gotten off on the idea that she didn't know, or maybe she did. The uncertainty turned me on.

Part of me wished Serena was here, even now. I wanted my secrets to come to light, so I wouldn't have to hide myself from her anymore.

I wanted her to know the real me. The murderer, the stalker, the bodyguard who controlled her. I wanted her to see my darkness and still love me.

His hard cocks pulsed in front of me, the tips dripping with precum. I stared in wonder, running my hand over the ridges that led to the bulbous base. Just as I remembered them, they were a dusty gray with silver veins that throbbed even in the darkness.

Ian's claws curled in my hair, and he dragged my head forward. The head of the upper cock bumped against my lips, and I mentally cursed.

I was going to hell. I was going to hell for submitting to him, but I couldn't stop.

"Open," he demanded. "Suck off your woman's husband, *slut*."

I started to say *fuck you* and instead got a mouthful of dragon cock. He thrust forward, and I moaned as he hit the back of my throat, my eyes rolling back.

"Good boy," he rasped. "Fuck, I forgot how good you feel. You suck cock better than most."

I reached up and gripped his scaled thighs, grunting as he dragged his cock back and then filled my mouth again. My head hit the wall, bumping with each harsh pump.

"Ten years with my wife, and you never fucking touched her?" he growled.

He pulled his cock back, and I looked up at him in a daze. "No," I said hoarsely. "I almost did after she killed your men. She was naked in my shower, her pussy right in front of me."

Ian bared his sharp teeth and yanked me up by my hair. The air crackled between us, the violent tension I'd felt becoming much more heated.

He shoved me back, and I fell onto the mattress with a grunt, my eyes widening as his wings spread behind him.

You're supposed to fight the dragon, not fuck him.

It was too late for logic.

"You're pathetic," Ian said softly. "If you loved her, why didn't you make her happy?"

"I did make her happy," I huffed.

He climbed onto the bed, straddling my thighs. His scales rubbed against me, the sensation making my cock throb. He grabbed my cock with his strong hand and leaned over me, rubbing it against one of his.

I blinked, focusing on his body, remembering that he had a pocket that kept his cocks in when he was in this form.

"Look at me," Ian snarled.

I huffed, my muscles straining. I propped myself up on my elbows, studying my cock against his. My mouth watered at the thought of sucking him again.

"Do you want to fuck me here?" Ian whispered.

I watched his claws glint, dragging my gaze to the slit his cocks came from.

Fuck.

"Say please."

"Fuck you," I whimpered.

"No, no. You have to say please in order to do that," Ian said. "I bet you're wondering what my wife would think of you right now, hmm? So needy for a monster's cock. Her knight in shining armor, begging like a little bitch."

"Gods damn it," I whispered. "She can never find out."

"Serena?" He asked, smirking.

"Yes. Promise me you won't tell her I fucked you."

"I promise."

That was too easy. I felt like I'd given my soul to the devil believing they were an angel. "I fucking hate you, Ian."

"Cute. Now, beg me like the desperate whore you are, Luca."

Chapter 17
Knight

Ian

I hadn't planned on doing this.

I had planned on attacking him. Punishing him. Doing something that would help me feel better after seeing the look on Serena's face.

Her finding that phone had pissed me off.

After fucking Serena two more times and filling her with my cum, I hadn't expected to be ready to turn Luca into my little bitch—but then he'd walked in with that gun. Acting like he was going to kill me.

As if.

He was a murderer, like me. He was also as desperate to be touched as Serena and I were. The three of us were ticking bombs, and his time had finally come.

I gripped his hair, looking down into his dark eyes. I could see the hate there. The way he despised me and how it wrapped around his lust for me, poisoning it. I could see the darkness of his obsession with Serena, and I understood it.

I was obsessed with her too.

In forty-eight hours, I had gone from hardly knowing her to making her the center of my fucking universe. I wanted her to have my children, to be my mate, to love me—and I was desperate to please her.

I was desperate to make her happy.

There was something alluring about her that drew us both in. Luca had been ensnared by her since his first meeting all those years ago, and now here I was, on the edge of caving to my most primal desires.

Like breeding her.

I couldn't tell Luca I'd fucked her, and I couldn't tell Serena I'd fucked him. It was a dangerous game of secrets all of us were playing, but at least I wasn't the one lying.

Luca had no idea that my cock had just been in the woman he'd loved for over a decade and that he'd tasted her for the first time now by sucking me.

I couldn't help but chuckle as he leaned forward, pushing his tongue inside the slit I was going to let him fuck. As I'd remembered, he was way better with his tongue than he should have been.

"That's right," I rasped. *Fuck.*

Luca grunted, his fingertips digging into my thighs. His hands were so much stronger than Serena's, making my muscles ache where he gripped me. It made me want to bend him over and remind him that he was submissive to me.

But not yet.

No.

I could be rougher with him. Harsher.

I gripped his hair harder, yanking his head back. I knew it

had to hurt. But he liked it, and I watched as he suppressed a moan.

"Keep worshiping my cocks," I ordered as I laid back.

Luca glared at me but straddled my legs, leaning down and taking one cock in each hand.

"To think they were all scared of you," I whispered. "All those men. Trained mercenaries who almost pissed their pants every time you walked by."

"I'm cruel," he whispered. "I hate everyone but her."

"And me," I teased.

"I hate *you* the fucking most."

"*Suck.*"

Before he could protest, I shoved my cock back into his dirty mouth. He glared as he began to bob his head up and down, taking me as far as he could while stroking the base.

He had no idea these sheets had been soaked in *her* cum only an hour ago.

I growled, closing my eyes as I lifted my hips, fucking his throat harder.

"Take it," I rasped as he moaned, trying to pull back. "You take it until I say otherwise, and then you get to fuck me."

His nails raked down my thighs, leaving streaks of angry pain, then I hit the back of his throat, holding his head down. Keeping him there for one, two, three—

I let him come up for air. He pulled back, gasping for it, before I dragged him back down.

"You're going to choke on my cock as punishment for pointing a fucking gun at me."

He tried to pull back, which was a mistake. I held him down longer, lifting my hips to force my cock down his throat. I held his head with one hand, sliding the other hand down to his throat.

Fuck I could feel myself there.

I grunted and let go of him. He raked in gasps, leaning back. His eyes closed, and I knew he was lightheaded.

His cock throbbed, cum dripping from it.

"You slut," I whispered. "Did you just come from choking on my cock?"

The liquid dripped, and I saw it pooling on the sheet.

"Bastard," I said. "And you're still hard too."

He opened his eyes, and the glare was gone, replaced by a look I'd never seen on this man's face.

"You know," he said. "I fucked you ten years ago to stay by her side, but I also fucked you then because you're a dragon. And you know what? For a dragon, you don't fuck much different than the rest of us."

I narrowed my eyes. Fuck, it was on the tip of my tongue. *Tell that to Serena.* But I wouldn't say it.

"You've never fucked a dragon," I said. "You've only fucked me like this. The real me would destroy that ass; you wouldn't be able to walk for days."

"Sure," he said, smirking. "Whatever you say."

"Do you want to choke again or do you want to be bred?"

"I want to fuck your stupid cock slit and come inside you, then get bred. So at least we're even."

Hardly my idea of being even, but I wasn't going to argue.

"Fine," I whispered. "Fuck me, then."

Luca straddled my thighs, and I leaned against the headboard, giving him an angle that would let him do what he wanted. He pushed both my cocks to the side, letting out a noise somewhere between a whine and a growl.

I watched as he pressed the head of his cock against the slit and thrust forward.

The two of us moaned together. He braced one hand on my chest, the other gripping my top cock, stroking it as he began to fuck me. I blew out a hot breath, embers floating around us as I felt him fill me.

I grunted as he thrust, pumping into me while he continued to stroke me. I reached up, dragging my claws lightly over him, tracing the scar that ran down his left rib cage. The touch had his hips bucking, the desperation infectious.

Our gazes locked, his lips tugging into a smile as he slammed into me, over and over, until I knew he was about to come.

He cried out, his head tipping back as his cock slid inside me. His cum began to shoot, covering me as he emptied every drop.

He panted, his chest heaving as he slumped.

"Good," I whispered. "If only our little queen was here to ride us both."

He stiffened, scowling. "Don't say that."

"Why? Haven't you thought about it?"

His expression gave him away.

I shoved him back onto the bed, grabbing his thighs and dragging his ass towards me. I shoved his legs back like I had with her, my intention to fill him and breed him too.

"Imagine," I said. "Her under me just like this. You thrusting into her pretty mouth, filling her throat with your cock while I fill her ass and pussy. I bet she'd love it."

"Fuck you," he rasped.

I grabbed the lube, pouring some onto his ass and my cocks.

"You don't want to think about it? I bet we could see the outline of my cock in her. And in my full dragon form..."

His cock was starting to perk up. I'd never seen Luca blush until now, and fucking hell—I wanted to see him do this every day.

I pressed the head of my bottom cock against him, pushing

his legs back further. "Just imagine," I said. "Maybe if you stop being such a prick, the three of us could live happily ever after."

Before he could say another damn word, I shoved my cock inside him, giving him every fucking inch. He cried out, his shout loud enough to wake Serena, which had both of us freezing.

My eyes slid to the door.

Fuck. I wished she'd walk in. I wished she would open the door and see me fucking Luca, making him moan and come. Her big strong bodyguard taking every inch of me.

He sucked in a breath, listening too.

"I wish she would walk in," I whispered. "I wish she would open that door, see you like this, and ride your ugly fucking face with that sweet princess pussy. Wouldn't you like that?"

"Fuck you," he rasped.

I pulled my hips back, grunting as my cock slid out. Luca gripped the sheets, his breaths uneasy as I pumped forward again. He let out a string of curses, and I reached back, grabbing a pillow and throwing it over his face.

"Shut up," I growled. "If you wake her up and she comes in here, I'm telling her everything. So either shut the fuck up and take it, or get out."

"I should have shot you," he huffed, grabbing the pillow and pressing his face into it.

I smirked down at him, pulling my cock back and slamming into him again. He groaned as I started to fuck him, my head falling back as pleasure curled through my body. Ten years of not fucking anyone, and now I had two partners that I never wanted to stop fucking.

My wings spread behind me, and I swallowed the flames I wanted to release, enjoying taking him more than I had the first time. My claws dug into his skin, leaving angry red marks as I thrust into him.

He groaned, his muscles rippling as he gripped the pillow tighter, muffling his cries.

I leaned over him, changing the angle and planting my hands on either side of him. I fucked him harder, closing my eyes. His scent surrounded me, drawing me in the same way Serena did.

Oh, fuck.

I opened my eyes and grabbed the pillow, yanking it away as I thrust all the way inside of him. I leaned down with a dark growl, grabbing his head and pushing it to the side.

"What are you doing?" he rasped.

His blood was calling to me. I grunted, still fucking him. I parted my jaws, baring my fangs.

"Ian," he whimpered.

"Be still." I sank my fangs into his shoulder, and he arched against me with a gasp, cursing and moaning my name.

His blood filled my mouth, and I knew.

I yanked back from him, letting out a low hiss.

He was my *mate.*

He was also my mate.

I felt the bond come to life, but I didn't want it. It wasn't supposed to happen this way, but it was too late.

I'd started a mating bond with Luca fucking Civello, my wife's bodyguard.

"Fuck," I growled. "Gods damn the fucking Fates."

"What the fuck is wrong with you?" Luca snapped.

I rolled my eyes, thrusting into him harder. I slid my clawed hand up his chest, gripping his shoulder. My magic zapped him, healing the wounds I'd just left.

I didn't give him my blood, so the bond wasn't complete. But still...

I could feel him.

"You're my mate," I snarled. "A fucking perverted body-guard is my mate."

I was angry about it, which only made me fuck him harder. Luca grunted, wrapping his arms around me as I pumped into him repeatedly, our breaths becoming harsher. The taste of his blood drove me wild. The knowledge that I had not one mate—but two—pushed me over the edge.

I groaned, coming hard. My hot cum shot out from both cocks, coating him inside and out. I grunted, staying there for a few moments as I filled him.

Fuck.

He was my mate.

What did that mean for us? For Serena? For Luca too?

I'd been alive so long, and I never imagined there would be more than one mate for me.

But I could feel the bond, the way he belonged to me. The way that my body and soul craved him.

His darkness, his anger, his passion, and his obsession. I could feel and see all of it.

I let out a breath, slowly pulling out of Luca. My cum coated his abs, leaking out of him too.

I wanted him again.

And again.

And I wanted Serena to watch.

I wanted her to join us.

Fuck.

"What was that?" he whispered.

"Fate," I muttered. "We're all fucked, Luca. I don't know what else to tell you."

"I don't know what you mean by mate."

"You belong to me," I said, staring down at him. "Monsters have mates. You're mine. When I tasted your blood, I knew it was true. It means we are bound together."

I had come so hard it was difficult to think straight, but I knew one thing.

Luca and Serena belonged to me—and I intended to make sure it stayed that way.

Chapter 18
Confession

SERENA

The next morning, I woke up, brushed my teeth, and contemplated murder.

I didn't actually want to kill Luca. But I certainly thought about it as I pulled my long hair into a bun and changed into a crimson dress. It was short, hot, and exactly what I wanted to wear, even though it was only 9 a.m.

I slipped on a pair of heels and studied myself in the bathroom mirror. Ian's ring gleamed on my finger, a reminder of everything we'd done last night.

I was falling for him. Fast. It felt right when I was with him. The problem was, I still wanted that with Luca, even if I did want to hit him in the head with a shovel right now.

Rage had me reaching for the crimson lipstick, and I swiped it on.

I was going to make him regret everything.

I relaxed my shoulders and held my head high, leaving the bedroom and going to the kitchen.

Luca was standing at the stove, cooking like he always did. His dark hair was tousled, and there were cuts on his face that hadn't been there last night. He looked up, raising a brow at me, and I felt the urge to run to him.

Even after everything. Even with what I knew.

I still felt that urge.

His lips parted, his eyes widening. "Are you going somewhere this morning?" he asked.

To your fucking funeral. "No," I said, forcing a bright smile.

He raised a brow. "You look nice."

"Thanks," I said, sauntering towards him. He stiffened as I came closer, and I fought the urge to laugh.

He'd always done that.

Now I knew why.

Now I knew why he looked at me the way he did. Why he liked to buy me clothes and pick out everything in my life.

It was all for him.

But what about me? What about what I wanted? I wasn't going to be his fucking doll, but he sure as hell was about to become my bitch.

"What about you?" I asked. "How are you this morning?"

I slid up next to him, listening to the way his breath hitched. He moved to the side, still pushing around the spatula in the pan. He was cooking what looked like a breakfast hash.

"I'm fine," he grumbled.

"Good," I said. "How was the errand for Ian?"

His jaw stiffened, his brows drawing together. I raised a brow and turned, leaning my lower back against the kitchen counter.

"That bad, huh?" I asked.

"I don't trust him," he said.

Of course, he'd say that. And, of course, he didn't trust Ian. Ian knew what I knew, and while I was certain Ian wouldn't murder Luca—I was sure Luca was worried about Ian finding his dirty little secrets.

"Really?" I asked. "He's grown on me. I appreciate him trying to protect me, ensuring I don't get murdered. Plus, leaving the castle was nice. A little getaway."

Luca cocked his head at my tone, frowning. "Are you okay?"

"Why wouldn't I be okay?" I asked. "I'm ready to conquer the world. Slay the gods."

He snorted, and that pissed me off. As if he doubted me.

I turned around, noting the butcher block within arm's length.

It was his turn to dodge knives.

"Hey, Luca," I said, feeling all the rage return. It burned in my veins, stinging like venom had been poured into me. "Are you right-handed or left-handed?"

His right hand was planted on the counter, his left stirring the potatoes.

"Right-handed," he said.

So that was the hand he'd used to stroke his cock while looking at pictures of me.

In one swift motion, I grabbed a knife from the butcher block, twirled like the murderous ballerina I was, and drove the blade straight through his hand, hard enough that it buried into the counter.

I'd never heard Luca scream until now.

He howled in pain, his knees immediately buckling as blood spurted. I held the knife there, seeing red. Seeing my anger, my rage, and the trust this motherfucker had broken.

"Serena!" he shouted, shoving at me.

I didn't budge. The blood speckled my dress, blending in

with the crimson fabric as he tried to get free. Squirming like a bastard.

I grabbed his hair and tilted his head, forcing him to look at me.

I'd never seen Luca cry.

"Confess," I whispered.

"Fuck," he rasped. "What the fuck is wrong with you? What are you—"

I ripped the knife out of his hand and stabbed it again. He screamed louder this time, his breath knocked out of him.

I hoped it fucking hurt.

"Tell me," I said. "Tell me the truth."

"The truth about what?"

"Is this the hand you've been stroking your cock with, Luca?"

"What? What the fuck are you—"

"The phone. The *ten thousand* photos you have on that fucking phone you took without my permission. Tell me about that, Luca!" My words ended in a shout, my vision darkening.

I could rip him apart. I felt the power flowing through me, the thirst for death. For suffering. For pain.

Yet, through it all, I felt love.

"I did it," he said, his dark eyes feasting on me. He knelt before me, blood dripping to the floor at my feet. "I've loved you forever. I've told you that. Ever since that day in the alley, I've loved you. My life belongs to you. My body, even if you wound me, belongs to you. You could slit my throat or stab me through the heart, and I would still belong to you."

"You kept me trapped in that house," I whispered. "For ten years. And you took photos of me fucking myself. Touching myself. Showering, eating, living in a cage you built for me. That's not love, Luca. It's obsession."

"Obsession," he whispered. "Yes. It's also that. I know I'm

fucked. There's a part of me that wants you to see my darkness and know that it's all for you."

"Oh, so it's my fault, then?" I snarled.

"No. No—"

I ripped the knife from his hand, planted my heel on his chest, and kicked him back. He hit the floor with a loud thud, his head cracking against the tile. I stepped over him, pointing my knife at him.

He was hard.

I could see his cock pressing against his pants.

"Is that for me, baby?" I asked sweetly. "Maybe I should stab your cock too."

He stared at me in shock, clutching his bleeding hand to his chest.

I lifted my heel, pressing it against his cock.

"Serena," he rasped.

"I should bust your fucking balls for what you put me through," I whispered. "So beg me for mercy. Beg me for forgiveness, and I'll tell my *husband* not to murder you."

"Please," he whispered. "I'm sorry. I'm sorry for hurting you."

"That's a very generic apology," I said, applying more pressure to my heel.

He gasped, his body tensing. The pan on the stove began to sizzle louder, more blood covering him. Covering the floor. Dripping from my knife.

"I'm sorry I took photos of you," he said. "I'm sorry I lied to you. I'm sorry I tricked you. I'm sorry that I made you think Ian hated you. I'm sorry that I trapped you in a house. And I'm sorry that I broke your trust, Serena." He sucked in a breath and sat up slowly, my heel still on his cock and my knife ready to strike. "But I'm not sorry for blackmailing *Don* Avellino all those years ago. I'm not sorry for fucking your newly wedded husband so I could stay by your side for ten years. I'm not sorry for fucking my hand every night, thinking about breeding your cunt over and over. And I'm not sorry for loving you."

What the fuck did he just say?

"You can hate me," he whispered. "That's fine. But either kill me or let me stay in your life, Serena. I can't live without you."

"I didn't ask you to tell me what you're *not* sorry for," I said. "I told you to beg me for fucking forgiveness."

We stared at each other. One beat. Two.

"Please forgive me," he whispered. His words were desperate. Hungry. Starved for what he wanted. "Please. I love you. I will make it up to you. Please show me mercy."

I took a deep breath, feeling the rage slowly melt away. I pulled my heel off his cock, instead planting it on his thigh. He stared up at me. My pussy fluttered as I felt his fingertips on my ankle, tracing up my calf to my thigh.

"I can promise you one thing," I said.

"What's that?" he asked.

"If you ever hide something from me again, I will kill you."

"Fuck," he whispered. "When did you become so fierce, *piccola regina*?"

"The moment I realized I don't have to obey anyone but myself," I said.

He nodded, swallowing hard. I held out my hand, offering it to him.

He leaned forward, lightly pressing his lips against it.

"You belong to me," I said. "Do you understand, Luca? Not my uncle. Not Ian. Me. You don't make deals for me. You don't control me. The only thing I want is for you to worship me."

"I can do that," he whispered.

"Good," I said.

"I'm falling in love with Ian. And I slept with him last night." I confessed.

Luca froze, his eyes widening.

"I already love you," I said. "Even though I hate you right now. The funny thing is that I slept with Ian for you. That's what I told myself, anyway. I struck a deal, much like the ones you've made–sleep with my monster husband so I can sleep with my bodyguard. So, that's what I did last night. Then I woke up this morning and realized I didn't fuck him for anyone but myself. And it felt *good*. So now you have a decision to make. You can leave and start a new life. I'll let you go, and you'll never see me again. Or you learn how to fucking share and become mine. Because I want you, Luca, but not if it means I can't have Ian too."

Ian had planted a seed in my mind last night when he'd asked if I wanted Luca to be there with us. It had grown, over-taking my dreams last night and sprouting blooms this morning.

I wanted both of them.

Luca and Ian.

Was that too much to ask for?

Luca stared at me for a moment and then *laughed*.

Fuck, he was losing his mind.

He let out a dark giggle, tilting his head back as tears began to stream down his face.

I glared at him.

He kept laughing, more tears streaming down his face.

"If that's what you want, then I guess I'm learning how to share," Luca said. "I will never leave you. Ever."

I swallowed hard, tears blurring my vision.

"Luca," I whispered. "I love you. I really love you."

He let out another noise and slowly stood, tugging me close.

I held onto him, tears now streaming down my face too. He pressed his lips against my forehead, letting out a breath.

"I fucked him last night, too," he whispered.

It was my turn to be shocked. I looked up at him, my big bodyguard. The man I had known for ten years. He'd cared for me when I was sick, cooked for me, and protected me.

He'd fucked my husband last night too.

"I fucked him ten years ago to be with you," Luca said. "It was part of a deal I made. I've done so many fucked up things, *piccola regina*. I shouldn't even touch you. I've sinned so much I'm scared the blood will rub off on you. And last night... last night, when I came home, I was with him again. I slept with your husband, the monster I've hated for so fucking long."

"So he slept with both of us last night?" I asked, my lips parting.

"Yes," Luca said. "Did he tell you about the phone?"

"No," I said. "I went to your room and was going to masturbate on your bed when I rolled over onto it. Then I guessed your password. My birthday, really?"

He slowly smirked. "You really guessed that?"

"Yes," I said. "Luca, I came from a mafia family, and I murdered three men last Tuesday. I'm not exactly Miss Perfect."

"You are to me," he whispered, cupping my face.

We both stared at each other, tears falling.

"You fucked a dragon so you could fuck me?" he whispered, his lips tugging into an arrogant smile.

"Shut up," I mumbled. "We need to bandage your hand. You're getting blood everywhere, and breakfast is burning."

"The blood matches your dress." He lifted his hand, thumbing away my tears. "You look pretty when you cry."

I sucked in a breath, not expecting *that* to turn me on.

"You look pretty when you're smiling. When you're laughing. But especially when you cry. But you know what will be even prettier? When you're sobbing my name while I fill you with my cum."

Fuck. *Fuck, fuck, fuck.* All the feelings I'd felt in the shower the other day came roaring back, followed by the lust that had been building for so long. My body froze against him, my breath hitching as my pussy ached for him.

"Ian can heal your hand," I said, stepping back from him.

I wasn't ready yet. Even though I wanted him so fucking much.

"I'll finish breakfast," I said. "Go have him heal you. Then we'll figure out the rest of our day."

"Morning."

Luca stiffened, and we both turned, looking at Ian as he entered the kitchen. He paused, arching a silver brow as he approached the coffee maker.

"Do I even want to ask?"

"Like you didn't watch on your cameras," Luca quipped.

He did nothing to hide his smile as he poured himself a cup of coffee.

"Can you heal Luca?" I asked. "With your magic."

Ian turned, taking a long sip of his coffee. He regarded Luca, the two of them having a staring contest.

"Yes," Ian finally said. "Come here, lover."

"Do not fucking call me that," Luca hissed.

I was amused. Did Ian call him that last night?

My entire body responded to that thought. Fucking hell.

I grabbed the pan on the stove and moved it while turning off the heat. Blood was everywhere, and I had ruined breakfast, but it had been worth it.

"I propose we either order breakfast or go out to eat," I said, wrinkling my nose.

I glanced up as Ian pulled Luca close, holding his hand. I

felt the magic, the rush of power filling the room, then it disappeared like a cool breeze.

"All better," Ian said. "I can kiss it too, if needed."

"Fuck off," Luca mumbled.

"I can order breakfast," Ian said. "I have to go to work today. My office is in the building so I won't be far. I need to check on some things and look into a shooting."

"A shooting?" I asked, alarmed.

Luca went to the kitchen sink and turned on the faucet, washing his hands. He sighed, glancing around the kitchen.

"I'll have it cleaned," Ian said. "Don't worry about it."

"Okay," he said. "Someone attacked me last night," Luca said, looking at me.

"What?" I hissed.

Not like I'd just stabbed him or anything.

"Why would someone attack you?"

"I don't know," Luca said. "I thought it was Ian at first."

We both looked at him, but he shook his head. "Not me." He grabbed his cup of coffee, letting out a soft hum. "It would have been much easier if it were. But no. Someone intentionally attacked you. Damon has sent me several heated messages about it since you were in contact with his mate moments before."

I felt a streak of jealousy, and Ian snorted smoke.

"No reason to look jealous. I'm sure you'd like Ashley, she's like you. Plus, Damon, Aaecus, and Minos would eat Luca alive if he ever touched her," Ian said. "I sent Luca to retrieve pomegranate seeds for me last night. They're useful for binding agreements, which I make when I bring certain men into my business."

Well, now I felt embarrassed.

Ian drained his coffee and poured another cup.

"You drink it black?" I asked, wrinkling my nose.

"Yes," he said. "So, aside from all the drama this morning... How'd you sleep, little queen?"

"Good," I said, sliding up next to him. He smelled good, looked good...

Fuck, I wanted to kiss him.

Ian leaned in, kissing the top of my head gently, before moving around the bar and taking a seat. He was already dressed for work, wearing a black turtleneck, pants, and a belt I wanted him to spank me with.

Fuck. I eyed the buckle, my thoughts running wild for a few moments. He set his coffee down, smirking at me.

The things I wanted to do with him.... All my sexual fantasies had been awakened, and I found myself wishing that I had all the things from that list... The handcuffs, the flogger, the lingerie. I wanted it all.

I wanted to be tag teamed by my knight and dragon, but the trick was making sure they didn't murder each other. Or that I didn't murder Luca.

"When are we getting ice cream?" I asked Ian, trying to focus.

Ian picked up a newspaper from the counter and opened it, which amused me. Who even read newspapers anymore?

"Ice cream?" Ian asked. "I was going to leave after breakfast."

Luca cleared his throat, looking around the kitchen at the mess.

"But you promised," I reminded him.

Ian peeked at me over the top of his newspaper. His coffee mug was steaming on the bar beside him, the paper hiding what I knew was a smirk. "Promised what?"

"That you'd take me out," I said.

"Serena, it's still morning. Both of you are covered in blood. The kitchen has been destroyed."

"It'll be brunch time soon enough," I insisted, pointing at the clock. "I can clean up by then."

He let out a low groan, a very annoyed one. "I'd rather order breakfast for us all."

I went around the bar, going up to him. I heard Luca chuckle from the kitchen as I all but cornered Ian, pushing his hand away so he'd move the newspaper. I pressed myself against him, giving him the sweetest look possible.

"Please," I said.

"You're killing me," he mumbled, giving me a thirsty look. "Even covered in blood, I want to devour you, little queen. But, no. It's not safe. Although, I do have a proposal."

"Do you?" I asked, narrowing my eyes.

He cupped my face and kissed me gently, making every thought pivot to one thing.

"I will order you a wonderful breakfast and then go to work for a couple hours. You can spend some time with Luca. Watch a movie or use the gym. Whatever you want. Then tonight, I will take you both out to dinner. Ice cream included."

I held my breath for a moment and then caved. "Fine," I said.

"Maybe we can take you shopping at some point so you can pick out a dress. There's an event on Sunday that I'd like to take you to."

"I'd like that," I said.

Ian winked at me and stood up. "I'm headed to the office," he said. "Be safe, have fun, and remember that monsters fuck better than men."

I snorted and felt the hair on the back of my neck prickle. I turned, meeting Luca's gaze.

I'd expected him to look angry, but that's not what I saw.

I could touch him now.

It started to sink in. Finally.

And Ian was leaving me alone with him.

"You look amazing in red," Ian said. "Like you're ready to conquer the world. But maybe you should shower off Luca's blood."

"Yes," I sighed.

"I'll see you later, honey," Ian chuckled, heading towards the door. "I'll be at the office if you need me. Luca, behave."

"I'll see you later," I mumbled. "Luca, come with me."

His eyes widened, and Ian let out a low, knowing laugh.

I left the kitchen and headed for the hall, pausing and turning to look at him. "What? Don't you want to see me naked? Or do you only prefer photos?"

Luca cursed, letting out a groan. "*Piccola regina.*"

I turned, hiding my smile before he could see how much I enjoyed torturing him.

Chapter 19
Obsession

Ian

I sat at the desk in my office and pulled up the camera feeds on my computer. I unzipped my pants, pulling out my cocks and fisting them. I began to stroke myself as I watched the knight finally claim his princess...

THREE FATES MAFIA

IAN

Chapter 20
Possession

Luca

She was finally mine.

I followed Serena down the hall, a lamb to the slaughter. She could stab me again, devour my soul, send me to my death —and it would all be worth it if it pleased her.

She'd punished me for what I'd done, and it had broken me.

I watched as she reached up and loosened her bun, unraveling the dark strands until they fell down her back in loose curls. She led me to my room and turned, her crimson lips drawing into a soft smile.

I fell to my knees in front of her, pleased by the way she gasped.

"Allow me to undress you," I whispered. "Please."

"Yes," she said.

I took in a breath, drawing her in. Her essence, her presence, the way she stood before me. I leaned down and unclasped her heels, letting her use my shoulders for balance. Her hands pressed against me as I slipped each shoe off, then I ran my hands up her smooth legs, hiking up the bottom of her dress.

I leaned forward, swallowing hard as I pressed my lips to her skin. She let out a soft moan, and my cock throbbed in response.

"I love you," I whispered. "I worship you. I need you."

I kissed my way up her inner thigh until my lips met the thin black lace she wore under her dress. I ran my thumb over her pussy, feeling how wet she was.

"Baby," I rasped. "Did stabbing me turn you on?"

She stiffened, the noise she made answering for her. My little rose had razor-sharp thorns. I groaned and looped my fingers under the delicate fabric, pulling it down to her ankles.

"So wet for me," I said. "I want to taste you, but not yet. I haven't even kissed you yet."

I rose to my feet and went around to her back, sweeping her hair to the side. I grabbed the small zipper at the nape of her neck and tugged it down slowly, enjoying how her eyes fluttered.

Every touch, every moment. All of it meant something to me.

She had discovered my secrets. She had seen my darkness.

But she hadn't pushed me away.

She had brought me closer.

She was a goddess who had granted me salvation, and I would spend the rest of my days showing her I could be worthy of her grace.

I'd show myself to her.

I pushed the shoulders of her dress to the side, letting the fabric fall to the floor. I unclasped her bra with one hand and smiled at her surprised squeak.

Now she was naked in front of me.

My cock was stiff and throbbing, desperate to be buried inside of her. My blood speckled her tan skin. She turned, looking up at me.

"Your turn," she whispered.

She ran her hands up my chest, and I groaned, my eyes never leaving her as she touched me. She smiled, pulling my shirt up and rising on her tiptoes to pull it over my head. Tossing it to the floor, her palms immediately returned to me.

"All your muscles," she said. "And your scars. I love every part of you. Even when you're a prick."

I chuckled.

Then her hands slid to my waistband.

"Serena," I said reverently.

She pulled my shorts down, followed by my boxer briefs. My cock sprang free, hard and pulsing.

"So hard, for me?" she taunted. "Do you like having your cock stepped on?"

I narrowed my eyes at her, letting out a low growl. I could only submit to her for so long before I needed to take control, to show her what it meant to be with me...but for now...

"When you're the one stepping on it, maybe."

She smirked and her hand circled my cock, drawing an involuntary groan from me.

Fuck.

Fuck.

"Serena," I rasped.

She stroked me slowly, our gazes locking.

"I've wanted this for so long," I whispered.

In one swift motion, I lifted her, enjoying her squeal as I pulled her over my shoulder and carried her to the bathroom. She let out a low laugh as I stepped into the walk-in shower and turned on the water, setting her down and pushing her against the wall.

Our lips met in a hungry kiss, her body warm against mine. The water pelted my back, the heat spreading through me all the way to my cold, rotten soul.

I pinned her arms above her head and turned her around, fitting my cock against her sweet ass. She pressed back against me, letting out a low moan.

"Luca," she whimpered. "I hate you."

That made me harder. I let out a low growl, pressing her against the tiles. I ran my hand down her side, sliding it over the curve of her hip and then lower.

"You said you were going to touch yourself on my bed," I whispered. "Is that true, *piccola regina*? Were you that unsatisfied after getting fucked by your husband?"

"I lied," she said, which was the actual lie.

I smiled, rubbing my cock against her ass. It fit so well. Her body was made for me. "Baby, I know it's true." I slid my fingers over her clit, feeling her tense against me. "You're so fucking wet for me. I'm going to make you come until you beg me to fucking stop."

"You can try," she said. "Ian has two cocks, you know."

"I only need one," I snarled. "And for that comment, I'm going to wash your mouth out with my cock."

I fisted her hair and pushed her to her knees, the thrill of seeing Serena kneel before me making me feral. A wild darkness had been unleashed, and her throwing Ian's name in my face was fuel for the fire.

"Open wide, little queen," I growled.

"Fuck you," she snarled.

I smiled down at her, pulling her hair tighter.

"I either force it in your mouth, or you open up like a good girl. We're going to wash your husband's name out of your fucking mouth, and then I'm going to show you what it feels like to be fucked by a real man."

She smirked, her crimson lips drawing back. "As opposed to my hot D.I.L.F. of a hubby?"

I let out a low growl and pressed the head of my cock against her lips. "I hope you choke."

She opened her mouth to argue with me, which was her mistake. I thrust forward, groaning as my cock slid into her mouth. She raked her nails down my thighs, the pain slicing through the pleasure. I yanked her hair, thrusting until I hit the back of her throat, and she let out a long moan.

I pulled back and pumped forward again—then felt her teeth on my cock.

I yanked out fast, letting out a snarl. "Don't you fucking dare."

She let out a low taunting laugh.

My cock throbbed in response and I pushed it back into her dirty little mouth, pumping harder. She let out a helpless moan, and I felt her start to choke.

"Good," I growled. "You belong to me right now. Not him."

I tipped my head back, holding her head in place, even as she struggled against me. I started to fuck her little throat harder, the hot water beating against my back. Steam surrounded us, curling around our bodies as I took her mouth.

I looked down at her. Tears streamed from her eyes, her expression reminding me of a little doe. I pulled back, allowing her to breathe. Letting her take a moment.

"Are you still thinking of him?"

"Always," she rasped.

A cruel smile slid across my face as I thrust forward and filled her mouth again. I hit the back of her throat hard, gripping her hair and making her take it.

She moaned, her body relaxing. I felt her give in, my cock

sliding back and forth, over and over again. I finally pulled back, and she let out a dark laugh.

"You drive me crazy, *piccola regina.*"

"Good," she said. "You deserve it."

"Are you still thinking about him?"

"I'm thinking about you, Luca."

Chapter 21
Princess and the Knight

Serena

I gasped as Luca gripped my hair and pulled me to my feet, our mouths meeting for our second kiss.

Finally.

I felt like I was dying and living simultaneously, every single part of me needing Luca in a toxic and surreal way. I ran my hands over his chest as he kissed me, a low growl leaving him when his hands fell to my hips. He reached around me and grabbed the soap, pouring some into his calloused hands and lathering it up.

I gasped as he washed me, his hands leaving a wave of heat following every touch. The patience was gone from us, and we only needed one thing.

Each other.

His blood washed off me, and our lips met again.

Luca lifted me and my legs wrapped around his hips, a moan escaping. He stole another kiss as he carried me out of the shower. Steam billowed through the room, clinging to the mirror over the marbled counter.

He set me on top, pushing apart my thighs. He cupped my face, kissing me as he pushed two fingers inside me.

I gasped and grabbed onto his shoulders, arching against his hand. His brows drew together, his dark eyes drinking me in as he offered me pleasure.

He pulled his fingers out and pressed them against my lips.

"See how wet you are?" he whispered. "Clean them off, baby."

I swallowed hard as I took his fingers into my mouth, tasting myself on him. A helpless moan left me, my eyes closing as I savored just how much he turned me on.

"You're mine," he whispered. "You may wear his fucking ring and ride his cocks, *piccola regina*, but you've always been mine."

"I know," I groaned.

Because, fuck, he was right. And while I did feel like I could belong to Ian as well, I'd always been Luca's.

He knelt between my legs and pressed his lips against my inner thigh. I groaned, arching my back as he moved up my leg all the way to my pussy, and that's when desperation flared through me like wildfire.

"Luca," I gasped. "I need you in me. Now."

"Not yet," he growled. "Not until I get a taste of this pussy."

"Luca," I moaned.

I'd never felt this electric before, every touch enhanced. He gripped my hips, dragging me to the edge of the counter. He placed my legs on his shoulders, making me scream as his tongue ran over my clit.

Fuck. Fuck. How many times had I dreamed of this exact

moment? Of being ravaged by him? Of him fucking me over and over?

He groaned as he began to suck on my clit, my screams growing louder. The sounds we made echoed through the apartment, but I didn't care. The idea of Ian listening to us...

I groaned, my eyes falling onto a camera in the corner of the room.

Or watching us...

I gasped, bucking my hips as Luca damn near made me see the gods. He drove his tongue inside of me, determined to suffocate himself on my pussy.

I gripped his dark curls, my hips bucking as he fucked me with his tongue. I closed my eyes, moaning as he edged me closer and closer. He growled against me, devouring me the way I'd always wanted.

I breathed harder, my head falling back as a cry tore from me. An orgasm overcame me, my thighs squeezing around his head. His grip on me tightened as I came on his tongue, everything zapped away by the intensity of it.

I laid back on the bathroom counter, gasping as I melted under him. Luca pulled his tongue free, licking his lips.

He looked hungrier now.

He lifted me with ease, throwing me over his shoulders.

"Luca," I gasped.

"Bed," he grunted. "I'm not fucking you for the first time in here. I want you on a bed."

He carried me out of the bathroom and into his room. He put me down, and I wrapped my arms around him again, our lips meeting in a kiss.

I could taste myself on him.

My hands ran over his body, pausing to feel his muscles. I drank him in, wanting to savor him as my hands lowered to his cock. He was so hard in my grip.

I broke our kiss, staring up at him as I slowly lowered to my knees.

"*Baby,*" he whispered, his voice breaking.

I wrapped my hand around his cock carefully, listening to his soft moan. His body had stiffened, his fingers sliding into my wet hair and bunching it up, keeping it out of the way as I leaned forward.

All I did was lick the tip like an ice cream cone.

He groaned, his hips bucking involuntarily. "Holy fuck," he snarled. "Fuck. I can't control myself with you."

"I've only done this for you," I whispered.

"*Fuck.*"

I grinned, stroking his cock up and down. I licked my lips and leaned forward again, taking the head into my mouth and gently sucking like I'd seen in every video I'd watched, imagining it was Luca and me.

It felt good to finally fulfill the fantasy.

I moaned and took him further into my mouth, gripping the base as I pulled back with a gasp.

"Take your time," he whispered.

I looked up at him as I swirled my tongue around the head, feeling a flush of embarrassment. What if I was doing this wrong? Earlier, he had taken control, but he was letting me explore, and I didn't want to fuck up.

"Serena," he said gently. "The only reason I haven't come yet is because I have an ounce of self-control. You can't do anything wrong to me." He read my mind.

I nodded, letting out a breath, and then took his throbbing cock back into my mouth. His fingers tightened in my hair, and I began to suck him, bobbing my head back and forth. He hit the back of my throat, and my eyes watered, but it felt fucking good.

Everything about him felt good.

He groaned, his breaths becoming ragged. "Look at you," he rasped. "My perfect little cock slut."

I'd never thought I'd feel proud of myself for being called his cock slut, but it melted me to my very core. My eyes watered as he hit the back of my throat again, and I moaned around him. He let me pull back, but...

I wanted to choke on him again.

I wanted him to wash away everything with his touch. With his demands.

I wanted him to possess me.

I pulled off briefly, looking up at him. "Choke me with it. Please, Luca. I want you to fuck my face."

Luca shook his head, but then he held me as he thrust his hips forward, filling my mouth with his cock. I yelped around him as he hit the back of my throat, but he didn't pull back or let me go.

I moaned, fighting him until I realized he wasn't going to let me go. In fact, he shoved his hips against me harder, forcing his cock down my throat.

I moaned again, and my fingers raked down his thighs. He let out a dark hiss and began to fuck my mouth, thrusting in and out. Spit dripped down my face, my eyes rolling back as I let him use me.

And fuck. It felt good to be used. There was a euphoric high that came with taking his cock like this, and I found myself relaxing into simply being his fuck toy.

I was so fucking wet too.

I slid my hand down to my pussy and realized I was dripping for him. He thrust hard, hitting the back of my throat hard enough to make me moan, and I felt my pussy clench in response.

I pushed two fingers inside of me, pleasure curling through my body.

Luca yanked back with a growl, and I sucked in a deep breath, looking up at him, my fingers still inside me.

"Does being used make you wet, princess?" he whispered. "Give me your slutty little hand."

With a gasp, I pulled my fingers free, and he took my hand. He leaned down, his eyes locking with mine as he sucked my fingers. He cleaned them with his tongue and then let go.

"On the bed," he commanded.

I got to my feet and turned, my head spinning as I moved to the bed. I crawled onto the soft blankets—the ones I'd been on last night. The same bed where I had discovered his darkest secrets.

Where I would take him for the first time.

I started to turn over, but Luca made a *tsk* noise.

"Stay like that," he said. "Ass up, head down, sweetheart."

My breath hitched as I did what he said. I felt the bed shift as he knelt behind me, his hand running over my body. He squeezed my ass cheeks, and I looked over my shoulder at him as he touched me.

"You're perfect," he said. "You belong to me."

"Yes," I whimpered.

He rubbed my ass more until he drew his hand back and slapped it. I squeaked as his hand struck, the brief pain followed by heat.

He whispered something I didn't quite catch and then spanked me again. I cried out, shocked that he would do this, but he didn't stop.

He spanked each ass cheek, harder with each hit, until I felt a plea almost slip free.

"Luca," I whimpered again.

The pain felt good. How did I tell him that?

He pushed my ass cheeks apart, and I squealed as he leaned forward, circling his fingers around my hole. I gripped the blankets, gasping as he did so, surprised to be touched there.

"Luca!"

He drew back, letting out a soft hum. "Did he fuck you here last night?"

"No," I gasped.

He pushed the tip of his finger in, making me cry out.

"So fucking tight," Luca said. "I'm claiming your ass after I fill your pussy."

He pushed me to the side, rolling me onto my back and positioning himself between my legs. I looked down between us, his cock slapping against my pussy and drawing a surprised moan from me.

Luca sucked in a breath, staring down at me. His touch became gentle, his eyes meeting mine.

"Please," I whispered. "Please come inside me. I've wanted this for so long."

"Me too," he said gently. "More than you could possibly know."

He pushed the head of his cock against my pussy, his hands gripping my thighs.

"Are you ready, *piccola regina*?"

"Yes," I whispered, tears filling my eyes again.

"You can cry," he whispered, smiling.

A tear slipped free, and I gasped as he thrust forward, filling me completely with every hard inch of his cock. I cried out, clenching around him. He paused for a moment, leaning down and planting his hands on either side of my head. Our bodies pressed together, his cock inside me. Throbbing, pulsing.

"You feel so good," he whispered. "Fuck. I should have done this so long ago."

We both leaned into each other, kissing again as he pulled

his cock back and thrust forward again. I wrapped my legs around his hips, moaning as Luca began to fuck me.

Luca was fucking me.

I closed my eyes as he began to pump in and out, his gentleness turning into something harder. Rougher. My nails raked over his shoulder blades, drawing a hiss from him as he slammed into me, his cock filling me repeatedly.

"Luca," I whimpered, letting out a rattled cry.

I didn't realize how much I had wanted him until now. My entire soul was shattering as we devoured each other, reforming into one piece. Sharp edges and all.

"I'm close," I rasped.

Luca grunted, keeping the same brutal pace, pushing me closer and closer to coming again. I could feel the tremors, edging until I cried out, squeezing his cock tight as I came.

"Fucking hell," he rasped. "You're choking my cock with your pussy."

I arched against him, panting as my orgasm tore through me, a hurricane of pleasure. Luca waited until I finished before lifting my hips, changing the angle so his next thrust was even deeper than before, pushing all the way into me.

I gasped, my body sensitive and hot like a live wire. His muscles rippled, his eyes closing as he took me, the noises he made dark and possessive.

"You—belong—to—*me*."

With one more thrust, he buried himself deep inside me and cried out, his hot cum shooting inside. I moaned as it filled me, feeling a satisfaction I didn't know I could feel until now.

Luca had just come inside me.

He slowly lowered my hips, collapsing on me. The two of us were a pile of heavy breaths and moans, a silence settling over us as we basked in the afterglow.

I stroked his hair, closing my eyes with a soft smile. Luca

laid his head between my breasts, letting out a soft contented sound.

"Mine," he whispered.

"Yes," I said softly. "I've always been yours."

But I was *his* too.

I wouldn't say that yet, though. I didn't want to hurt Luca.

Luca lifted his head, letting out a gentle hum. His hand slid up my body, cupping my breast next to his face.

I let out a giggle. "Hey."

"I didn't worship these enough," he said, running the pad of his thumb over my nipple.

I gasped, his touch sending an electric shock through me. It split through the heavy haze of sated lust, rekindling the need.

He lifted his head, his other hand cupping my other breast and doing the same. He circled my nipples with his thumbs, pushing my breasts together until they almost touched.

Then he took both nipples into his mouth. I cried out, surprised by the amount of pleasure that gave me. His tongue flicked over them, then he sucked them hard enough to hurt, but the pain turned me on in a way that left me wanting even more.

There was a very dark and perverted part of me that wanted him to mark me. Bite me, pinch me hard enough to leave a bruise, something that would leave his mark on me.

He lifted his head, frowning. "What?"

"What?" I whispered. I knew he couldn't read minds, but fucking hell, he knew me too well.

He raised a brow, making me blush. "Your mind did something. I felt you stiffen under me. What's wrong?"

"Nothing's wrong," I mumbled. "I just..."

Luca let out a low growl.

I looked away, fully blushing now. "I want you to bite me. Or... leave a mark."

"Aside from my handprint on your ass?"

"Yes," I said.

"Are you embarrassed by that?"

"Maybe," I said sheepishly.

"Do you know how many times I've thought about biting your tits, Serena?"

"What?" I asked.

He leaned down and sank his teeth around my nipple, making me gasp. The pain sharpened as he bit harder and sucked, his eyes never leaving mine, even as I squirmed against him. He held on a minute longer, tears springing to my eyes, and then he let go.

Fuck. The pleasure that followed, the rush. I looked down, seeing the mark he'd left, and whimpered.

"The other one," I said.

He swirled his tongue around the bite he'd left, nipping my nipple before he moved on to the other. He squeezed my breast hard in his hand and bit down, shaking another sharp cry from me. He sucked again as he bit, the pain sending electric shocks straight to my pussy.

"Fuck," I cried.

He sucked harder and then let go, leaving an angry ring of teeth marks around my nipple. He flicked his tongue over it, sucking and kissing me softly.

My eyes fluttered, a moan leaving me.

I could stay like this forever with him. In this bed, touching him, sucking him, being fucked by him. I smiled to myself, enjoying the feeling of being claimed more than I ever could have imagined.

He leaned back and sat up, cocking his head. "Stay put," he said. "I need to go get lube."

"Lube?" I asked.

"For your ass, princess. Your pussy was fucking dripping

for me so we didn't need it, but your ass will, especially since you could barely take my finger there."

I swallowed hard, watching as he stood. His cock was hard all over again, his naked body perfect. He ran his fingers through his dark hair, smirking.

"Where are you going to get lube from?" I whispered.

"Your husband."

Chapter 22
Bounty

IAN

Cum covered my keyboard and desk. I leaned back in my chair, letting out a frustrated groan.

Watching the two of them together had made me lose it. I was supposed to be working, running my businesses, calling some of the stupid mafia bastards I had to work with to remind them that they worked for me—but instead, I had watched my mates fuck, and wished I was there.

I zipped my pants and readjusted my belt, letting out a soft growl.

My phone lit up on the desk, and I grabbed it, seeing I had several new alerts.

I switched to the app and pulled up my email. Every leader of the Three Fates Mafia had one specifically for the Three Fates—an idea that Ashley had introduced. Modernizing us monsters and demigods. I'd been against it at first, but it had some uses.

Why they still insisted on sending me a letter with a wax seal instead of an email was beyond me, but the Fates did what they wanted. Most of the time, it felt like theatrics. A way to remind me they were the boss.

There was an email at the top of my inbox from Jason, one of the demigod mafia heads, that turned my blood to ice.

Wanted: Luca Civello.
Award: 150 million dollars and the Golden Fleece

"What the fuck?" I whispered.

Fuck.

The Golden Fleece?

I felt rage curl through me. That had been stolen from me ages ago by Jason, and I'd never recovered it. By the time the mafia had formed, he'd sworn up and down that it had also been stolen from him, so he couldn't return it.

Jason was offering *the* Golden Fleece and 150 million dollars to whoever brought in or killed Luca. If that wasn't a slap in the face, I didn't know what was.

The email was short, straight to the point, and ominous.

Fuck. This was bad news. I'd brought Serena to Moirai and worried about her, but now Luca...even if we weren't sure what we were yet, I knew he was my mate.

He was mine as much as Serena was. Which meant that Jason attacking him was an attack on me.

At least now I had a good idea who attacked him last night. Shooting at someone outside the Helm was rash. Jason had always been a thorn in my side and in the side of all the other monster mafia leaders, but this was outrageous.

He was playing a deadly game.

There was a general 'no-kill' rule when it came to the ten of us. But a year ago, Ashley had beheaded and killed Hercules, and since then...

That rule didn't feel like it mattered anymore.

I would have to fight him. I would have to start a war, potentially against other mafia leaders too, if they decided that bounty was worth it.The annoying part was this would bring out the rats, the ones hungry for money. Assassins who wanted that bounty.

How fucking dare Jason do this.

I would end him.

I was tired of demigods like him thinking they deserved the entire world. They resented that they had to share a city with the same monsters they had hunted for so long.

I felt a streak of rage, smoke curling from my mouth. I squeezed my phone and then hit the reply all button.

Ian Colchian: Luca Civello is in my custody. Any attempts on his life, warranted or unwarranted, will be seen as an act of war.

This bounty is null and void.

Not So Kind Regards,

Ian

I pressed send before my logic could kick in.

Everyone in our mafia would see that. From the monsters, to the demigods, to the Fates—and anyone else who might have been on that list. Assassins and whomever else.

Fucking hell.

I didn't care.

"Good," I growled.

I would burn anyone alive who touched him or Serena.

Embers and smoke exhaled on a breath, floating around me.
I needed to call Jack. We needed to organize our men. I needed

to call Cerberus and ensure that they would side with me. Medusa, the Hydras, and Chimera as well.

The good news was all of them hated Jason as much as I did.

But Jason had other allies. Perseus was the only demigod who might align with me. She'd never been afraid to stand up to the others.

Are you really going to start a war over Luca?

The answer was yes.

He was mine. Even if he didn't want to be. Even if he fought it. He belonged to me the same way Serena did. I hadn't lived this long without my mates, only to lose them the moment I found them.

I would do anything to keep them safe.

I stared at my phone a little longer, then jumped as a number flashed across the screen. I raised a brow.

It rang in my hand. I stared for another moment, then pressed the answer button.

"Who is this?" I snarled.

"Is that how you answer a phone call from a dear old friend?"

Jason.

"Hardly a friend," I said, my jaw stiffening. "I don't know what game you think you're playing, but you won't win. This is an act of war, Jason."

"Is it? I'm asking for a mortal in exchange for 150 million dollars and the Golden Fleece. A mortal. No one cares about the life of someone like him, not even your monstrous friends."

"You will not touch him," I said. "You will not go near him."

Jason let out a humorless laugh. "Bring me Luca, Colchian," he answered. "You have him in your custody, as you said. We have an event this Sunday. Bring him with you, and we'll make a nice tidy deal like you always love. Luca's life to save Serena."

To save Serena.

My hearts beat a little harder.

"I thought you said the prize was the Golden Fleece and 150 million dollars."

Silence. The kind that made my skin crawl.

"I'm trying to be nice," Jason whispered. "Trying to save your little wife from a horrible death. I'm sure she would scream so well for me."

Rage ran through me. The kind I hadn't felt in thousands of years.

"I will slaughter you," I whispered back. "I will rip you apart over and over again. I will torture you until you can't remember your name. You're a demigod, so you could take it, right?"

"Can the same be said for Serena?"

My blood ran cold.

"Bring the bodyguard with you on Sunday, Colchian. Enjoy your week, as it's the last you'll ever have with him."

The line went dead, and I gripped my phone hard enough that it shattered. Then hurled the shards across the room.

"*Fuck!*" I roared.

How long had I lived? How long had I fought? For centuries, I had been searching for my mates. I'd never found them, never had been gifted a fated mate's love. And now I had two mates, but one of them was being stolen from me.

I couldn't let it happen.

I had to keep him alive.

And I had to keep myself alive too. Which meant I needed to work off some of my temper before I fucked everything up.

I went to my desk and opened the drawer, pulling out a new phone. This wasn't the first one I had destroyed, nor would it be the last. Within a few minutes, I activated it and sent Luca a text.

I'll be home late. Let Serena know. And tell her not to worry. Do not open the door for anyone. Keep it locked. Don't go anywhere.

Also, get her a phone so I don't have to fucking text you all the time.

The motherfucker texted me back a thumbs up.

I swallowed hard and left the phone on my desk. Leaving my office, I took the elevator downstairs to the parking garage, ignoring the glances I got from the men I had stationed everywhere. I made it to my car and got in, needing to escape.

I needed to fly.

I needed to let my monstrous self free.

Occasionally, I would drive outside of Moirai and transform. I'd let my entire dragon free, would feel the wind on my massive wings and body. Even though I had designed all of my homes to accommodate my dragon form, I needed to fly.

If only I had something to burn, too.

My hearts pounded faster as I left the parking garage and weaved through the busy city streets.

Within an hour, I was zooming through the hills outside the city limits. I pulled to the top of a hill and parked on the side of the road, tucking my car between several trees.

I moved in a blur, plunging into the woods that separated the road from some of the hills and cliffs I always went to.

Breaking the tree line, I stopped on the crest. Overlooking the valley, the sun started to set. I could see the amber dots of different homes, the neighborhoods still part of Moirai.

Fuck.

I was going to murder Jason.

The Fates could punish me. I didn't care.

I wouldn't let him hurt Serena or Luca.

Does he know she's a demigod?

I wasn't sure how he could possibly know anything. Serena had always been my greatest secret.

I'd given her that castle, far away from Moirai and my entire world. But now I wished I'd kept her close instead. Maybe then, I would have been able to ensure she could defend herself.

I didn't think she was helpless by any means.

But I was worried.

I worried she would face a monster far worse than me.

Demigods were evil. They had a darkness in them that could be twisted the wrong way, and once it was, there was no turning back. Serena had that darkness, but she had too much goodness to become a monster like Jason and the others.

I stepped off the cliff, letting myself fall.

My blood burned, my body craving to break free. The monster inside me needed to let loose, or else everyone around me would suffer. I didn't stop myself from changing, instead allowing my bones to crack and muscles to snap.

It was a relief, like going to the chiropractor and getting the best adjustment imaginable. My groan became closer to a growl as wings burst from my shoulder blades, and I kept growing as I plummeted toward the ground.

Skin turned to scales. My eyesight changed and my sense of smell heightened. My wings caught the wind, and instead of becoming a ground pancake, I became a massive fire-breathing dragon.

Chapter 23
The Dance

Serena

I curled up on the couch, watching the city come alive beneath me. The lights and sounds were so different from the castle on the coast, and while part of me missed it, I was enjoying this too.

Luca was asleep. We'd spent all day together, and it had been perfect.

Except for one thing.

Ian hadn't come home.

I should've been asleep by now, but I had worried when Luca told me *not* to worry about Ian.

I closed my eyes, allowing my thoughts to flow. I was starting to feel this nagging sensation like everything I'd received would be taken away. That at any moment, the curtain would lift—and I would be shown that the love I was beginning to feel was a lie.

The door to the apartment opened, and I raised my head,

peeking over the back of the couch as Ian came in. Relief flooded me.

He was in his more monstrous form, and I realized I had missed seeing him with scales. He looked up, his iridescent gaze meeting mine.

"It's 1 a.m., little queen," he said softly. "You should have gone to sleep. You didn't need to wait for me."

"I couldn't sleep," I said.

Ian shook his dragon-like head and came over to me. He smelled like wood smoke and fire. He leaned over the couch, giving me a gentle nudge that I equated to a kiss.

"Hi," I whispered, smiling. I leaned into him, glad he was home.

"I missed you today," Ian sighed. "You smell like Luca."

"I'm sure I do," I teased.

We'd been very *active* throughout the day.

I slid off the couch and walked to him. He extended a clawed hand, and I took it, allowing him to tug me close. I reached up and ran my fingertips over his scaled jaw, admiring how they glinted.

He was warm. I clung to that, pressing my hand to his chest. "Your clothes didn't shred," I whispered. "In your form."

"No. I have some that can be manipulated with a bit of magic," he said. "I was flying outside of the city."

"As a dragon?" I asked, enamored.

"Yes," he said. "A big fire-breathing dragon with silver and black scales and claws that could tear you in half."

"So scary," I teased.

Ian offered a soft smile, but it didn't reach his eyes. Even in this form, I could tell something was off.

"Is everything okay?" I asked.

He let out a low hum, his wings wrapping around us. It was

strange and comforting, and I found myself leaning against him and closing my eyes.

"It will be," he promised. "Just...mafia problems."

I snorted. "You make it sound so normal."

"It is normal to me," he sighed. "I wish that it weren't."

"I'm not even sure how the mafia works," I whispered. "Well, this one compared to the one I grew up in."

"There are ten of us," Ian said. "Five monsters and five demigods. All of us work under the Three Fates."

"Oh," I whispered.

"The city is divided, and different businesses belong to different mafia leaders. Most of the time, we play fair."

"And now?"

Ian was quiet for a few moments, long enough to try and evade the question. "Are you ready to sleep?" Ian asked.

Should I let it go? Or press for answers? I wanted to know what was going on, but... "Not quite."

"How about a dance then?"

"A dance?" I asked, looking up at him.

"Yes," he said. "A dance. How about you pick out a bottle of wine and come back here, and we'll have a midnight dance."

A midnight dance. "Okay," I said softly, my throat constricting.

I went past Ian before he could see my expression. Tears sprang to my eyes, my emotions getting the better of me. No one had ever asked me to dance before.

Some of the things that happened this week were things I didn't know I had missed—it turned out that being asked to dance was one of them.

I went to the kitchen, letting out a deep breath. I opened one of the cabinets, not surprised to find a rack full of wine bottles. Rolling my shoulders and forcing myself to relax, I plucked a cabernet out and took it to the counter.

Music began to float from the living room, soft and classical. It was gentle and soothing.

I uncorked the wine and poured each of us a glass. Once I returned to the living room, I froze in the doorway, looking around wide-eyed.

In the time it had taken me to pick out a bottle of wine, Ian had managed to light dozens of candles around the room. The flames flickered, creating a warm golden atmosphere that made me want to swoon.

Ian sauntered up to me, stealing his glass. He winked as we both took a sip.

"Now, would you dance with me?" he asked.

"Yes," I whispered. "I'd love to."

He took our glasses and set them on a small table, then turned back to me. He gently tipped my face up, and I held his gaze as his hand slid to my lower back. The warmth between us was comforting. Slowly but surely growing into something that belonged in an inferno.

He swept me to the center of the living room, the two of us swaying to the music.

"You're beautiful," he said. "Stunning. Smart. Fierce."

"A murderer," I mumbled. "An orphan. Someone who has powers from a godly parent she doesn't know."

He swept my dark hair back, his claws running over my scalp, causing my breath to hitch.

Fuck. I'd do anything to feel him do that again.

"Can.... Can you do that again?" I whispered.

"This?" he asked, running his claws through again.

I couldn't stop the moan that left me, my eyes fluttering.

"My, my," he murmured. "You're so sensitive to my touch, princess."

"Maybe that happens when you wait so long to be with someone."

He nodded his heavy head, his iridescent eyes burning in the dark. "I regret that it's taken this long for me to get to know you. I wish I had kept you close to me instead of sending you away. I think that it would have been better for Luca too. I'm sorry. For everything."

His apology was heartfelt and had me pausing for a moment. I hadn't expected him to ever apologize for anything, but hearing it...

"I'm going to make things right," he whispered. "I'm going to make sure both of you are protected."

"Did something happen?" I asked again, concerned. "Is everything okay, Ian?"

"It will be." That ominous phrase again. I didn't like it. "I want to make you happy. I'm falling for you. I can't help it. I'm falling in love with you. Hell, I've been in love with you since I first saw you all those years ago. I've never loved anyone before."

"Never?" I whispered, shocked.

"Never."

Ian began to sway back and forth, guiding me as we danced. He tugged me close, our bodies pressing against each other. His warmth wrapped around me, his confession making my mind spiral.

He was falling in love with me.

"I can't be with just you," I finally said.

"I know that."

"And I haven't fallen in love with you...yet." Maybe that was a lie. I couldn't tell. I certainly wanted him, and I didn't want him to leave anytime I was with him.

He chuckled, our bodies pressing tighter together. "All I can do is hope that you do."

"I love Luca. I have for a long time. And even with everything I've learned, I still want him."

"Even knowing that you've been his captive for ten years?"

"Yes," I whispered. "What I choose to do with him is up to me, not you. If you and I are going to have a healthy relationship, then you have to be able to trust me and respect my decisions. I need the people in my life to not stand in my way once I choose my path."

His eyes softened, his hold on me tightening. "Will he respect that?"

"Will you?"

He was silent for a moment, searching me. "Yes," he whispered. "I will. I worry about you. I worry about him too. But I want you in my life, Serena. I've already gone too long without you in it."

I nodded, relaxing some. I wanted him in my life too. More than I knew how to express. "I expect the same from him going forward."

"Good," he sighed. "I worry for your safety. I brought you here to keep you safe. I can't let you loose in the city, especially this one. But... if you tell me what you want or need, I will do my best to make it happen."

"I don't want you to do anything for me," I said. "I want to do things for myself. That's what I'm trying to say. For example, you mentioned us shopping for a dress. I want to go into the city and buy a dress I pick out for myself. I don't want you or Luca to drive me, and I don't want either of you to pick my dress out. I want to do it myself."

"I can't let you go somewhere by yourself right now."

I started to pull back from him, but he held me tighter.

"Serena," he pleaded. "This city is dangerous. It would eat you alive. Not because you're weak but because you belong to me. I know you are capable of anything and everything you set your mind to, but I can't let you loose, baby. I can't."

"You can't stop me," I said, pulling away from him.

His gaze darkened. "I could."

"You wouldn't," I snapped. "What are you going to do? Tie me up? Spank me?"

I glared at Ian and stepped back, only to feel another set of arms wrap around me. I gasped and spun, looking up at Luca.

"You're not going anywhere alone," Luca said. "I woke up to you two arguing about whether you can go out alone in the city, and you're smarter than that. Just because we do stuff for or with you doesn't mean you aren't capable."

That pissed me off. "Both of you can fuck off," I said. "What? You're two peas in a pod now that you've found a common chauvinistic asshole opinion?"

Both of them growled like cavemen.

I crossed my arms, returning their glares. Luca and Ian crossed their arms too, facing me.

"If Luca and I have one thing in common, it's your safety, little queen."

"Are you forgetting that I was shot at?" Luca asked. "Or that you're a new demigod? Or that your husband is part of the mafia?"

"Okay, enough. Both of you can stop," I seethed. "Seriously, you can both fuck off."

That made them bristle.

"I'm leaving."

I started to turn, and Luca was the one who reached for me first. I slapped his hand away, watching as his eyes darkened.

He lunged for me, but I was ready.

I stepped back, spinning out of the way—only to be caught by Ian and hoisted over his massive shoulders.

"Let me down!" I shouted, my temper unraveling. "Let me fucking go!"

Ian ignored me, carrying me down the hall toward his

room. Luca trailed behind him, both exuding the same pissed-off energy.

"Fuck you, Luca," I snarled. "Fuck both of you. I'm not your fucking pet!"

"Keep screaming," Luca growled as he stalked after us. "I'm starting to like it."

"Fuck you," I said again.

Ian carried me into his room, and Luca kicked the door shut behind him. I was thrown onto the bed, bouncing at the center. I sat up, looking from Ian to Luca and then back to Ian.

Ian began to strip, his eyes never leaving me. "Are you done throwing your tantrum, little queen?"

"I hate you," I whispered. "I should have run away from our stupid marriage long ago. And you," I growled, looking at Luca. "I should have sent you packing the moment I found out about the photos. Both of you can kiss my ass."

Luca's jaw ticked, his rage emanating from him. He looked at Ian, arching a brow. "I think we can both agree she's being a brat."

"I can agree," Ian said, tossing his shirt to the floor. "I also think we can both agree that brats get punished."

"I can agree to that," Luca said.

"Excellent," Ian said. "Maybe give her mouth something to do besides complaining about how terrible we are."

"You can kiss my ass," I repeated.

"You know both of us would enjoy that."

I found myself smirking; I couldn't help it. I was pissed and frazzled, but damn it, they were both hot. They were a distraction.

"I hope you rot in—"

My sentence faltered as I felt a surge of electricity throughout the room, the air causing the hair on the back of my neck to stand up. Ian and Luca both froze, confusion washing over their faces.

"Oh fuck," Ian said. "Fuck. That's god magic."

I saw fear in his eyes.

He moved for me, reaching out his hand—but it was too late.

The magic surrounding us became thick, and I felt my entire body start to burn. Suddenly, I found myself falling, Luca and Ian disappearing.

Chapter 24
He Had It Coming

SERENA

My ass hit the asphalt hard.

"For fuck's sake," I rasped, the pain jarring me. I let out a soft groan, looking around. "What the fuck?"

I was in a dark alleyway between two buildings I didn't recognize. I was barefoot and still wearing a chemise. Someone or something had literally plucked me out of Ian's bedroom.

"Hello, Serena."

I scrambled to my feet and turned to see a massive man standing behind me. He was *huge*, like a pro wrestler and a bear morphed into one man who looked like the leader of an evil motorcycle club. He had a black mullet and a beard, tan skin, and wore a leather jacket and jeans.

He felt familiar, but I couldn't quite place where I knew him from. One of my uncle's men, perhaps? But no, that wouldn't make any sense.

I drew in a deep breath and squared my shoulders. I didn't

care that I was barefoot and wearing fucking pajamas; I wouldn't cower.

"Who are you?" I asked, tilting my chin up. He towered above me by at least three feet. "What are you?"

"You can call me Ares," he said, stepping closer. "It's been some time since we've seen each other, and I figured that would be more comfortable than calling me Father. Or Dad. I think humans use Dad more often, no?"

My fucking father was Ares?

I refused to retreat from him. I was already pissed at everyone in my life, and Ares the god-who-was-also-my-father had managed to steal spot number one.

"You know what? Fuck you," I said. "I was about to have hate sex with my dragon and my bodyguard. I'd like to go back home now."

Ares winced, making a face. "I don't want to hear about that."

"Well, I don't want anything to do with you," I sneered. "Really, the balls you have suddenly showing up in my life."

He narrowed his eyes, the air shimmering around him. "I hope you know I could kill you with the snap of my fingers."

"Then do it," I said. "Also, why should I believe that you're my parent? What was my mother's name? What—"

"Your mother was named Giana. She was a beautiful, calm, and stubborn woman who made me question everything about myself. And that's saying something, considering how old I am."

I froze at the mention of my mother's name. My heart skipped a beat, the blood draining from my face. "She's dead," I whispered.

"I know," Ares said, his voice straining. "She was killed."

"By who?" I whispered.

My uncle claimed she died in a car accident, but I knew that wasn't true. I always suspected it was something more.

The last time I saw her, she made me promise not to cause any trouble.

That promise had ruined my life.

It wasn't until recently that I had grown tired of upholding that promise. Good girls didn't get into trouble, but I didn't want to be a good girl any more.

Ares shook his head. "I'm not telling you. You would go after them and then you'd die."

"Who killed her?" I growled, stepping closer until I was toe to toe with him.

The god of war stared down at me, his eyes burning. "They will kill you, Serena."

"WHO FUCKING KILLED HER?"

"Your uncle," Ares whispered. "*Don* Avellino. He was forced to by one of the other demigods. They killed Giana before her time because they wanted you to be ready."

"Ready for what?" I asked, tears springing to my eyes.

"To keep you from your own fate as a demigod."

"But they married me off to Ian," I whispered.

"They did. They've done everything they could to stop you from reaching your full potential because they fear you. You're my daughter, a woman of war. A woman of courage. Men will fear you, Serena. And they should. You are deadly. You are fierce and angry." His voice softened and he lifted his hand, pressing it against my cheek.

"*Who* is the other demigod?" I whispered. "Tell me who."

"Jason," Ares said. "Or as you know him—J. Your uncle's right-hand man. Although he only stayed in that position long enough to get what he needed before moving on."

Jason. J.

My wedding day replayed in my mind. The man who had

arranged my marriage to a monster with a cheerful smile on his face, an evil one.

He was supposedly a demigod, like me.

He had orchestrated my fate.

But why?

"What destiny am I supposed to fulfill?" I asked.

"You're supposed to kill him," Ares said. "That's all I can say, Serena. I have to go now, but I have a parting gift. I'm sorry that I could never know you. You are everything I could ever wish for in a child."

He pulled his hand away and stepped back, his eyes starting to glow. I looked away as he burst into light, taking away the warmth of his presence.

When I looked back, I saw a knife on the ground. I leaned down and picked it up, feeling the metal buzz against my fingertips. The silver blade had a golden stripe down the middle, the handle molding perfectly against my palm.

A thrill ran through me as I gripped it.

I was bewildered by everything. I had met Ares, found out he was my father, and that someone from my past was a demigod.

Was he one of the demigods that Ian had mentioned?

Was he the reason my dragon had been so tense?

I let out a long breath, staring down at the knife.

Men will fear you, Serena. And they should. You are deadly. You are fierce and angry.

He was right.

Fuck.

I really was a demigod.

My dad really was a god.

And my uncle had murdered my mother.

Tears trailed down my cheeks at the thought of her. She

had been too good. She hadn't deserved to be hurt by anyone that way. To think that man had raised me after killing her...

Evil. He was fucking evil.

I let out a soft cry and then screamed.

I screamed as loud as I could until I could feel the rage vibrating in my bones, the pain and sadness burning in my blood.

I screamed until I felt numb.

Then I wiped away my tears and gripped my knife, taking a measured breath. Exhaling everything until I felt somewhat calm again.

"What's a pretty thing like you doing here? We heard you screaming."

I turned, my heart skipping a beat as two men came down the alley. They eyed me hungrily.

This was not going to be their day.

"Leaving," I said, keeping my tone cold.

I needed to get the hell out of here. Hell, I needed to get back to Ian and Luca before they razed the city trying to find me.

The knife warmed in my hand as I tried to move past the two men, but one of them stepped in front of me with a dark laugh.

"You're not going anywhere," he said. "Looks like we have ourselves a treat."

"Right. We can fuck her together," the other laughed. "Make her our little bitch. We already know what she sounds like when she screams."

Disgust rolled through me, followed by a wave of anger. All the rage for every man in my life who had fucked me over. My uncle, my father, J, Luca, and even Ian.

Ares had been right. I *was* angry.

I remembered the day I met Luca. I remembered being a

child in an alley, clinging to a little boy who wasn't able to defend himself.

I remembered the look on that criminal's face, the same as the two men attempting to corner me now.

I was not a little girl anymore. And I certainly wasn't weak.

I didn't need someone to rescue me.

Not a bodyguard.

Not a dragon.

"Listen, I'm not having a good day. And I've murdered men stronger than you," I said, keeping my voice firm. "Get the fuck out of my way."

"I don't think so, princess," the other man said.

Princess.

I wasn't a motherfucking princess. I was a gods damned queen.

Everything happened in a blur. One of them jumped toward me, grabbing onto my arm and attempting to tackle me to the ground. The knife moved by itself, drawing my hand with it. I plunged it straight into his gut, his crimson blood splashing over me as I stabbed him.

I yanked it out.

And stabbed him again.

Then I moved, a warrior with grace, a killer in motion, and drove my blade into the neck of the other man. More blood sprayed me, the red bleeding through my chemise. Coating my skin as I stabbed him until he was nothing more than a lifeless corpse in an alley.

My chest heaved, the rage slowly receding.

Normally, I would feel panic.

Normally, I would feel guilt.

Not this time.

I blinked, realizing that I was kneeling on the ground. My

knees stung from the grit of the asphalt, blood dripping down my skin.

"Oh good," a smooth, feminine voice said. "I found Ian's little wife."

I looked up, my eyes fluttering as I took in the presence of a woman wearing a white suit. She was tall and beautiful, her heels giving her several more inches in height.

It was the middle of the night, yet she wore sunglasses. Her skin was smooth like glass, and her lips were painted red. She wore a headscarf with bright colors, her hair hidden beneath it.

"I killed them," I whispered, the numbness already setting in.

"Well," the woman said. "What is it they always say? They had it coming. Maybe they should have chosen to walk a different way. Or maybe they should have thought about it before showing off their necks to your pretty knife."

I let out a soft, dry chuckle despite the circumstances.

"I'm a murderer," I said.

"And I'm Medusa," the woman snickered. "You can call me Madeline, though. That's what this world knows me as. Now, come on. Your husband has moved heaven and earth to find you. He even bribed me. I'll send someone to clean up the bodies."

"You're not going to call the police?" I asked.

She laughed, her voice reminding me of chimes. "Honey, the chief of police is on my payroll. I can have him pick up the bodies and dump them if needed. Now, come on. Your dragon is breathing fire down our necks. I've never seen him so angry before. He called up each of us monsters and offered us favors. The Colchian never offers favors."

I slowly got to my feet, wincing as I looked down.

"Oh dear," she said. "Hmm. If I had known how gorgeous

his wife was, I would have bartered for him to let me have a date with you."

I laughed, stepping over the body and going to her. I liked her. "I have two boyfriends already. Well, a husband and a boyfriend? It's complicated."

"Hmm. Well, if you ever get tired of playing with boys, come find me," Madeline said. She smirked, arching a brow. "Don't beat yourself up too hard for murdering them. They wanted to hurt you. And besides, I go through at least four men a week. All because they don't follow instructions well."

My eyes widened. "You kill four men a week?"

"Sometimes more." Madeline grinned voraciously, holding out a perfectly manicured hand. "Let's go, princess. Your dragon and knight need you."

Chapter 25
Enemies to Lovers

IAN

"We will find her," I said for the thousandth time.

Half of those times, I'd been talking to Luca. The other half to myself.

Luca and I stood in the living room, reviewing a map I had spread out on the floor. I had three cell phones, two laptops and was waiting to hear anything from the people I'd sent out. The sun was starting to rise outside, the sky slowly turning dark pink.

"What if she's dead?" Luca whispered.

My head snapped up, a low growl leaving me. "Do not fucking say that, Luca. She's stronger than that. You taught her how to fight."

"I taught her how to fight men, not gods," he hissed, raking his fingers through his hair.

I drew in a breath and crossed to him. Grabbing his shoulders, I forced him to look at me.

He swallowed hard, his dark eyes widening as they met mine.

"We don't deserve her," he whispered. "Neither one of us does."

"Then we have to be better," I said. "Starting with not treating her like a breakable object and instead the woman we know she is. The woman we both love."

His jaw ticked, but he nodded, my words visibly sinking in. "You love her."

"I do," I said. "I think I could love you too if you'd let me."

Never mind there were people trying to kill him. Or that I hadn't told him or Serena about the bounty.

I'd barely had time to digest any of that information. The fact that Jason was out to get Luca...Part of me feared Jason was the one who'd taken Serena away, not a god.

But the level of magic that had filled the room was more than any demigod could manifest.

"I'll find her," I said darkly. "No one can hide her from us, Luca. Not a god. Not the Fates. And certainly not one of the demigods."

Luca nodded and surprised me by yanking me down for a kiss.

Fuck. It was rough. It was harsh. Both of us were tired, worried, angry, and wishing that the woman we loved was safe. We felt like failures. That was what I felt in our kiss.

I leaned into him, our lips sliding across each other. My hearts pounded a little faster, my blood rushing as we devoured each other.

A knock at the door had us each taking a step back and trying to regain our composure. "Come in," I growled.

The door opened, and in stepped Medusa, followed by Serena.

"Serena," Luca whispered.

The breath was knocked out of me, and my body felt weak. I looked up at Medusa, giving her a nod.

"Thank you," I said.

She held up a hand. "Remember, you owe me. And I want the seeds, Ian. I was supposed to be riding a pretty little thing from one of my art shows, and instead I rescued your wife."

"Fine. Stay there for a moment."

I stalked to my room and grabbed the vial of pomegranate seeds. Though I used them to enforce contracts, I could always acquire more. It was a small price to pay for Serena's safe return, plus bribing Madeline worked to my advantage.

I gripped the vial, walked back to the living room, and handed the seeds to her. "Get out."

She smirked and waved her hand. "Bye, Serena."

"Bye," Serena said, smiling at her as she left.

I didn't like that. In fact, I didn't like anything about this situation. The control had been yanked from under me.

Serena had been taken by a force I couldn't stop.

It made me fear losing her.

The three of us stared at each other for a moment. Serena was barefoot, her legs skinned up with bits of asphalt, and her night dress was soaked in blood. She held a knife in one hand, the other curled into a fist.

"Are you okay?" Luca asked.

She nodded, her shoulders slowly relaxing. "I uh... murdered two guys in an alley."

Luca and I both nodded slowly.

"Kind of hot?" Luca offered, wincing.

Serena let out a strained laugh. "No. Not at all."

Luca and I stood still, waiting to see what Serena would do. Then the tension broke, and we both rushed to her. Neither one of us had slept. Both of us were angry. I had called everyone. I had pulled on favors, demands, promises. I had used every resource I had. Every man, every monster that knew me. Everything. We had turned every fucking stone over in the city, but it was Medusa who had found her.

"Serena," I rasped.

I picked her up and dragged Luca in close too, so we could both touch her. Both hold her. There was a desperate edge to both of us that had shaken away our hate for each other.

"I'm covered in blood," Serena whispered, wiggling against us. "But I'm fine. You can put me down."

"We were worried," Luca said, pressing his lips to the top of her head. "You're fierce, *piccola regina.*"

Serena leaned into us, finally relaxing some. It was like watching a balloon deflate slowly. "I met my father," she whispered. "It's Ares."

I was torn between surprise and anger. I hated that he had been able to simply whisk her away.

"My father is the god of war, and apparently a demigod named Jason has been trying to keep me from ever reaching my full power. He has been since I was a child."

Fuck.

Fuck. I had almost forgotten about the phone call I'd received from that bastard.

I tensed, and it was visible enough that Luca and Serena turned their attention to me.

"Who's Jason?" Luca asked.

"J," Serena said, raising a brow. "Do you remember him?"

Luca pressed his lips together, his face becoming stoic. He took a step back from us, drawing in a breath.

"You do," Serena said. "You know who I'm talking about."

Luca ran his fingers through his curls, his heart beating loud enough I could hear it clearly.

"What do you know about him?" I asked quickly.

Was there a different reason that Luca had a bounty on his head? One that I wasn't aware of?

"I need to sit down," Luca whispered.

I gestured to the couch. "All of us do."

"I'll get blood on the couch," Serena said.

"I don't care," I said. "Sit. I have... some things to reveal as well. It sounds like all of us do."

The three of us moved to the sofa. Luca sat on the edge of the cushion, letting his face fall into his hands. His muscles were tense, his distress visible.

"J, or Jason, was someone who joined your uncle's mafia right before we left," Luca said. "He was also someone who had information on your uncle. It was how I was able to blackmail your uncle and leave their mafia with you, Serena."

"What did you do in exchange for that information?" I asked.

Luca was silent for a moment.

I knew this wasn't good.

"Just so we're clear," I said. "Jason is cunning. He's evil. He is the only demigod I've fought with regularly over the last few thousand years. He almost always gets what he wants and will play the game for years. For decades. And he has..." I said, thinking about the Golden Fleece.

"I need whiskey or something," Luca muttered.

"What did you do, Luca?" Serena asked, glaring at him. I could feel her mistrust, her anger.

I could feel his fear.

I didn't like either. They were both my mates. I didn't want them to feel distressed.

Hell, I wanted to protect them. To keep them locked away from my world. But that was slowly becoming more and more impossible the longer we were together.

Maybe returning to Serena had been a mistake. Maybe I had damned us all.

"In exchange for the information I used to blackmail your uncle, I had to keep Jason, or J, updated on any of your outbursts. He asked me to make sure I never let you leave the castle. He claimed it was for your protection. He told me Ian was evil and wanted nothing more than to hurt Serena. And I believed him. Because why wouldn't I? At the time, I trusted him."

Serena jumped up from the sofa, glaring at Luca. "Is that the reason you kept me locked up? Why you lied to me this whole time? And you never fucking thought that would be an important thing to mention in the ten years we were together? That J, the man who arranged my marriage to Ian, wanted you to keep me locked up?"

"Whoa, hold on," I said. "J did not arrange my marriage to you."

"Oh? Then how did we become married, Ian?" Serena seethed, crossing her arms.

I found my gaze settling on her breasts and on the blood there.

Fuck.

Thoughts. Brain. Problems. I had to make myself not think about bending her over and fucking her in that night dress.

I thought back to all those years ago. To when Serena was a fresh eighteen year old, to when I had made a deal to marry her.

All of the secrets the three of us had were finally coming to light tonight.

"I dreamed of you," I whispered, looking up at her. I held her dark gaze, basking in the heat of her rage. "I dreamed of you for years. The dreams began before you were born. I would see us together. A mate who belonged to me. You were always followed by a shadow, and now I know why," I said, glancing at Luca. "Your uncle reached out to me and wanted to create a partnership through our businesses. I flew to Italy to meet with him, but we were ambushed by his men. They killed three of my own. I did not take kindly to being attacked," I said.

No.

That night had been one of blood, and I'd demanded penance for being attacked. For being betrayed.

Serena had been my prize.

"We retaliated, of course. I murdered thirty of your uncle's men that night."

"I remember," Luca whispered. "At that time, I didn't know it was you."

"It was me," I said solemnly. "I gutted them like animals and left their bodies on the docks where *Don* Avellino kept his boats. I was going for his family next. I snuck into the villa where your family lived, and that's when I saw you, Serena. You had no idea," I whispered. "No idea I was even there."

Her expression slowly changed, her rage melting into something unreadable.

"A year later, we were wed," I said. "You were my prize. I don't know what they told you. Maybe they said Jason arranged it. Maybe, in some ways, he had. But I saw you and claimed you as mine."

"Then why did you send me to the castle?" she whispered. "If I was the woman you dreamed about, why did you abandon me?"

"I didn't want my world to hurt you," I said. "I'm a dragon, princess. I hoard what is most precious to me. And after I saw your face on our wedding day, I didn't want to force you to be mine. I thought about it. But I wouldn't do it. And it became easier to keep you away than embrace my dreams."

Serena let out a sigh, pressing her lips together. "And you,

Luca? What do you have to say for yourself? Was everything a lie, then? All of it?"

"No," Luca said. He looked like a man on the edge of despair, ready to sink to his knees.

Hell, I'd be right there next to him.

"I did what I had to do to keep you with me," Luca said. "To protect you. J didn't reach out very often. Only once a year or so. He would call and ask for updates. Most of the time, I told him nothing had happened."

"But?"

"He called earlier this week," Luca whispered.

My hearts squeezed.

Fucking hell. This was a mess. A web of lies and secrets, all of us doing what we hoped was right when it was the furthest thing from it.

"Jason called me today," I said. "He put a bounty on your head, Luca, for 150 million dollars and the Golden Fleece."

"What?" Luca's eyes widened. "On *me*?"

"Yes," I said. "Your life in exchange for keeping Serena safe."

"That's a load of bullshit," she whispered harshly.

"It is," I agreed. "But as I said, Jason is cunning. He knows the three of us have been keeping secrets from each other. And he used that knowledge against us. To think that we would hide so much."

"I told you," Serena said, looking at Luca. "Not to lie to me again. Do you not remember?"

"I..." Luca trailed off. "I'm sorry I didn't disclose everything to you."

"I need a shower," she murmured.

"We'll shower," I said. "All of us."

"And then sleep," Luca offered.

"You're sleeping alone tonight," she said, glowering. "So

what now? Luca has a bounty on his head. I have a magic knife from my long-lost god parent. And Ian has been dreaming about me since before I was born."

"Well," I said. "I imagine Jason has gone through this much trouble to ensure his safety and power."

"Ares said that my destiny was to murder Jason," Serena said. "And that was all he *could* say."

"I think Jason probably wants one of us dead then," I said. "Since we are your mates. And since Luca was manipulated to hate me, it would stand to reason that I would send him away, even if it upset you. He's betting on us being enemies. He's betting on us hating each other."

Luca nodded, sitting up. He sighed, shaking his head. "I'm tired of hate."

"I am, too," I said.

"I'm tired of feeling trapped," Serena said. "And now I know who created the cage in the first place. How could the Fates allow something like this?"

"The Fates are fickle," I said. "And they wouldn't interfere."

Serena mumbled something under her breath and ran her fingers through her dark hair. Sunlight poured into the living room now, the city coming alive below.

"I have a proposal," I said gently. "I know you're probably pissed at both of us, understandably so. But Luca and I have been worrying about you for hours."

"I was only gone for an hour," Serena said, frowning.

"No," I replied. "You were gone most of the night, baby. I had half of the Three Fates Mafia looking for you. Time moves differently in the presence of a god. That's why the sun is rising right now."

"Oh," she whispered.

"I think we should all shower and sleep in my bed. Maybe

even cuddle. And when we wake up, we can plan how to murder Jason."

Serena was silent, studying me. "Fine," she said. Her lips slowly pulled into a smile, her shoulders finally relaxing. "Shower, cuddles, sleep, and plotting murder."

"Just your average Saturday," Luca chuckled dryly.

Serena laughed softly and reached for him, surprising him by cupping his face. "You're lucky I love you," she said.

"I am," he agreed, tugging her close. "Seeing you covered in blood turns me on."

"Fuck," she mumbled.

"Maybe we can help wash it off," I offered, my cocks already stirring. "Ares did rudely interrupt us. What awkward timing."

"At least I was clothed," Serena giggled. "Fucking hell. I can't believe my father is Ares. And I can't believe I'm dating a dragon and my stalker."

"Hey," Luca and I both said.

"We're already married, wifey," I said. "Need I remind you, sugar?"

"Do not start with the pet names," she laughed, giving me a light shove.

"Honey tits. Sugar lips. Apple of my eyes."

"Gods, I'm going to gag," Luca said.

"I can come up with names for you, too," I said sweetly. "That stalker guy. Pervert. My little bottom—"

All words faltered as Serena gripped the hem of her night slip and pulled it over her head, revealing her very naked body.

Both of my cocks hardened.

"I have a proposal," she said.

"I think you have our attention," Luca whispered, his voice breaking.

She slowly smirked.

Fuck.

I loved it when she wielded the power she held over us.

It did things to me.

"How about we shower, have some fun, sleep, and then plot murder. And somewhere in there, eat some food and buy me a dress for the event." She ran her hands up her body, cupping her breasts.

Fucking hell.

My cocks throbbed against my pants, my hearts beating harder.

She licked her lips, squeezing her perky nipples for us.

"Please," Luca whispered.

"Even if I want both of you together?" she taunted. "You think you can share your little toy?"

"Yes," Luca and I both growled.

"Good boys," she said.

Oh no.

"You better fucking run to the shower," I growled, narrowing my gaze on her.

"Why? Are you going to punish me for calling you a good boy? Should I call you daddy instead?"

"You call me sir," I grunted, leaning forward. "Unless you want me to fuck your cunt with that blood on you, get your ass going."

She winked and twirled, taking off down the hall.

I grabbed Luca by the cuff of his shirt and gave him a push. "You too, boy. Before I fuck you so hard you forget your name isn't 'Ian's bitch'."

Chapter 26
Mated to the Dragon and Knight

Serena

All of the tension, all of the hate, love, and frustration, every ounce of it drove the three of us together.

And it was explosive.

Ian shoved me against the shower wall as Luca cranked it on, the hot water hitting our skin. I groaned, grabbing Ian's face and running my fingers through his silver beard. He kissed me, and I remembered the night he had just told us about.

The night he first saw me.

I had no idea that a monster was waiting for me in the dark.

Or that one day, I would love him.

I melted against Ian as I felt Luca's hand touch me. Running over my hips, up my sides, and around to my breasts. I gasped as they pressed me between them, their cocks hard, their hunger driving them both.

Ian kissed down my throat, letting out a low growl. Luca kissed the other side.

I couldn't believe that they hated each other. Not when they worked so damn well together.

"Oh fuck," I gasped.

My head fell back on Luca's shoulder, a moan escaping me as he scraped his teeth over my neck. The sensation was ethereal, and I realized that spot did it for me.

Both of them realized that too.

Luca let out a deep groan, kissing me there. I gasped, my pussy pulsing as he nursed my neck.

"Your body craves the marks," Ian whispered at my throat.

"What marks?" I panted.

Ian slid his hand down to my pussy, rubbing his two fingers over my clit. I cried out, bracing my palms on his shoulders.

"Mating," Ian grumbled. He gripped my jaw, forcing me to look at him. Steam surrounded us, the blood on my skin washing down the drain, taking my sins with it. "Do you want to be mated, little queen? Do you want to be ours?"

"Yes," I rasped.

Luca let out a growl, his teeth scraping my neck again. My body reacted like I'd been struck by lightning.

I was so fucking wet. So turned on.

"I want this," I groaned. "Please."

He slowly exhaled, running the pad of his thumb over my bottom lip. His gaze darkened, and I watched my husband give in to his desire. Into the primal needs that plagued him, the darkness that drew us all together.

"You have to bite her," Ian whispered to Luca. "And she has to bite you. She's not a mortal like you, but she can bond to you. So can I. But then..."

"Do it," I said.

"If we do this, then we will always be connected," Ian said.

Luca let out a soft hum. "I think that's already the case, Ian."

"That means you'd be bonded to me, little knight."

Little knight. The nickname made me smile.

Luca pulled me closer to him, his cock fitting against my ass. He rested his chin on my shoulder , looking at Ian. Taking him in.

"Why not?" Luca whispered. "You know I belong to you too."

Ian's expression softened, and I realized he wanted this more than either one of us could fathom. How long had he been waiting for his mates? He'd been alive for so long, and he'd just now found us...

"Okay," Ian said softly.

"Mate me," I said simply. "I love you. I've fallen for you in a matter of days, and I wish we wouldn't have waited so long to get to know each other. But we're here now, and we can be together," I said. "I can be with both of you. And you can be together too. We can finally get our happily ever after."

"The dragon, the knight, and the princess," Ian teased, swallowing hard. "I think we might be meant for each other."

I leaned up on my tiptoes, kissing Ian again. This time it was softer, deeper, and filled with longing. With need.

He broke our kiss and reached for Luca, pulling him in for one too. Luca tensed for a moment, before relaxing into it. I ran my hands over Ian's chest and leaned forward, swirling my tongue over one of his nipples.

"Holy fuck," he growled.

I grinned like I'd struck gold, but before I could do anything else, Ian leaned down and sank his teeth into my shoulder.

"Fuck," I gasped.

There was an initial pain, but it was swallowed whole by the pleasure that followed. My eyes closed as I felt something

I'd never felt, like the strings of fate were snapping to life inside me.

I could feel him. His thoughts, his emotions, and how fucking much he wanted me. How much he cherished me.

Ian slowly pulled his teeth free, swiping his tongue over the wound. It started to heal, the edge of his magic bleeding through me.

Luca nuzzled the other side of my neck.

"Please," I whispered. "I want to feel you too."

"Claim your princess, little knight," Ian murmured.

He kissed the soft spot of my shoulder and then bared his teeth, sinking them in hard. His teeth weren't as sharp as Ian's, but I still felt the bond come to life.

It was magical. It was wonderful. Beautiful. I gasped as Luca became one with me, our souls melding together like precious metals. He whimpered as he took my blood, his hands holding onto me.

I felt his fear, worry, and anger at anyone who might harm me. I felt his devotion. His love. His obsession for me.

I felt it all.

His darkness. His light. The ugly parts of him and the parts I wished the whole world could see.

"Luca," I whispered.

He pulled away, holding the back of his hand to his mouth, his eyes wide. "This is..."

"Weird?" Ian chuckled.

"Amazing," Luca whispered. "But also strange, yes. Normal people don't bite people and feel their souls."

"Well, we are hardly normal," Ian said, smirking. "It's your turn, little queen. Where do you want to bite?"

A dark giggle emerged. I got to choose. Where was I going to leave my mark on him? On Luca?

I pushed him back against the shower wall, enjoying how

smoke curled from his mouth and his eyes lit up. I slowly lowered myself, my knees hitting the tiled floor.

"Serena," he rasped.

"Are you going to bite his cock? Because I would pay to see that," Luca snickered.

"That's like me paying her to do it," Ian growled.

"Not your cock," I said, kissing the line of his hips.

But I did want to stroke them while I did it.

I gripped his top cock, stroking him as I pressed my mouth against the V of his hips. I listened to his groans and growls, then sank my teeth straight into his skin as I continued to pump my hand up and down.

"Fuck," he rasped.

I felt the connection solidify and knew the mating bond was complete. A circle meeting itself, all three of us welded together. I swiped my tongue over the bite mark on Ian and licked the head of his cock, watching as my dragon husband cried out.

His pleasure surrounded me, turning me on further. My pussy pulsed, my heart beating faster.

I rose up and turned, raising a brow at Luca. His dark gaze roamed over me, his lips tugging into a smirk.

"Come here, *piccola regina*," he whispered.

I went to him, kissing down his entire body until I came to the same spot I had with Ian. Luca's cock throbbed, hot water streaming down his body. I gripped his shaft and leaned forward, biting him on his hip.

Luca gasped, his fingers gripping my hair and holding my teeth to his skin. He groaned, any pain replaced by pleasure and need. I stroked his cock as I tasted him, letting out a soft groan.

He gripped my head as I pulled back, guiding my mouth to his cock.

I knew what he wanted. What he needed.

I parted my lips, taking the head of his cock between them and sucking. Luca grunted, thrusting his hips forward and filling my mouth completely. He hit the back of my throat, drawing a soft moan from me.

I looked up, watching as Ian leaned forward and kissed Luca. I slid my hand down to my pussy, rubbing my clit as I took Luca's cock over and over. I groaned around him, his grip tightening in my hair hard enough that it stung.

Just like I liked it.

Ian and Luca broke apart, and I was pulled to my feet, my lips meeting Luca's right as I was lifted. My legs wrapped around his hips and he turned, pressing my back against the wall. I felt the head of his cock against my pussy, and let out a gasp when Ian pressed his body against Luca's.

"You're going to feel me fuck you through him," Ian growled.

"*Oh*," I whispered.

Luca moaned and thrust forward, his cock sliding inside of me. I cried out, pleasure gripping me. Luca cursed, his cock pulsing inside of me.

"You're so wet and tight," he rasped. He let out a low moan, his head falling back as Ian thrust his hips forward.

We all cried out together, Ian burying his cock inside Luca as Luca's cock filled me. Ian pressed his palms against the wall to either side of my head, thrusting his hips again.

His thrust made Luca thrust, drawing a gasp from me.

I could feel our bonds, the strings of fate binding us together.

"You're so big," Luca groaned.

"You can take bigger," Ian groaned.

Ian began to pump his cock in and out of Luca, and Luca did the same to me. We fell into a rhythm, one that was edged with passion and need. I cried out, gripping Luca's shoulders as the three of us fucked.

"Harder," I whimpered.

Ian gripped Luca's hips, his eyes shining like jewels as he buried himself into our mate over and over again. Luca huffed, his cock hitting that spot—the one that had me screaming.

"There," I cried. "There! Please don't stop!"

"We won't, little queen," Ian growled.

Luca's cock thrust in and out of me, and I felt an orgasm creep up, overcoming me quickly. I gasped, arching my back as I came on his cock, my pleasure echoing through our connections.

"I'm going to come," Luca rasped. "Fuck."

"Me too," Ian groaned.

The two of them fucked harder, Luca holding onto me tight as he let out a shout. I felt his hot seed fill me, his cock jerking as he came inside of me. Ian let out a similar sound, and I watched as he came inside Luca, feeling his pleasure. His ecstasy.

The three of us melted against each other, the hot water starting to run cold.

"Fuck," Ian mumbled.

Luca let out a chuckle, looking at me and then back at Ian. "I think it's time for the actual shower, then sleep."

I nodded and whimpered as Luca slowly pulled out of me, his cum dripping from me.

Being with the two of them was...

Perfect.

It was everything I wanted.

We washed off quickly, and I was climbing into Ian's giant bed a few minutes later.

"In the middle, *piccola regina*," Luca teased.

I moved to the center as Ian and Luca climbed in next to

me, our bodies molding together. Ian pulled the blankets up, tugging me closer.

I let out a happy sigh, my eyes already closing. "Just a nap," I murmured. "We still have a murder to plot."

"Get some sleep," Ian chuckled. "I love you. Both of you."

"I love you too," I whispered.

Luca made a noise, but didn't argue with Ian. "I love you too," he mumbled quickly, as if we wouldn't hear it.

I felt Ian smile against me, and that made me happy.

If only we didn't have a demigod trying to destroy the three of us.

Chapter 27
Afternoon Delight

Luca

The three of us slept in Ian's bed until the sun set. I woke up slowly, realizing I was spooning Serena, and Ian was spooning me.

I was in the middle.

How in the hell had I ended up in the middle? We'd gone to bed with Serena between us.

Ian's arm looped around my waist, his warmth wrapping around me. We were all naked, and I could feel both of his cocks against me.

I let out a low groan, my blood boiling, not with anger or rage, but with need.

Pure need.

Losing Serena last night had sent me over the edge, and Ian had been my anchor through it all. Realizing I had unintentionally harmed her and all of my guilt about Jason weighed heavy on me.

Yet she still loved me.

I could feel the bite she'd given me, our bonds alive. It was like having her under my skin, as close to me as possible.

Ian moved behind me, his head nuzzling mine. His voice was low, that barely awake crackle sending a bolt of pleasure through me. "Afternoon, little knight," he whispered. "You feel good against me. When are *we* going to mate?"

I swallowed hard, closing my eyes. "When do you want to?"

"Now," he grumbled, his cocks pulsing against me.

"Do it," I whispered.

He pressed his lips against my neck, kissing me until he came to the soft muscle where my neck met my shoulder. I inhaled right as he bit me.

He moaned, bringing his hand up to my face and offering me his wrist. I didn't hesitate, biting him as if I was a vampire.

The bond to him felt much different than the one I had with Serena, but I enjoyed it all the same. There was a dark obsession that we shared, a stain on our souls.

Serena moved against me, letting out a sleepy sigh as her ass pressed against my hardening cock. I mentally cursed as Ian and I completed our bond, all while she started to move against me.

I pulled my mouth free. "Serena," I rasped.

Meanwhile, Ian slipped his hand down my body.

"Ian," I whispered, my voice barely heard.

His hand slid down my ass, his top cock pressing against me. He pulled his teeth free, his tongue swiping over the wound.

Fuck.

Serena wiggled against me again, her ass rubbing against my own throbbing cock.

"*Piccola regina*," I groaned. "Fuck. Both of you..." I trailed off as Ian pushed two fingers inside of me, making me groan.

Serena stirred more against me, then I felt her hand wrap around my cock. A low groan left me as she turned her head, giving me a sleepy wink.

"Morning," she whispered. "I could feel the two of you."

"Could you?" I rasped, my eyes fluttering as she began to stroke me.

"You're so hard," she murmured.

"He's needy," Ian said, his voice gruff. "I think he needs some attention, don't you?"

"Ian," I growled.

He chuckled and sat up. "Roll over onto your stomach and let her get on top of you. I think I can fuck you both at the same time."

I let out a low hiss, but Serena nodded, biting her lip. "Yes please," she said.

"Fuck," I muttered. "That puts me on the bottom."

"Right where you belong," Ian teased. "Roll over."

I wanted to tell him to fuck off, but I rolled over onto my stomach, groaning as my hard cock pressed against the blankets. Serena ran her nails over my back and straddled me, balancing herself on me. Her pussy rubbed against me, her soft moan driving me wild.

I heard the crack of Ian's hand against my ass cheek before I felt it. An involuntary cry tore from me, then one was pulled from Serena as he spanked her next.

Fuck.

I looked back over my shoulder, watching as Ian started to shift into his half-dragon form.

"Oh, yes," Serena said. "Please."

"Now that you're my mates, I could take you in my full form too," Ian huffed as he straddled the back of my thighs. I buried my face into the pillow as he opened a bottle of lube, dripping some onto me, then Serena.

The idea of him fucking us as a full dragon ran through my mind. My cock pulsed in response, my heartbeat speeding up.

Serena leaned over me, her breath warm against my neck.

And then she bit my ear.

"Fuck," I moaned, trying to lean up, but Ian shoved me back down.

Holding me in place.

I felt the head of his cock against my ass and Serena bit me harder, a sultry laugh leaving her.

"You're a monster," I mumbled to her, even though it turned me on more than I had words for.

"You like it," she huffed. "Fuck, I can feel my husband's cock against me."

Husband. I groaned, wishing I could bury my aching cock into her too.

My ear stung as she cried out. I felt Ian thrust inside her and then me.

Both of us at the same time.

I gripped the blankets as I cursed, his cock filling me completely. Serena whimpered, her body warm against mine.

"You both feel so fucking good," Ian grunted. "My little mates."

He pulled back and thrust forward again, drawing cries from both of us. He let out a soft curse as he found a rhythm, his thick cock sliding in and out of me.

Fuck. I was getting fucked by Serena's husband and was relishing it.

Fuck. I really loved him.

He pumped in and out of us. Serena moaned on top of me, her hands intertwining with mine as we took him.

Over and over.

The bed squeaked under us, his breaths becoming hurried as he fucked us harder. I felt my cock jerk against the bed, aching against me.

"I'm going to come," I moaned. "Fuck."

"I am too," Serena cried.

"Come for me," Ian rasped. "Both of you. I want to feel you squeezing my cocks with your little cunts."

He thrust into us, and I couldn't take it anymore. I let out a roar as I came, feeling my cock release all over the blankets. Serena cried out, her body tensing on top of mine as her own orgasm overcame her.

I squeezed Ian's cock, cursing as I came.

He groaned, thrusting harder. "I'm going to fill both of you."

"Please," I whimpered.

Serena let out a little gasp. "I like hearing you beg," she said.

I smiled into the pillows.

I liked begging.

Sometimes.

Ian pumped in and out until he finally let out a growl, shoving his cock all the way inside of me. I felt his cum pour into me, heat spreading as he shuddered against me.

We all collapsed into a sweaty heap, his cum pumping into me for another minute.

Ian slowly pulled out, sliding off my thighs. "Clean our little queen up," he commanded.

Serena rolled off me, and I leaned up, seeing the mess of cum on the blankets and my stomach. With a low growl, I grabbed her thighs and dragged her to the center of the bed, pushing them apart.

Her husband's dragon cum dripped from her pussy, her cheeks flushed.

"I like seeing his cum drip out of you," I admitted.

Even though I'd just come, it turned me on.

She let out a helpless gasp as I buried my lips between her thighs, circling her swollen clit with my tongue. She tasted perfect. I looked up at her body as I licked her, watching as Ian leaned down and sucked one of her nipples into his mouth.

Her soft sigh melted into another moan as I sucked her clit, watching the way he played with her breasts. My cock began to pulse again, need making my entire body stiffen.

I needed to bury my cock inside her. To fill her with my seed and his. To make her mine.

Ian let out a low growl and kissed her. I pushed my tongue inside her, the taste of her mixed with him making me feral.

"You're so fucking perfect," I groaned, before driving my tongue back into her.

She cried out, her hips bucking. "Luca," she moaned.

I loved hearing my name on her lips.

"Make her come again," Ian growled. "I need her to be ready for my dragon cocks."

She tensed at the mention of his dragon form, and so did I. The thought of her taking his full monster cock made my own jerk in reaction. I reached down and stroked myself as I drove my tongue inside her, wanting to drown in her pussy.

Her thighs squeezed my head, her sharp cry edging me further. I lapped her up, cleaning up the mess Ian had made.

Would I be able to see the outline of his cock inside her?

The thought nearly made me explode.

I pulled my hand away and pushed her thighs apart, resting my thumb over her clit and rubbing it quickly as I tasted her.

"Drown him, little queen," Ian commanded, his baritone voice sending a thrill through me.

Serena trembled against me, her breaths becoming faster as I swirled her clit. She let out a sharp cry, her body trying to arch up. I held her in place, holding her to that pleasure that curled through her. Her cry turned into a yell, her orgasm crashing into her.

Her pussy flooded with her essence, and I licked up every delicious drop, a man starved.

Desperate for her.

I leaned back, licking my lips. I watched as Ian grabbed Serena's face, letting out a low growl as he forced her to look at him.

I was possessive of her. I was obsessed with her. But seeing the way he touched her, the way he touched me...

I could share.

Serena leaned up, the two of them sharing a kiss. Ian cupped her face, his hands beginning to change. I watched as his fingers started to turn into claws, his face turning into that of a dragon.

I watched as my little queen took his forked tongue down her throat. Her nipples hardened, her chest rising and falling.

Fuck.

I leaned down and pressed my lips against her clit. I kissed her there, then kissed up her stomach, trailing kisses all the way until I came to her breasts. She groaned as I cupped them.

Gentle. Sweet. All while our dragon ravaged her in a hungry kiss.

My tongue flicked over her nipple, teasing her.

I felt Ian's clawed hand grip my curls, yanking my hair. I grunted as he pulled me back, sucking in a breath as he broke his kiss with Serena and kissed me.

"Fuck," Ian growled, letting out a low hiss. "I want to shift completely. My primal side is calling to me. Can we go downstairs?"

"What's downstairs?" Serena rasped.

"A room big enough for me to be a complete dragon," Ian explained. "And one with a nest..."

"A nest?" We both asked.

Serena let out an excited giggle, grinning at us both. "Sure. I want...I want to see you. *All* of you. Luca?"

I thought about it for a moment. But I already knew the answer. "Yes," I said.

"Good," Ian said. "Let's take an elevator ride then."

"What if someone sees us?" Serena asked.

"It's the weekend, little queen. We're the only ones in the building besides the guards, and they know better than to watch."

"Let's go then," I said, sliding off the bed.

Chapter 28
Dragon Nest

The room Ian was talking about was massive. The ceilings were tall and there was no furniture because almost every inch was covered in mounds of gold.

Gold.

I stared, looking around us in awe.

"You have...a lot of gold," I whispered.

"I do," Ian chuckled.

He led us through literal piles of it. Gold coins, blocks, jewels, necklaces, and treasures. It rose up above us, mountains gleaming around us.

"Is this a hobby of yours?" Luca asked warily. "Hoarding?"

"I'm a dragon; it's in my nature. I've been collecting for hundreds of years."

At the center was the nest Ian had mentioned. It was a mound of pillows and blankets in the middle of all the treasure.

"I'm going to breed both of you amidst all my treasure," Ian said. "My cum is still dripping from both of you. My wife and her little knight in shining armor."

I'd already seen stars twice in the last hour, but fucking hell. When he said things like that...

Luca drew me close, tugging me into a kiss. I groaned as he pushed me down into the center of the nest, wrapping my arms around his neck. His body pressed against mine, heat binding us.

I could feel Ian watching us, searing us with his gaze.

I liked being his wife, I realized. It was hot. There was something about him saying it that drove me wild.

The elevator ride down to this room had only left me wanting more. I had already come so fucking hard, but I needed to be filled by both of them.

Luca let out a low growl, drawing back. We both looked up at Ian.

He stood, both of his cocks hard and dripping with precum. His wings spread behind him, his iridescent gaze burning into me.

I needed him.

"Show us," Luca whispered.

I'd never seen Luca submit to someone else like this, but it turned me on. Seeing my big bad bodyguard give in like this...

"If I shift, I'm going to take both of you again," Ian whispered. "You are my mates, so I can use my magic to make... make it fit."

"Make it fit," Luca echoed. "Fuck. How big are your cocks?"

"Big."

Luca exhaled audibly, looking at Ian and then back to me.

"I want it," I said. "And I'm curious about this magic."

"As am I," Luca said. "I'm very curious."

Ian snickered, giving Luca a dark smile. "I think that's Luca saying he might be falling for me," he teased.

Luca gave him a look but didn't deny it. That made me smile.

"I've fallen for both of you," I said, grinning like an idiot.

They looked at me, both smiling.

Gods, all three of us were so far gone for each other.

"We both love you more than anything else, Serena," Ian said.

"Truly," Luca echoed.

I felt my heart skip a beat, my stomach twisting from the excitement that burst through me. The happiness.

How long had I imagined falling in love? Being in love with someone, creating a life with them? I had fallen for both of them. I saw exactly who they were and loved them completely.

I wanted this. I could feel our mating bonds tying us together and the warmth that emanated through them.

They both looked at me like I was the center of their world. My dragon and my knight.

Ian's gaze flickered to Luca, and I could see it.

It was the same way he looked at me.

"Ian," I said, raising a brow. "So..."

"Ah, I suppose you want to see me, little queen," he said.

I nodded, my eyes drifting back down to both of his cocks.

The things we could all do together...Dirty thoughts drifted through my mind, and I squeezed my thighs shut, biting my lower lip.

Luca let out a low growl, pulling them apart. "I want to see how wet you get for him when he changes."

"Fuck," I whispered.

The bastard knew me too well. There was no hiding when Luca was with me. Or Ian, for that matter.

"Even if she kept her thighs shut, I would smell her arousal," Ian chuckled.

His body began to change, his already half-dragon form growing. His muscles grew, and the sound of bones snapping and reforming made me worry. Did becoming a full dragon hurt him?

All of my concern melted away, though, as he kept growing. I gasped quietly as he filled the room, his massive wings spreading around us.

He was enormous.

He was beautiful.

"Fucking hell," Luca whispered. "You're huge."

Ian let out a sound that reminded me of a chuckle. It was loud enough that I could feel it in my bones. He shook his head, the spikes lining his long neck gleaming in the light.

He moved closer to us, parting his jaws. Rows of teeth faced us, and I let out a nervous giggle.

It's not too bad, right?

Luca and I gasped in surprise at the same time.

"I can hear you in my head," I said.

That's right, little queen.

His voice was still the same.

He stepped over us, planting his claws into the blankets above my head. Luca reclined next to me, his hand slipping into mine as we looked up at our dragon.

His body reminded me of a serpent with a long tail. His wings were sheer with spiny branches covered in scales. My eyes roamed over him in awe, then fell onto his cocks.

Like in his half form, he had a pocket that held him.

Like what you see?

"Yes," Luca said, his voice husky.

He squeezed my hand, surprising me when he moved onto

his knees. He reached up, running his hand over one of Ian's hard cocks.

Ian let out a long groan, a shiver running through his body.

"How will that fit?" I whispered, thinking about taking him.

I was a demigod, right? An immortal? But even my body had its limits.

"What's the saying? Faith, trust, and dragon cum?" Luca teased.

"That's definitely not the saying," I said.

"Come touch his other cock," Luca said. "Unless you're scared, *piccola regina*."

"Fuck you," I whispered.

I wasn't scared. I was fucking turned on.

I sat up and crawled towards Luca and Ian's cock. Ian moved his head, his neck long enough that he could curl around himself.

"Fuck," I whispered.

Luca started to stroke Ian's cock, watching me with a smirk. "You're scared."

"If you keep saying that, I'm going to peg you," I mumbled.

Don't threaten him with a good time, Ian snickered. *I think I have a strap-on—*

I leaned forward and licked the head of his bottom cock.

Ian groaned, his hips jerking. *Fuck.*

I wrapped both my hands around his cock, stroking him in the same rhythm that Luca did. Ian growled, his entire body vibrating with the noise as we played with him.

Luca leaned over and I met him in a kiss, both of us moaning. He pulled away, winking at me.

I'm going to cover you both in my cum if you keep going, Ian warned.

"Maybe that's what I want, sir," I replied, smirking as I said the last word.

Luca snorted. "You call him *sir?*"

You call me daddy.

"I do not," Luca growled, narrowing his eyes. "I've never called you daddy before. Shut the hell up, Ian."

Ian and I both laughed. I ran my hand down his shaft, reaching for his knot. "There's no way," I whispered. "No way it will fit."

I will use my magic.

My breath hitched, the thought of him fitting this massive cock inside me made my pussy throb. My heart beat a little faster, heat flushing over my skin.

You want my dragon cock in your little demigod cunt, princess? Do you want your knight to watch too?

"Yes," I whispered.

My head was spinning with the thought. I let out a low groan, turning to look at Ian's head. I could see the mischief in his eyes. He couldn't smile like a human, but I could feel it. The monstrous desires that plagued all three of us.

"Please, sir," I rasped. "I want you to breed me. Fuck me."

Luca let out a low noise. "Fucking hell, Serena. You have a dirty mouth."

"And you love it," I quipped.

"That I do."

Alright, little queen. Spread your legs for me.

Chapter 29
Lay not Slay

Ian

I wrapped my claws around Serena and lifted her, enjoying how she squeaked as she realized how big I was. Luca continued to stroke one of my cocks, letting out a low hum as I placed our mate on the pillows and blankets and lowered my head between her legs.

She let out a soft breath, her dark-brown eyes wide with anticipation. Her skin was flushed from coming, and I loved it.

I loved everything about her.

Her scent filled me, drawing me closer. I parted my jaws, lapping my forked tongue over her pussy. She cried out, arching against my nest as I tasted her.

I began to draw on my magic, feeling the bonds connecting us buzz to life. The magic was an entity unto itself, a spell deep-seated in my monstrous soul drawn forward by my mate.

She would take my dragon cock.

Luca seemed to sense this and stepped out from under me,

running his warm palm over my scales. I licked Serena between her legs, her cry rocketing through the room. The taste of her was like a drug in my veins.

My mate, I told her. *You're going to take my cock so well, little queen.*

I drove the tips of my tongue inside her tight pussy, her cry echoing around me, her body squeezing me. Milking me like it soon would be doing to my cock. She was wet and still full of my cum, her body ready for me.

The spell came forward, a soft whisper. I felt her body begin to change, aided by the magic to be able to take my cock. She groaned as her pussy changed, her body becoming the perfect breeding hole for me.

"Ian," she rasped. "Fill me. Please. I'm aching for you. I need you inside of me, sir."

Sir.

A growl reverberated through me and I lowered myself, gripping her body with my claws and lifting her again. I was going to hold her and use her like my personal fuck toy.

Are you sure, Serena? I asked as I positioned her. I looked up at Luca, holding his hungry gaze. His hand wrapped around his cock, his eyes pinned on us like we were the only drop of water in a drought, the only thing that could quench his thirst.

"I'm sure," she rasped. "I'm sure, I'm sure. Please, Ian. Please give me your cock."

I moved my long neck, turning my head so I could see my cocks, could see the top one pressing against her entrance. The magic that bound us snapped with an electrical charge, her body ready for me.

How long had I dreamed of this moment? To be able to take someone entirely, for them to accept the monstrous part of me that everyone hid from? She wasn't scared of me. She loved me.

And I loved her.

You're next, Luca, I promised him.

He let out a strained noise, his breath hitching.

Serena relaxed in my clawed grip as I pressed the head of my cock against her pussy. She was so fucking wet for me, her body aching to be filled. I growled as I pushed into her, slowly, carefully, letting her adjust around the shape of me. To how big I was. She gasped, her pussy immediately clenching me like a closed fist as I fit myself into her.

"Oh fuuuuck," she moaned, her voice low. She raised her head with a pant, looking down at her body. "Fucking hell."

My perfect little fleshlight, I groaned.

"Fuck," Luca said, watching in awe. "You're really taking him, *piccola regina.*"

All she did was groan. I continued pushing inside of her until I simply couldn't anymore. I filled her as much as her body could take, and still, half of my cock was untouched. But it didn't matter.

Fucking her like this was unlike anything I'd ever experienced in all my time.

I pulled her up, her cry urging me on as I pushed her back down, maneuvering her like my own fuck toy.

The two of us groaned in pleasure, and I could feel her through our bonds, a mirror to my own ecstasy. It was beautiful and wild and—

She suddenly came hard around me, her cry driving my clawed hands to use her body, to push in and out of her as she saw the gods and heavens and everything I would see the moment I filled her with my seed.

I thrust in and out of her, feeling cum drip from my bottom cock. I gasped as I felt Luca touch me, his little tongue working at the slit and lapping up every drop.

I'm going to come, I groaned. My other set of claws tore into the blankets, shredding the fabric as I bore down, jerking my little queen up and down until I couldn't stop myself.

I roared as I came, the floor trembling and my wings spreading behind me. Gold clinked as it fell to the floor around us. She and Luca both cried out as my cum shot out, coating her insides and Luca's chest. My cum spilled out of her, dripping from her pussy as I held her on me, looking down as she bloated with my seed.

"You look pregnant," Luca whispered, running his palm over her stomach.

"Would you like that?" she huffed. "Do you want me to get pregnant, Luca?"

"Yes. From him and then me."

She let out a groan. I slowly pulled her off, my cum spilling out of her as I laid her down.

Then I grabbed Luca.

"Hey," he gasped.

I was hard. I was still so fucking hard. I'd come so much, but I needed more.

I whispered the spell and he groaned as I turned him over so he could look down at Serena.

Her eyes widened and she watched as I pressed the head of my cock against his ass.

I'm going to fuck you, Luca.

"I can feel the magic," he groaned. "I can feel it changing me."

"Getting you ready for his dragon cock," Serena rasped. "It feels so fucking good."

"It does," he grunted.

The two of them kissed. I leaned over both of them, lowering Luca enough so he could pin Serena beneath him.

Fuck.

I need them both at the same time. I'd just fucked her so

hard, but I wanted to fuck her again. To give them my cocks, to breed my mates over and over again.

That primal part of me took over. I let out a low growl, smoke curling from my nostrils.

Put your cock inside her, Luca.

He turned his head, glancing up at me as I changed our positions, getting ready to do what I wanted.

I watched as he turned his attention back on her, their bodies grinding against each other. She wrapped her legs around his hips, letting out a soft whimper as he shoved his cock inside her, groaning.

The sounds they made together were hot.

My claws dug into the floor, and I reached down, adjusting the head of my cocks against them. One against her pussy, feeling his cock inside her...the other against his waiting hole.

"Ian," she whimpered. "You're going to take me together?"

Yes. I want to fill you both at the same time. You're going to take your mates' cocks, little queen. Both of us.

I looked down, watching them as I slowly pushed forward. Both of them groaned as their bodies stretched around me. I could feel Luca's cock throbbing inside her tight cunt, his ass squeezing me as I pushed into him. I stilled, allowing him to adjust. Waiting for him to realize my magic would let his body take me, that he would feel good being bred by me.

She already knew. She raked her nails over Luca's back, gasping in pleasure as she adjusted to the two of us.

Luca let out a long groan. "Keep going," he whined. "Please. Please fuck us."

I let out a low growl, my chest rumbling as I pulled back and pumped back into them.

Their cries rang through the room.

The need to fill them overcame me, but I held on, willing myself to wait. To fuck them until they came first.

"Ian," he groaned.

Only a couple days ago you wanted to slay me, and now you're taking my dragon cock.

Every thrust made him fuck Serena too, the three of us moving together. I pumped harder, growling as I took them. Their bodies glistened with sweat and my cum, the two of them taking me over and over again until they both screamed.

I felt them come around me, and I couldn't hold on any longer. I tilted my massive head back, a roar rumbling through the entire room as I gave my mates my cum, filling them both together.

Chapter 30
Round 2

Luca

Ian's cum filled Serena and me as I came inside her. I could feel the ridges of his cock against mine, her pussy tight around us. I panted, pressing my forehead to hers as we came down from the high of our orgasm.

But even after coming, I was still hard.

I whimpered as he slowly pulled out of us. I could still feel the effects of his magic, lust pumping through me. Serena leaned up, trailing kisses down my neck. She bit down, drawing a hungry groan from me.

"Your magic has broken me," I rasped.

I felt his long dragon tongue along my spine, heat blowing from his nostrils.

*I don't know how long it will last...*he admitted to us.

I didn't care. I was between the two people that meant the most to me, sharing pleasure with them that was decadently carnal.

"You feel so good on top of me," Serena whispered against my skin. She continued to suck and bite my neck, and I hoped she left her mark.

Ian let out a dark chuckle as he moved to the side, spreading out next to us. His massive body curled around us, leaving enough room in the middle for the two of us to spread out if we wanted.

I want to watch you fuck her, Luca.

His words went straight to my cock. Serena sucked in a breath, her hands running up and down my body.

Fuck. I knew exactly what I wanted to do.

"Do you want more, Serena?" I asked.

"Yes," she answered.

"Will you say 'red' if you need me to stop?"

"Yes," she whispered eagerly.

I cupped her face for a moment, kissing her tenderly as I slid one hand back. I curled my fingers in her dark hair and gripped hard. In one swift motion, I rolled her onto her stomach, pulling her head back with her hair.

"Luca," she gasped.

"Does the pain feel good, little queen?" I whispered.

I needed this right now. To dominate her in front of him, even as his cum dripped out of us. There was a possessive part of me, the part I had fought for so long, that craved to own her. And as I yanked her hair, I felt myself giving in to that desire.

"Yes," she moaned. "Yes, this is so good. I love the pain."

I pulled her onto all fours, her ass pressing against my cock. I let go of her hair and sat back on my heels, squeezing her ass cheeks. She was stunning like this. Her skin flushed, our cum trailing down her pretty thighs, her body shivering with anticipation.

I leaned down, my eyes meeting Ian's over the curve of her ass. He let out a low noise, watching us intently. I squeezed her cheeks,then bit one of them hard. She cried out and I gripped her hips, holding her in place before she could crawl away.

I bit harder until she was whimpering and crying. The noises she made had my cock dripping more precum. I sat back, bringing my palm down on her ass cheek. She gasped as I slapped her, her ass jiggling from the impact.

"Look at him," I whispered, rubbing the spot I'd just spanked. "Look at your monster, princess. I want you to watch him while I make you scream."

"Luca," she whimpered. "More. I need more."

"Insatiable," I teased, spanking her again.

I spanked one cheek several times in a row, harder than the last, until she squeaked, her back arching. Then I switched to the other, watching her skin bloom red, my handprints burning as I spanked her. She gripped the blankets beneath us, cursing as I switched.

"Fuck!" she screamed.

I expected her to tell me to stop. But she just lowered her torso, pushing her ass up in the air as I spanked her again and again.

I glanced up, seeing how Ian's cocks hardened from watching us. His body was large enough to curl completely around us.

"Crawl to his cocks," I told her, giving her a light shove.

Serena moaned and did as I asked, crawling to Ian. Her ass swayed back and forth as she moved. Once she was in front of him, she looked back over her shoulder at me.

"What do you want me to do with his cocks?" she asked.

"I want you to suck him while I fuck your ass." I kneeled behind her and watched as she reached for his cock, running her hand over the ridges as I spread her cheeks.

I pressed two fingers against her hole, slowly easing them in.

"Oh," she grunted, pushing back against me.

I slapped her ass, letting out a low growl. "So eager."

"I need your cock in me," she whimpered.

"Suck his dragon cocks, little queen," I reminded her.

I glanced behind me as Ian raised his large head, curling in closer so that his cocks were in front of Serena's face, with his head right behind me.

Fuck her.

His command sent a bolt of pleasure through me.

I replaced my fingers with the head of my cock. She began to lick him as I slowly pushed in, taking my time.

Tipping my head back, I exhaled and thrust inside her. I gripped her hips as her ass took my cock, her body squeezing all eight inches. She whined as I began to fuck her, pumping in and out.

Over and over.

Desperation rolled through me. I looked down at her, slapping her ass as I fucked her harder.

And then I felt Ian's dragon tongue against me.

Don't stop fucking her, Luca.

I cried out as his tongue pushed inside my ass, as big as a cock. He began to tongue me, pushing it in and out in the same rhythm I fucked her, in the same rhythm she sucked his cock.

The three of us moved together, a perfect synchrony of pleasure and lust, each of us giving everything to the other. I got lost in the waves of desire, feeling myself dragged deeper into the carnal need.

His tongue hit just the right spot and I couldn't take it anymore.

I let out a low grunt, pushing all the way inside her before releasing the last of everything I had. Every fucking drop I could possibly have, pumped inside her.

I cursed, collapsing against her, completely spent. Ian

pulled his tongue free and she collapsed into the blankets, panting.

I rolled to the side, spreading out as Ian began to change back into his human form. The three of us ended up laying side by side, all of us catching our breaths.

"Damn," I finally whispered. "So that's what fucking a dragon is like."

"I feel like I just died and went to orgasm heaven," Serena said.

The three of us broke out into a fit of laughter and I closed my eyes, thinking about everything.

Things I wished I didn't need to think about.

"Already?" Serena murmured, her hand sliding over my chest. I felt Ian's hand slip into mine, giving me a gentle squeeze as the worry began to creep in. "Can't we wait a little longer before we start thinking about tomorrow?"

I drew in a long breath, trying to relax, then released it.

"Shower and food first," Ian said. "We'll worry after that, little knight."

COLCHIAN

Chapter 31
The Ball

S ERENA

"You look like a goddess," Luca said.

I smiled at him as I ran my hands over my dress. It had a sweetheart neckline and glittered, the sequined fabric hugging my body. My long dark hair fell around my shoulders, and he was right.

I did look like a goddess.

I drew in a nervous breath. "I don't know how I feel about attending an event like this."

"It'll be okay," Luca promised. It was easy coming off his lips, but I still had my doubts. How could it be okay if we didn't know what might happen? "I'll be there too. You'll be safe."

Safe.

I drew in a breath, attempting to settle my nerves. Aside from the fact that we were going to a mafia ball, which would have made me nervous anyway, we were also going to confront the man who'd been using me like a puppet in his fucked up play.

And I was done being a puppet. The Fates might pull my strings, but Jason would not. Not anymore.

We'd spent this entire morning talking through everything. Ian had been working since midnight, organizing his men. I'd learned that one of the leaders, Jack, would be part of the team protecting me.

There would also be a team protecting Luca.

And a team hiding, waiting for a command from Ian.

It could either be a swift mission or an all-out bloody war. Regardless, I also knew both Ian and Luca were trying to keep me far from it, even though I was the demigod daughter of Ares. Fighting should be in my blood.

Well, it was in my blood. I'd already killed five men this week; what was twenty more?

Luca cupped my face, his fingertips pressing into my skin. His eyes searched mine, brows drawing together.

"Will you be safe?" I whispered. It was a redundant question, but I couldn't convince myself to let it be.

Less than a week. That was how long I'd had my happy ending, and hell, it hadn't actually been *happy* until the last forty-eight hours. Luca and Ian were mine as much as I was theirs, and I would do anything to keep them now that we were together.

Blood would be spilled tonight.

My stomach clenched with anxiety, and I felt sick.

"Hey," Luca whispered. "I will be okay. Jason won't get me. Ian will snap him in half. And you have your knife, right?"

I nodded, holding up my clutch. Inside it, I had my knife, a small gun, and lipstick. I felt like a spy or an assassin.

"After tonight, we will be able to put all of this behind us,"

Luca said. "It's silly that Jason is using me as a bounty anyway. He's trying to get to us."

He had gotten to us. Or at least, he had gotten to me. Now that I knew this mysterious Jason was J, and that he had been using Luca and me for over a decade, I was ready to hunt him down and kill him.

"Are we ready?"

Luca and I both looked up as Ian came out of his room. He looked like a silver fox, wearing a black tux with a bow tie, his hair slicked back, and his beard neatly trimmed. He paused in the doorway, taking us in as well. "Both of you look delicious," he said.

Luca and I smirked. He was right. We did look good. Luca wore a tux as well, his dark curls combed back.

Fuck, both of my mates were hot as hell.

"We look great," I agreed. "And so do you."

Ian smiled, walking toward us. He tugged each of us close, stealing a kiss from Luca and then me.

"Everything is going to be okay," he said softly, his gaze darkening. "That Jason wants to meet at this event is ridiculous. No one will want anything bad to happen, not when we're all together. We will use it to our advantage."

I nodded. His reassurances soothed my nerves, but I still worried something could go wrong.

I couldn't lose Luca or Ian.

"Serena will distract the partygoers, and Luca and I will handle Jason."

"I don't like it," I said. "I'm strong and can kill as well as you can."

"If you're with us, we'll do anything to protect you," Luca said. "We need you to play your part, *piccola regina*."

"I know," I said, feeling a flare of frustration. "I don't like being put in the corner."

Ian let out a soft sigh. "Serena, you are precious to us. We need to know you are safe while this happens. People will die tonight."

I swallowed hard, holding back any tears. I couldn't ruin my makeup, and I fucking hated crying. "Alright," I said. "Let's go."

"Alright," Luca said softly. "We have our plan. Jason will be dead by midnight, and tomorrow we'll get to start our new life. One where we don't have to worry about death threats."

It almost sounded too good to be true.

* * *

I'd never been to an event like this in my entire life.

When I lived in Italy with my family, there would be large events, but those had been lively, loud, and fun. People might have dressed up, but the air was filled with happiness.

This felt different.

Everyone in the room wore a smile, but they were masks hiding their vicious fangs. The energy was different than anything I'd experienced before. It moved like a snake, consuming you entirely within its dark grip. An undercurrent of mistrust and greed.

Ian guided me through the front doors of a historical building in downtown Moirai. The floors were polished, gleaming from the chandeliers above us. Waiters darted around with trays of champagne, and I took everything in as we descended a set of stairs.

It will be okay.

Even though Ian was not in his dragon form, I could hear him in my mind, and I loved this new connection. Being able to speak without anyone hearing us brought me some comfort.

Luca made it to the balcony. Look up slowly.

I did as he commanded, my gaze sweeping over the dazzling crowd to a balcony on the right side of the room. I couldn't see Luca there, but I could feel him in the shadows, blending in. Staying out of sight.

I swallowed hard.

"Ian!" a voice called.

I looked up as a blonde woman practically ran towards us, her bright blue eyes shining with happiness. She wore a crimson red dress that hugged her body, her hair swept up into a chignon. She was stunning.

Three massive men followed behind her like hawks, carrying an air of power with them. People parted for them out of instinct as they followed the woman.

"Hi," she said as she met us, grinning. "You made it. You must be Serena. I'm so happy to meet you. I'm tired of all the ancient people here."

"Ashley," Ian chuckled. "It's good to see you."

"Hi," I said, offering her a smile.

It had been way too long since I'd talked to someone my age. Even though I had occasional calls with Mia, I was happy to see someone like Ashley.

"It's okay if you're nervous," Ashley said. "I am too. There aren't any gods here tonight, but there are monsters and demigods, and some of them are assholes. Not to mention, supposedly, the Fates are here for the auction. I have no idea what's being auctioned, though."

"Ash," one of the men grumbled. "Everyone can hear you."

"Let them," she said, giving him a sharp look. He stared at her momentarily, and I watched him visibly fight a smile. "This is Damon. That's Minos, and that's Aaecus. My husbands."

"Oh," I said. I'd never met someone with multiple husbands before, but it made me relax. "Hi," I greeted them.

Minos, the middle one, winked at me—while the other two offered tight smiles.

"Is Jason here?" Ian asked tightly.

"I haven't seen him yet," Damon answered, giving Ian a look I couldn't quite read. "I heard he may arrive fashionably late with an item for the auction that *no one can resist* ."

My stomach twisted in knots. I gave Ian a nervous glance and felt him urge me to stay calm through the bond. To stay collected. I found myself glancing back up to the balcony, wishing Luca wasn't here.

For once, I wished that he was far away from me.

Ashley raised a brow and then reached out, offering me her hand. I took it and gasped as I felt an electric shock run up my arm. She inhaled sharply, her eyes lighting up.

"*Oh,*" she breathed.

She was like me.

I knew it, even though no one had said it aloud.

Ian tugged me back, letting out a low growl, but she ignored him. Her expression became concerned.

"We should keep moving through the crowd," Ian said. "Greeting some of the other leaders. You haven't met the Chimera twins or the Hydra men yet."

"She's not missing much," Minos quipped.

Ashley snorted. "They aren't that bad."

"Once again, I'd like to remind everyone that most people here have amazing hearing," Damon hissed. "So please do not insult other mafia brethren. I'd prefer to keep this suit pristine. The dry cleaning bill to get blood out of it is unbelievable."

"I'm ready to rip off my suit," Aaecus muttered.

"I'm also ready to rip off your suit," Ashley teased.

The looks on her husbands' faces made even me blush.

I wanted to get to know her. She was a demigod, no doubt about that. I had so many questions for her, so many things I wanted to know. Had she always known she was one? How had she met her husbands?

"I could stay with Ashley," I offered, looking up at Ian. "If you'd like to keep speaking to other leaders." *If you'd like to hunt down Jason.*

Ian looked down at me, holding my gaze for a moment.

He didn't want to leave me alone, but he would have to eventually. That was the plan.

He tore his gaze from me, looking at Ashley's men. "Keep her safe."

The three of them bristled, especially the bald one. "Ian," Damon said. "How about I accompany you?"

"No," he responded, turning me to face him and kissing my forehead. *You can trust them. Ashley's mates are a fierce monster known as Cerberus. If anything happens, I'm confident they'll keep you safe. Stick with her.*

"Okay," I whispered.

You're the distraction, he reminded me.

Right, but how would I distract anyone here? Fucking hell.

Ian pulled away, taking his warmth with him. I watched as he weaved through the crowd, heads turning as he left.

And then I felt the eyes on me.

Ashley moved closer, looping her arm in mine and pulling me close. I was thankful for that.

"I'm okay," I said, even though she hadn't said anything.

"Yeah," she said. "But we can stick together, right?"

"Yes," I said.

"We can pretend to be girlfriends," she teased.

"Ashley," all three of her husbands growled.

That made us both snicker.

"Do they always growl?" I whispered.

"Oh, always," she said, grinning. "Monster men do that.

Maybe monster women do too, but I've only ever met one monster lady."

"Medusa? I mean, Madeline?" I asked.

"Yes! Have you met her?"

"I have," I said, thinking back to Friday night. Medusa didn't seem all that bad.

"I hate this shit," Aaecus muttered, looking around. "I hate the food. I hate the champagne. This ball is dumb."

"How about you go get us drinks?" Minos said.

"How about I fuck you in the bathroom?"

"Aaecus," Damon hissed. "Fucking behave."

I laughed again. They were something else.

"How did all of you meet?" I asked.

"Oh, I broke into their home to steal a painting, and they caught me and forced me to sign a contract to be their sex slave," Ashley nonchalantly explained.

"Ashley," all three of them growled again.

She let out a dark laugh and winked. "It's okay. In the end, I stole their hearts."

"Yes, she did," Damon mumbled, looking around us. "It's tense in here, more than usual."

I nodded in agreement, feeling the tension he spoke of. I'd been to other formal events before, only twice in the last ten years, but neither had felt like this. There was an electric buzz in the atmosphere that made the hair on the back of my neck stand up.

I looked around for Ian, my gaze finally finding him.

And the three men who approached him.

Even though there was no outright hostility, I knew those men were not friendly.

Fuck.

I looked around for Jack or anyone who was supposed to be on my team but spotted no one.

When I looked back to where Ian had been, he was gone.

My heart began to pound in my chest. The three men and Ashley instinctively stepped in closer.

"What is it?" Damon whispered. "You can be honest with us. We've known Ian for a long time, and you're his mate. We will help."

I sucked in a breath, feeling nauseous again. What if they hurt Ian? If they managed to hurt him, then there'd be no saving Luca. I'd lose both of my mates, and everything would—

"I need to create a distraction. Something big. Something that will make everyone look at me or us. It's important. And then I need to leave. My mates are in danger."

"Oh, we can definitely make that happen," Ashley said, looking at her husband with shoulder-length dark hair. "Minos..."

He raised a brow and sighed dramatically, looking at Aaecus.

Damon gave a slight nod. "Serena, right?" he asked.

"Yes," I said.

"When this stupid ball is over and whatever shit is going on is done, you owe us a drink. We'll handle the distraction, and Ash will sneak you out."

"Alright, deal," I said, nerves fluttering through me.

"And what Ashley will not do is run off into a fight that isn't hers," Aaecus said, staring pointedly at Ashley.

"No promises," she teased.

"The things I do for love," Minos added, rolling his shoulders.

"Ready?" Ashley whispered. I nodded, despite feeling not ready at all. "Let's go," she said.

Her three husbands began to shift, their very expensive suits shredding as they became creatures that looked like werewolves. Then they began to morph together into one giant monster. The newly-formed monster let out a fierce roar, making the chandeliers tremble as people screamed.

Ashley pulled me along, guiding me through the crowd as Cerberus began creating absolute chaos. Shrieks and cries surrounded us as we made it to the far wall and dashed down a hall. When I looked back, I saw blood dripping from one of the balconies.

Fuck. Fuck, fuck, fuck.

It couldn't be Luca's because I would feel if something happened to him, right? I would know, through the bond.

Panic crept in, but I swallowed it down, trying to calm the fire burning my soul.

I'd save them. I'd save my knight and dragon.

"What's going on?" she asked, tugging me into a small room.

We slammed the door shut and looked around, making sure we were alone. We were.

"Hi. I'm a demigod, the daughter of Ares, and Ian is my mate. You probably already guessed that much. We have another mate, Luca, and Jason put a bounty on his head. So, we're here to murder him tonight to stop him from murdering Luca." I said it all in one breath and watched as she registered everything.

"Got it. Well. Okay. Jason is a bastard, so I'm on board with this plan," she said. "Where did Ian go?"

"To find Jason, but I saw three men surrounding him and I didn't see where he went."

"And Luca?"

"He's supposed to act as bait, but I'm scared our plan won't work."

"Who made this plan?" Ashley asked.

"Ian did."

Ashley sighed, squeezing the bridge of her nose. "And they

didn't include you because they love you. I swear to the gods, these monsters. They're protective to a fault."

"They are," I said. "But, I have to save them. I can't lose them."

Ashley nodded and was already kicking off her heels. "Alright. I think we should kidnap two waiters, steal their outfits, and then go find Ian and Luca. Their men won't pay attention to waitresses since they'll be looking for us."

I stared at her for a moment and let out a low giggle. Maybe a slightly panicked one. "You're exactly the kind of girl I want to be friends with."

She grinned. "Ditto, babe. Girls that kidnap together, stay together. I'll get you to your mates Serena, and after Jason is dead, we can get drunk on frozen margaritas."

Chapter 32
Bait

Luca

Everything seemed to be going fine until I felt a hand on my shoulder. I turned around, and proceeded to be knocked out by a man twice my size.

And hell, I could take a punch.

But this was different.

I blinked, forcing my eyelids open as I slowly came to. The light in the room flickered, pain burning through me. I could handle the pain, but the light was fucking annoying.

I blew out a breath. We'd known this could happen, but I had hoped everything would work out. Fuck, Ian and I had done everything we could to make sure it would. Until that man snuck up behind me.

I hoped that Ian would get to me before Serena tried to intervene.

"Luca, Luca, Luca."

I lifted my head, looking to my right.

"Wow," I said. "You're as ugly as you were ten years ago."

J, Jason, glowered at me. He wore a tux, his hands covered by leather gloves. Two men stood next to him, both with hollowed-out expressions one would expect from the henchmen of a cunt.

"You're not so cute either," Jason said, stepping closer. "You took that punch poorly."

"It was weak to sneak up like that."

"It was even weaker to not be alert," Jason sneered. "Here's something for you to think about. All you are is bait."

"Indeed," I said bitterly.

Jason smirked, cocking his head. "Oh, did your dragon boss tell you to act as bait, too? Did he also tell you I have my men searching for your pretty princess? And that they all know how to kill a demigod?"

He was fucking with me. I glared at him, forcing my expression to remain unaffected. Forcing myself to not give anything away.

Jason stepped closer to me and leaned down. His eyes shone with hatred, his lips pulling into a sneer. "I'm going to slaughter her," he whispered. "She's going to die, then I'll kill you and Ian. I'll finally have one less thing to worry about. The Fates are wrong," he said. "She won't be the death of me."

"Haven't you lived long enough?" I asked. "Aren't you tired of this world?"

"Spoken like a stupid mortal," Jason snickered. "You have no concept of time or how vast it is. I've seen the rise and fall of empires. I've killed countless monsters and done what the gods created me for. I've gotten everything I've ever wanted, and that isn't changing today because of some fresh demigod bitch. She's not supposed to exist. It's against the rules the Fates themselves made."

"If the Fates didn't want her alive, don't you think they

would never have intervened?" I bit out. This guy was a motherfucking nutcase. Power-hungry and insane. "Or do you really think you're able to escape fate?"

"I've been escaping fate my whole life, Luca Civello," he chuckled. "The things I've done. I'm meant to rule this entire fucking mafia, to be the best of the best. Everyone, even monsters, will submit to me. These new demigods are worthless. Like that Ashley woman."

I had no fucking idea who he was talking about.

"She murdered my brother. And Serena will try to do the same, but she won't make it anywhere close to me. And I'm going to make sure she feels her mates die before I kill her too."

"You won't keep us apart," I said. "You've tried for so fucking long. You used me to keep track of her. And you knew that Ian would keep her out of his world. You convinced me to hate him."

"And you wanted a woman you aren't good enough for," he chuckled. "I may plan on killing her, but even I think a demigod loving a mortal is absurd. You're below her. She has the blood of the gods, of beings who created you. Her power is unfathomable compared to the likes of you."

He grabbed my face, his gloved fingertips sending spears of pain from where he gripped me.

"You will die," he whispered. "And I hope you scream. Ten years of listening to you cry and snivel like a whipped child over a toy you couldn't have. Ten years of you confessing all your dark secrets to me. And finally, *finally*, I get to kill you."

"You can try—"

His blade came out of nowhere, burying straight into my gut. I gasped, my body slouching forward as the pain spread through me.

I felt my connections to Ian. To Serena. I felt them tighten. I felt their pain, their worry, their absolute terror.

Fuck.

"What?" Jason whispered. "I can monologue with the best of them, but I follow through." He stabbed me again, blood gushing over me, spilling onto the floor. "Nice and slow," he sighed. "Knowing that your mates are fighting to get to you. But they won't make it. Do you want to know what I'm selling tonight at the auction?"

I made a noise, my vision beginning to dot.

"I'm going to sell your princess' heart. Cut straight out of her chest, bloodied and still beating. I'm sure someone will buy it. Who wouldn't want a piece of her?"

He yanked the knife out and stood, turning to walk away. "Let's go," he said to his men. "Let him bleed out here. No one will find him anyway."

My vision continued to darken, the pain almost unbearable. But all I could feel was the sadness.

I'd failed her again.

Even after all these years, I hadn't been able to protect my little queen.

All I could do was hope that our dragon would be able to save her.

My eyes shut, the world around me disappearing. My thoughts turned to Ian and Serena.

I'd been able to love them, even if it had been brief. That was more than I thought I would ever have.

A soft feminine voice cut through the darkness and the pain. "It's not your time yet, Luca."

A hand touched me, warmth filling me, surrounding me. The pain began to dull, a soft sigh coming from whatever being stood before me.

"Everyone has their time. Their beginning and their end. But the end doesn't always have to be sad, though mortals believe it is. My sister is sometimes gentle when she cuts the thread."

My eyes fluttered, my lungs filling with a deep breath. I raised my head, blinking.

A woman stood in front of me. She wore a silver dress, her hands coated in my blood. One of her eyes was golden, the other pale lilac. She offered me a gentle smile.

"Who are you?" I croaked.

"Lachesis," she said. "Do not worry, little warrior. You aren't dying today."

"How can you..." I drifted off as I felt the stab wound start to heal, my heart pumping as energy began to return to me.

She smiled, and it was brilliant. I felt the urge to look away, fear curling through me. She was like an angel.

And then she was gone.

Chapter 33
Gift from the Gods

IAN

The three men who had planned to lead me to Jason were dead.

I stared at the blood on the floor, my hearts pounding so hard I could feel it in my temple.

I had felt Luca's pain.

I had felt him die.

My chest heaved, blood dripping from my claws. Tears streamed down my face.

There was no place in the universe where Jason could hide from me now. The pain that tore through me was immense. The cutting of the bond had hurt unlike anything I'd ever felt, and for a moment, I had wanted to die too.

Then I thought of Serena.

Jason couldn't take her too.

It would end me.

I took a calming breath, my wings spreading behind me. I

realized I was still crying, so I wiped away the tears. I cracked my neck and swallowed down the fire in my throat, the burn settling in my gut.

I had to keep going.

I had to keep moving.

I willed myself to take a step forward, then I was running. Tracking. I could breathe in Jason's scent, could feel him close by.

The historical house where the ball was held had four stories. I made my way up to the third floor, noting that no one was around.

It was silent.

My rage and heartache over losing Luca propelled me forward.

There stood Jason, the Golden Fleece draped around his shoulders. He was at the end of the hallway, his eyes burning with malice. I noticed a glimmer around him that emanated power.

"Did you feel him die, dragon?" Jason asked.

"I'm going to murder you," I said, my voice cold.

"No," Jason chuckled, taking a step towards me. "You won't. In fact, you're exactly where I need you to be."

I heard a sound before I felt it, and by the time I felt it, it was too late. I looked down at my chest, where a knife jutted out from one of my hearts, and I could feel a poison bleeding from it. Some sort of magic that brought me to my knees.

I couldn't move.

Fuck. Fuck, fuck, fuck.

Panic followed, my nostrils flaring as Jason walked down the hall toward me. He wore that stupid grin, the grin of someone who believed they had won.

He stopped once he came toe to toe with me. "One of the perks of being the son of a god is that you receive gifts," he whispered. "They favor us, you see. They want us to kill all of you wretched monsters."

"Why are you doing this?" I whispered.

"To thwart Fate," he said. "And to fuck you over . After all these years, I've never forgotten our battles. I've never forgotten my hate for you, dragon. And I can't wait to see your mate's face when she realizes she can't save you, like the two of you couldn't save Luca."

Chapter 34
Queen of Blood and Blades

Serena

Ashley helped me fight and held back a group of men trying to stop us from entering the theater. But I had made it.

The auction.

The place Jason waited for me.

I stepped into the theater, looking over the heads of everyone who sat and waited for the curtains to open. There were at least 200 people, and despite the fact that Cerberus had interrupted the event earlier, they seemed to have stuck around.

Here for the show.

Rage rolled through me. I'd felt my bond with Luca snap, which nearly killed me, but then I'd turned all my pain into anger. For now.

I gripped my knife, blood dripping from it.

All I saw was red.

I took a step forward, and a spotlight blinked on, shining

directly on me. I glared, ignoring how all the attention in the room shifted to me. A few shocked gasps and murmurs followed, along with a few growls. Some people stood up, but I ignored them.

I knew what I looked like.

Ashley and I had never managed to kidnap any waiters, so I was still wearing my silver dress. Only now, the sequins were sticky with blood. My hair had unraveled amidst the fighting, and my blade was slick with death.

Power burned through me, leaving holes in my heart.

There was only one person I wanted.

"Serena Avellino," a voice called.

That voice belonged to *him*.

I still recognized him. Even after ten years, I remembered the face of this slimy bastard at my wedding. The curtains drew back, and Jason stood center stage.

The crowd gasped in horror.

"*Jason*, what are you doing?" someone called out. A woman I didn't recognize.

Ian was on the stage too, a knife sticking out of his chest. I knew he was still alive, I hadn't felt the loss of his bond like I had with Luca's.

He raised his dragon head, but I could tell he wasn't fully conscious.

"Reclaiming our future," Jason hissed. "We've let monsters live for too long."

That statement was not met well. Three vicious-looking men stood from their seats, followed by Medusa and two other men I had yet to meet.

I didn't see Cerberus, but if Ashley was still fighting, I was sure they had gone after her.

I felt a flicker of guilt. I hoped she was okay. I hoped I'd be able to fulfill my promise to buy her and her husbands' drinks.

"This is absurd," one of the monstrous men roared. "You're breaking our laws! The ones put in place by the Fates themselves!"

"And do you see the Fates here, Chimera?" Jason snarled. "None of us have seen the Fates. Not in ages. They don't decide what happens to us, we do. That girl there—" he pointed at me as I made it to the edge of the stage. "She's destined to kill me. But not if I kill her first. Right after I murder the Colchian dragon."

Jason raised his hand as I tumbled onto the stage, a knife gleaming in his grip.

"No!" I shouted.

I felt the word with every part of my being, my power bursting from me. The knife flew from his hand, and he let out a snarl.

I rushed toward him, gripping my own blade.

"You stupid girl!" he yelled.

The two of us met in the center, in front of everyone, a torrent of violence. I lunged forward, backhanding him across the face.

I aimed for his gut and tried to drive my knife into him, but the fabric kept it from piercing him. *Fuck*. It looked sheer, but it was tougher than armor.

He laughed, lunging forward and knocking me back.

"Stupid girl," he said. "As if you could kill me. You've been nothing but a housewife for a decade."

"And?" I hissed. "That makes you nothing but a weak demigod who's scared of a housewife."

His lip curled, sneering. He lunged for me again, and I moved, twirling out of the way.

The fabric didn't cover him entirely, which meant he had weak points.

The two of us fell into a violent dance, each dodging the

other. He leapt forward as I swung my knife, and I cursed as the blade was deflected by the Golden Fleece again. Jason grabbed me by the throat, slamming me onto the stage floor and pinning me beneath him.

My head smacked, pain radiating through me. Jarring me. My knife clattered out of my grip. I shot my palm out and struck him in the throat like Luca had taught me, and then grabbed him and headbutted him. He grunted, distracted long enough for me to roll to the side. I snatched my knife and pivoted as he reached for me again.

I grabbed his hand and brought my knife down on his wrist.

It was horrifying how easily the knife went through, like cutting soft butter. Jason howled as his hand was severed, gold blood gushing out, not red.

I was so focused on that, I didn't see his other hand swinging with his own weapon. I gasped, unable to move out of the way, then a body shoved between the two of us, taking the blow.

I stumbled back, my mouth falling open as a woman took the knife straight through her thigh.

"Percy," Jason wheezed. "What are you—"

The air crackled around her, every hair on my body standing up as electricity surrounded them. She raised her hand and a lightning bolt appeared, a jagged shape that flashed erratically.

Golden ichor dripped onto the floor, her arm poised to kill.

Jason had gone silent, his eyes wide.

"Do you wish to kill him?" the woman, Percy, asked.

Did I?

I didn't hesitate. I gripped my knife and moved around her, driving my blade straight through his heart. He cried out, his breath becoming a sickly rattle as he continued to bleed.

"A demigod can't die from a stab," he rasped.

"This is a knife from Ares," I said, twisting it.

"It is your time, Jason, son of Zeus."

I looked up, and everything around me seemed to stop. The pounding of my heart, the people around me, the woman who was bleeding.

A feminine figure stood over us, crimson strings draping from her slender fingertips. She reminded me of a ghoul, with dark gray skin and long silver hair. One of her eyes was missing, replaced by a golden ball that gleamed in its socket.

"Atropos," Jason wheezed.

The woman lifted a string, one that had come undone, fraying. In the other hand, she held a simple set of scissors, but the blades gleamed in a way that made my very soul shiver.

She snipped the loose thread in one swift motion, and Jason collapsed.

I pulled back from him, blinking at her. "You're one of the Fates," I whispered.

"I am," she said. "You will not see me for a very long time, child. I wish you well, daughter of Ares."

With that, she vanished, and everything resumed.

Percy yanked the knife from her thigh, letting out a low hiss. I felt hands on me and looked up, startled to see Ashley. "Your man is alive," she rasped. "I found him. He was trying to get to you."

I got to my feet quickly and looked across the stage, seeing Luca hobbling towards Ian. A blade was still stuck in our dragon's chest.

I ran to them, tears blurring my vision. "Oh my gods," I cried.

Luca pulled me into his arms, squeezing me tight. "I thought I was dead," he rasped.

"You were," I whimpered. "I felt you die."

We broke apart, our attention turning to Ian. I cut his

bonds and he fell forward, letting out a low grunt as Luca caught him.

"Pull the knife free," he huffed.

Luca yanked it out and Ian immediately began to move, color returning to his cheeks as the wound began to heal. "That knife was keeping me in place," he said. "It's a blade from one of the gods, although I don't know who. Gods and their fucking gifts."

"Ian."

The three of us looked up. I realized we were definitely not alone. What seemed to be the entire monster mafia surrounded us on the stage, along with Percy and Ashley. The demigods.

"Jason can't be dead," one of the monster men was saying. "She only stabbed him."

Had they not seen Atropos?

"One of the Fates took him," I interrupted them.

That caused a lot of uneasiness.

Ian let out a breath, pulling Luca and me close. "We would like to leave," Ian said coldly. "We can meet another time."

Ashley yanked the golden fabric wrapped around Jason's body off, bringing it over to us. "Here's the Golden Fleece," she said, eyeing it before ultimately handing it to Ian.

He took it carefully, his eyes softening. "I've been parted from it for so long," he sighed.

Ashley nodded, giving the three of us a soft smile, then turned on her heels. "Alright. Everyone, leave. Someone take Jason's body; I want nothing to do with him."

"He was our leader!" one of the demigod men roared.

"Orpheus," Percy snapped. "We will hold a burial for him, but shut the fuck up."

He scoffed at her and picked up Jason, leaving quickly. I watched him go, followed by the other demigod I didn't know.

"Well, well," one of the monster men chuckled. "It seems like the Fates are picking all of you off."

Percy gave him a flat look. "And you could be next, Chimera. Who knows what they have planned."

With that, she turned, descending the stairs and leaving.

Ian sighed. "Let's get home," he said gently. "I need both of you in my arms, in my bed, and safe."

I nodded, relief spreading through me. I dragged him into a kiss and then Luca again, never wanting to let them go.

Chapter 35
One Week Later

"Bend over, little queen."

My breath left me as I bent over the edge of Ian's bed, my pussy wet and dripping.

It had been a week since all hell had broken loose, and the three of us had survived. We'd survived Jason's crazy antics and, as Ashley and Cerberus had done, combined the mafia branch I suddenly inherited with Ian's. It would be a slow process, a lot of work, but...

I'd gotten everything I wanted.

I had Luca. I had Ian. And I was a motherfucking demigod queen.

"Go ahead, little knight," Ian instructed.

Luca brought a paddle down on my ass cheek, drawing out a sharp cry from me. The pain strung, but it was accompanied by a wave of pleasure that came from being with them.

This entire week, we'd either been working or fucking.

Or both at the same time. One day, I'd taken Ian's cocks while he was on a phone call, and that had been very rewarding.

"Good girl," Luca huffed. "Fuck. I need a picture of her like this."

The paddle literally said 'good girl' on it, and it left the words printed on my ass in angry red marks.

"Yes, but get the other ass cheek first. Then we'll get a picture and hang it in the living room."

"Fuck you both," I swore, but there was no heat to my words.

Luca and Ian chuckled, both absolute devils together.

My other ass cheek was smacked hard, and I hissed as the sound cracked through the air. I looked back with a moan as Luca rubbed his palm over it, his cock straining against his pants.

"Is that for me?" I whispered, licking my lips.

"Not yet," he said.

I heard the sound of a camera snapping a photo and felt myself get even more wet, my pussy pulsing.

"Take off her thong," Ian said.

Luca knelt behind me, and I felt his warm breath against me. A low moan left me as he suddenly sank his teeth into my ass cheek, the pain sending waves of pleasure through me. He leaned down, the tip of his tongue dragging over my pussy before he pulled my thong off.

Excitement ran through me, melting into pleasure as Luca ran his rough fingertips over my skin.

We heard the camera again, and Luca simply let out a soft moan.

"You're going to have a whole album from today," I mumbled.

Luca chuckled. "That's the goal."

"Alright, little knight. You can fuck her. I'm going to take pictures and join when I please."

"Yes, sir," Luca said, spreading my cheeks.

I groaned as he pressed his tongue against my pussy, driving it inside me.

"Luca," I gasped.

His fingers slid up between my thighs, pressing against my clit as he thrust his tongue in and out of me. I was so fucking wet, my body buzzing with heat. With pleasure.

He pulled his tongue free right before I came.

"You bastard," I growled, looking back at him,

Click. Ian smirked as he took a picture. "I like it when she's feisty."

"So do I." The sound of his pants unzipping had me sucking in a breath. I felt his cock spring free, slapping against me.

"Luca, please." I was desperate for relief. I needed him to fill me up, to give me every inch of his cock.

Ian let out a low grumble, and I heard him move. He came to the bed, holding up the camera.

"I want to see her face as you thrust into her, little knight."

"Fuck," Luca muttered.

He pressed the head of his cock against my pussy. In one swift thrust, he filled me all the way, a cry of pleasure tearing from me.

Click.

"You'll like that one," Ian rasped.

He set down the camera, crawling onto the bed as his form began to change, his wings spreading behind him. Luca grunted as he began to fuck me, his cock sliding in and out of me. I was so fucking wet, so incredibly turned on. Pleasure pulsed through my body, my eyes fluttering as my mate took me.

I felt another cock slap my face and looked up. Ian knelt in front of me, precum dripping from his glorious dragon cocks. He slid his claws into my hair, the feeling of them scraping over my scalp making me moan.

"Open up, little queen."

I parted my lips for him. He thrust into my mouth at the exact moment Luca pumped into me, their cocks filling me from both ends.

"Such a good girl," Ian groaned. "You feel so fucking good."

"She's our perfect girl," Luca said.

The two of them praising me was almost enough to make me come.

"Her little cunt is squeezing me so tight," Luca gasped.

Ian hit the back of my throat. I groaned around him, my eyes rolling back as I succumbed to absolute pleasure and need. Luca gripped my hips, fucking me harder, his groans filling the room.

I melted between the two of them, feeling the pleasure begin to build.

Fuck.

I was getting closer and closer to coming.

Ian fucked me harder, tears streaming down my cheeks.

"Her throat is taking me well too," Ian huffed.

"If we switch, then all holes would be filled..."

They both suddenly pulled out of me, and I gasped, dragging in air. In a matter of seconds, Luca's cock was pressing against my lips, and Ian's cocks were against my pussy and ass.

"Oh fuck," I cried.

Luca took the chance to thrust into my mouth, and Ian did the same to my pussy and ass. Both dragon cocks speared me, the ridges rubbing against me in a perfect way.

I moaned around Luca as I took them. They fell into a

rhythm again, a brutal one. I screamed around his cock as an orgasm crashed into me, but they didn't stop.

They kept going. Harder. Faster.

Luca leaned forward, pushing my head down on his cock with one hand while the other reached under. His fingers slid against my clit and he began to circle me quickly.

Another orgasm tore through me, my scream muffled. He grunted, his breaths shortening.

"I'm going to come," Luca groaned. "Fuck. I can't stop."

"Come on, baby," Ian crooned. "Hold out a little longer and come with me. We can breed her little cunt together."

Luca growled, and I could feel him barely holding it together. The two of them kept going, until Ian finally let out a loud growl.

"Now!"

The two of them cried out as they came, their cum filling me in all holes. I swallowed down Luca's seed, the taste of him bringing me a different sort of pleasure. Ian's cum pumped inside of me, shooting until he was finally spent.

They both slowly pulled out, cum dripping from me. I gasped, collapsing forward on the bed.

"Fuck," I groaned.

I heard Ian move, then heard the rustle of him picking something up.

Click.

Luca let out a dark chuckle and I smiled, melting into the blankets.

"I love you," Luca said, kissing me. "And I love tasting my cum on your lips."

"I love you, too," I said, smiling.

Ian came to me, leaning down to spread my legs apart. I gasped as I felt his tongue against my pussy, lapping up his seed. He moaned, his forked tongue cleaning me up.

"I love you, too," Ian said. "And I love tasting my cum in your pussy. And I love you, Luca."

I looked up as the two of them leaned forward and kissed.

"Perfect," I breathed.

And it was.

The three of us were meant to be together. All of the hate, all of the secrets—everything bad had disappeared, revealing the kind of love I'd always grown up dreaming of.

I'd finally gotten my happy ending.

Six Months Later

SERENA

"You look stunning," Ashley said, sliding into the seat beside me. "We look hot as hell. We could have any man, woman, monster, or demigod in the world."

I giggled, arching a brow. "I'll be sure to tell your husbands that."

The two of us had become best friends. Not only because we were both demigods, or that we both loved monstrous men, or that we were both badass mafia ladies—but because we worked.

"Thanks," I said, grinning at her. "It's nice to have a girls' night. Forget about running our *businesses* for a bit."

"Indeed," she sighed. "I literally bribed my men to not follow me tonight. Meanwhile, I'm sure the Cerberus crew is keeping watch."

I snorted. "I'm sure they are. I'm sure my crew is, too."

"All because we want to have a girls' night. Like we can't protect ourselves."

I smirked. My kill count had luckily slowed since the week Ian, Luca, and I had come together, which was nice. As good at killing as I had become, I still wasn't the biggest fan of it.

Ashley and I had decided to meet at a bar that Percy supposedly ran. Slowly, the two of us had found ourselves talking to the odd demigod more and more. She was older, like the others, but obviously didn't share their beliefs. I was convinced she didn't hate monsters either, which was nice.

"Margaritas, ladies?" The bartender asked. "They're on the house from the Mistress."

"The Mistress," I echoed.

He gave us a nod, his lime green eyes fixing on us. I studied him, blinking a couple of times. A purple mist clung to him, one that seemed to hide what he truly was. I had no idea what he was though, definitely not human.

"Yes, please." Ashley said eagerly. "A frozen swirl margarita with a cherry sounds fantastic."

"Excellent," he said, grinning. "And you, my Queen?"

"I'll have a water," I said, a slow smile spreading across my face. I hadn't told Ashley the news yet, but she would be the first to know aside from Luca and Ian.

"Ice and a lemon?" He asked.

"Yes," I said. "Thank you."

That Luca and Ian had even let me go out since our discovery this weekend showed how much progress we'd all made in the last few months. They could still be protective and overbearing, but gods, I loved them more than anything.

The moment he stepped away, Ashley grabbed my hand. "You always drink," she said, studying me. She leaned in, narrowing her piercing blue eyes. "Are you pregnant?" she whispered.

I nodded, feeling the excitement rise up, a welcoming tide.

"Oh my gods!" she squealed, throwing her arms around me. "Oh my gods! This is going to be the cutest baby to ever grace the face of the entire planet."

"*Babies*," I corrected her.

She damn near toppled out of her chair. I laughed as she bounced up and down.

"HOLY FUCK," she squealed. "TWO. TWO IN ONE!"

"I found out this weekend," I said. "I wanted to tell you first. Well, aside from Ian and Luca."

"I'm getting shit-faced tonight in celebration," she laughed, planting a kiss on my cheek. "I'm so happy for you, Serena. I really am."

"Thank you," I said, smiling. "I'm nervous and excited and hoping that everything will be okay."

"Why wouldn't it be?" Ashley asked.

"Well, I'm a demigod. And Ian is a dragon. And Luca is a mortal man. Well, I suppose not entirely mortal any longer. The bond with me and Ian will change his lifespan, which I am thankful for."

"Right," Ashley said, pressing her lips together. "It will be okay, Serena. They will be loved and protected. And they'll have a cool ass aunt and uncles, too."

I grinned. "That they will."

The bartender returned with our drinks and then left us with a wink.

She smiled, then her expression turned wistful. "Man," she sighed, picking up her margarita. "When that happens to us, I don't know what I'll do. Imagining Damon as a Daddy...outside of the bedroom..."

I damn near choked on my water. "Ashley," I hissed, laughing. "Oh, my gods."

"I'd need them to call him papa instead or something."

The two of us stared at each other for a split second before breaking into another fit of giggles.

"The two of you sound like you're having fun."

We both looked up, our instincts kicking in fast. Orpheus, one of the demigod men who definitely did not like us, was standing at the bar. His dark eyes roamed over us with disgust.

"We are having fun," Ashley said. "What do you want?"

"A favor," he said.

"You dare approach us here?" I asked. "At a bar? One you obviously don't fit in at."

"Yes," he said. "I needed to speak to you both."

Ashley shook her head. "Speak, now. Then get the fuck out."

"I wish to collect a blade that belonged to Jason," he said. "It was never his to begin with. It was mine, a gift from my father. I would like it back."

I knew what knife he spoke of. The one that had rendered Ian's magic useless and practically turned him into a living doll. The strangest thing happened when we brought it home, it had turned into an umbrella of all things. Now, it lived in Ian's office, in a safe.

"We don't know what you're talking about," Ashley said.

"Serena does," Orpheus looked at me. "I need it back."

"What do I get in exchange?" I asked.

His eyes flashed, but his demeanor remained calm. "Whatever you want, daughter of Ares."

"That's a high price to pay," I said, my voice unwavering. "Fine. I will discuss it with Ian and Luca."

He nodded and turned, leaving the bar.

"The audacity," I muttered.

"He sucks," Ashley sighed.

"Let's forget about him and enjoy our evening."

Ashley nodded, and the two of us did just that. We spent

the next several hours talking about everything in our lives— from the monsters we loved to the future with children to how much we'd both changed.

And I felt happy. Truly happy.

I had my dragon, my knight, my friend.

I had a family.

I wasn't sure what the Fates had in store for me, but I knew I was right where I was meant to be.

Also by Clio Evans

CREATURE CAFE SERIES

Little Slice of Hell

Little Sip of Sin

Little Lick of Lust

Little Shock of Hate

Little Piece of Sass

Little Song of Pain

Little Taste of Need

Little Risk of Fall

Little Wings of Fate

Little Souls of Fire

Little Kiss of Snow: A Creature Cafe Christmas Anthology

WARTS & CLAWS INC. SERIES

Not So Kind Regards

Not So Best Wishes

Not So Thanks in Advance

Not So Yours Truly

Not So Much Appreciated

FREAKS OF NATURE DUET

Doves & Demons

Demons & Doves

THREE FATES MAFIA SERIES

Thieves & Monsters

Killers & Monsters

Clio's Creatures

Hello Creatures!

My name is Clio Evans and I am so excited to introduce myself to you! I'm a lover of all things that go bump in the night, fancy peens, coffee, and chocolate.

IF you had the chance to be matched with a monster- what kind would you choose?!

Let me know by joining me on FB and Instagram. I'm a sucker for werewolves (and plague doctors ;)) to this day.

Thank you

There are so many people that I would like to thank! WENDY-YOU ARE THE BEST editor I could ask for. Sarah, thank you so much for all of your feedback, you are the best. Lo and Kim — thank you so much for all of your support on this book.

Milton Keynes UK
Ingram Content Group UK Ltd.
UKHW021313130923
428604UK00022B/383

9 798398 602760